devotion

michelle herman

Outpost19 | San Francisco
outpost19.com

Herman, Michelle
        Devotion / Michelle Herman
        ISBN 9781937402815 (pbk)
        ISBN 9781937402822 (ebk)

Library of Congress Control Number: 2015919178

Cover art: Glen Holland

Portions of this manuscript appeared in somewhat different
forms in *The Yalobusha Review* and *American Literary Review*.

OUTPOST19

ORIGINAL
PROVOCATIVE
READING

Also by
Michelle Herman

Fiction
Missing
A New and Glorious Life
Dog

Nonfiction
Like A Song
The Middle of Everything
Stories We Tell Ourselves

For children
A Girl's Guide to Life

devotion

For my brother

one

Esther Savaris was halfway through her senior year of high school, a pretty girl, seventeen years old and still growing (according to the doctor, who had known her all her life— who had *delivered* her into her life—and who, on the morning she turned up in his office, tearful and pleading with him to keep this visit a secret from her mother, measured her as if she really were still just a child and then announced that she had grown three-quarters of an inch since her last visit), when she ran away with János Bartha, her singing teacher, who was nearly seventy then, and by whom Esther, Dr. Azogue had confirmed, was three months pregnant.

When she turned eighteen, Bartha married her. By then, they were thirteen hundred miles away from Esther's family and the studio on Ocean Parkway where Bartha had been giving singing lessons for more than twenty years—as far away as Esther had ever been from Brighton Beach, from the apartment she had lived in all her life above her parents' candy store, from Abraham Lincoln High School and the glee club, the girls' chorus, the Drama Society, and her girlfriends (there were no boyfriends; she was not allowed to date, not until after her high school graduation—"and now I'll *never* be allowed," she had said cheerfully to Bartha, trying to cheer *him* up, for he was grim and silent as he sat beside her on the train that was to carry them halfway across the country): they were in Omaha, Nebraska, where there was a cousin, Vilmos Bartha, who had offered to help them get settled. It was October, 1965. The baby, Alexander, was fourteen weeks old.

1

The marriage ceremony was brief and disappointing. Esther had been thinking of it as something like the graduation she had missed in June, something official that would mark the start of her new life. But as the justice of the peace mumbled his few words, with Vilmos and his stern, blonde, Middle Western wife acting as witnesses, and Alexander sleeping in his carriage in a corner, she could see that she had expected too much.

Nothing had changed. It was like a magic trick at a birthday party, when the magician, who was really just somebody's uncle or next-door neighbor, said *Abracadabra* but nothing happened. Then some of the children would laugh, and others would shift around uncomfortably in their folding chairs and sneak glances at one another: *Was this supposed to happen? Was this a joke?*

Toward the end of the ceremony, Esther almost asked, "Is that it? Are you sure?" It seemed to her that the justice of the peace, a plump little man with a long fringe of uncombed reddish hair, in a too-tight brown suit, no tie, and black, exhausted-looking penny loafers (a penny in the left shoe only, Esther noticed; the right one was empty), looked as if he might be absent-minded, as if he really might have left out some important part. Even the exchange of vows, so familiar to her from movies and novels, went by too quickly. The promises that she agreed to make seemed as routine as the pledge of allegiance she had recited every schoolday morning of her life. It did not seem possible that she was meant to take them seriously.

To have and to hold, for better, for worse, for richer, for poorer, in sickness, in health.

But if she didn't take them seriously, she worried, she could not expect that *she* would be taken seriously. And this was the point, after all. Proving that she knew what she was doing, that she was a serious person. Because even Bartha seemed sometimes in doubt of her ability to understand what she "had done." As if she were too stupid to see clearly the results of her own choices! "Stupid, no," he had said when she'd made this accusation, in the first days after they'd arrived in Omaha. "Not stupid in the least— indeed, too smart, some would insist, to give away your future as you have." "Not *give*," she told him. "You must mean throw away." At that time she was still in the habit of correcting him when he misused—when she assumed he had misused—an idiom in English. Lately she had come to think that he said, always, what he meant, and if it sounded odd it wasn't his fault but the fault of her own listening, that language (*usage*, as it was so unpleasantly called in school) was more complex and interesting than she had been taught.

This was her chance to make it clear that she had made decisions, that she had not just let things happen, and also that she was willing, that she *wanted*, to stick by them.

And his chance to prove the same.

This was a startling thought, because it had never crossed her mind before that Bartha had anything to prove (and prove to whom? she asked herself. Only himself, since she had never doubted him—since it had never crossed her mind, either, that he might not have known what he was doing).

It was all done with now. They were on the street outside the office of the justice of the peace, and Vilmos was shaking Bartha's hand and beaming. His wife, the imperious Clara, was looking bored and impatient. "We must make a celebration!" Vilmos said. "Clara and I will

3

take you to lunch! Where shall we go? Esther, what is your choice?"

"You choose," Esther said. "Wherever you like will be good."

Bartha looked at her curiously. She usually claimed to like eating at restaurants, and she liked being asked which restaurant—and more often than not Bartha forgot to ask her, and then she would have to point this out to him later. But she couldn't think about restaurants now. She was busy with the idea that had come to her—that today's ceremony was nothing but the two of them, her and Bartha both, proving that they were serious, that they were *grown up*. She remembered what her father had said (not said, but bellowed, fists pounding the kitchen table) on the night she broke the news of her pregnancy, of her relationship with Bartha itself. The night before they'd fled. "Half a century he's got on you! He should know better, should know how to act, how to be. A grown man, an elderly man, and he's acting like an idiot boy."

No—she would not let herself think of her father.

Not her father. Not anyone. No one but the two of them. No one else mattered. There was no one to whom it was necessary to prove anything—no one but themselves.

No one in all the world except Vilmos and Clara and Mr. One Penny even knew that this marriage had taken place. And no one but she and Bartha—and perhaps Vilmos, who, out of kindness, would insist he did too—cared that it *had* taken place.

It struck her now that this must be why people had elaborate, extravagant weddings. They *forced* other people to care. (And even if the fifty or a hundred or more relatives and friends attending, all dressed up and bearing gifts,

4

could not in fact be made to truly care, the commotion was sufficient so that the private cares of the two people at the center of it *seemed* to be important, at least for a few hours.)

It was not as if she'd wanted, even if she'd had a choice, that other kind of wedding—what her friends at home would have called *a real wedding*, with a white lace dress and veil, music and flowers and a tall, many-tiered white cake, a ring-bearer and a flower girl and bridesmaids in taffeta, dancing until past midnight, and finally a fat leather-covered book of photographs on the coffee table. But all in all, *this* wedding, in that too-small, poorly heated, poorly lit, windowless room in what passed for an office building in Nebraska (both she and Bartha had made jokes about this on their way in, and Vilmos had smiled and sighed and rolled his eyes, as he did every time they made their "New York bigshot joke remarks," and Clara had, also as usual, been offended), *this* wedding had less resembled the private commencement exercises she had had in mind than it did the meeting she'd had with her "guidance counselor" the first week of senior year, when she was lectured briefly in the woman's tiny office, under a fluorescent light that buzzed and flickered, about the importance of choosing the right college and then asked a few irrelevant, obviously memorized questions, the answers to which the counselor did not even bother to pretend to listen to before she wished Esther luck with her applications and called for the next senior waiting on the bench in the hallway, who shrugged and rolled her eyes at Esther as she passed.

How foolish she had felt for being disappointed, for having hoped for anything resembling guidance.

The restaurant Vilmos chose, the Bohemian Café, was

a favorite of Vilmos and Bartha's. The four of them settled themselves into a booth there, and Esther readjusted the baby (still sleeping, miraculously, although now in her arms), laying him across her lap, her left hand tucked beneath his head, her right hand on his chest so that she could feel the lift and fall.

Vilmos accepted a menu from a waitress in a Czech costume even as he smacked one hand on the table. "Wine!" he said. "I believe wine is called for on such a day. Shall we all have some?"

"Wine?" Clara said. "At this hour?"

A menu was set before Esther but she did not pick it up. She watched Vilmos, who smiled a little, nodding, then answered his own question, "Yes, I believe we will have some wine."

Ever since she'd met them, Esther had been waiting for Vilmos to get angry with Clara. He never even seemed to be annoyed. Esther couldn't understand it, and she watched him carefully now as he turned to Bartha: "And some dumplings, too? For everyone? Because they're homemade here, you know, and they're not bad. You've tried them, János, have you not?"

"Of course," said Bartha. "And you're right, they're not bad. But the noodles also are homemade, and they are better than the dumplings."

"Esther?" Vilmos said. "Do you also prefer the noodles?"

Esther nodded. It made no difference to her. She liked going to restaurants, but not for the food. She liked the eventfulness of a trip to a restaurant. She liked being served; she liked being asked what she wanted. It was still a novelty to her. Her father did not believe in restaurants.

"A waste of good money," he had always said. "I do not understand how such places stay in business."

But mostly, going to a restaurant was interesting now because it was the only place she did go, the only place Bartha ever took her. There was nowhere else to go, nothing else to do.

"Yes," Vilmos murmured, thinking aloud, "it's true that the noodles might be even better...."

Esther tried not to smile. She could not imagine thinking about such a thing long enough to make a choice about it, to have an opinion about it. She wondered if Vilmos meant what he said—if he'd really just rethought the dumplings. Vilmos loved Bartha as much as she did. Certainly he cared as much as she did about pleasing him, or at any rate not *dis*pleasing him.

Clara cleared her throat. She often did, before she spoke—it was her version of a drumroll, to introduce whatever new disagreeable thing she meant to say. "No noodles for me," she said, "and no dumplings either. It's too early in the day for something so heavy. I'll just have a little soup."

"And a glass of wine?" Vilmos said. "You'll have wine with us, to celebrate?"

"No," Clara said. "No wine. If I drink, I'll fall right to sleep."

"Not even a single glass, or half of a glass, to make a toast?"

There was not a hint of irritation in his voice. Esther wondered how he managed it. She could not have done it, could not have remained amiable day after day, year after year, to Clara—who responded to her husband now with a look so empty of expression that if Esther hadn't already been used to it she would have been alarmed.

She had no doubt that Clara hated her (though Vilmos swore she didn't, swore she "only disapproved" of her— "and even that, believe me," he insisted, "just a little bit. She'll get over it in time, I promise you. You only must have patience").

"No wine," Clara said again. "I'll have a glass of water."

"Soup and a glass of water," Vilmos said. He said it thoughtfully, as if he were memorizing a difficult line of poetry. "All right, then." He picked up his menu. "For the rest of us, however…let's see.…"

Esther could not begin to guess what had made him want to marry Clara. She wasn't pretty and she had no sense of humor, she wasn't talented or clever—she wasn't even interesting, the way some plain but smart girls were at school (though Clara was smart enough, Esther supposed; still, she was not quick-witted, which was the attractive part of smartness). She was always angry or dissatisfied—*always*. Esther could not recall a time when she had heard Clara say something kind, or when she had seemed happy—and at twenty-nine she was already every bit as harshly finished-looking as the stout, tired, middle-aged Midwestern women Esther saw each week at Hinky Dinky pushing cartfuls of canned vegetables and cellophane-wrapped meat.

"János, you must choose the wine," Vilmos said, without taking his eyes off his menu. "Unless of course you would prefer some beer. They have Czech beer, you know, in this place."

"I prefer wine, always," Bartha said. He didn't look up from his menu either. This was how he and Vilmos always behaved in restaurants. It mystified Esther, their fascination with these lists of things to eat and drink. They would argue tirelessly about the merits and demerits of a given restaurant, a dish, a method of food preparation. "If Esther also will have wine, let's have a bottle."

"Good. Will you have wine then, Esther?"

She looked from one to the other. Neither of them had looked at her. Each was studying his menu as if he would be tested on its contents later.

"Esther? Will you drink wine?" Bartha said.

She knew she should say, *Yes, I'll have wine*, or else, *No, I don't think so, thank you*. No—she knew that what she *should* say—what Bartha wanted her to say—was yes, she'd have some wine, *of course I will*. But really she could have wine or not have wine, it made no difference to her. And Bartha must know that it made no difference to her—noodles or dumplings, wine or no wine. He must know that she only pretended, for his sake.

A moment passed before he looked up, eyebrows raised—puzzled, not impatient. He wasn't accustomed to having to wait for her to answer him. Whenever he asked her a question, she was grateful, for it wasn't so often that he asked her anything, and no matter what it was— how serious or trivial, or even if she knew it was only rhetorical—she'd reply immediately, sometimes without pausing to think about what she was saying.

But she was thinking now. What she was thinking (she told herself this, told it to herself as if she were telling someone else a story) was that she was angry. This had only just occurred to her, as she considered him while he considered her—his head cocked, his eyebrows raised (as if she were a menu, she thought; as if he were contemplating and discarding possibilities). His eyebrows, like his hair, were perfectly, brilliantly white, and so unruly that he looked, always, as if a ferocious wind had just blown by him.

They looked at each other steadily. He—her *husband*, Esther thought—was still waiting for an answer. She knew she was being stubborn, knew it wasn't reasonable to refuse to answer. But she found—and this was a surprise—that her stubbornness pleased her.

"Take the baby from me, will you? My arms are getting tired."

This was true enough—her arms *were* tired—as she had been holding Alexander since they'd left the office of the absurd little Mr. One Penny. But she expected Bartha to point out that she could not blame him for this, that he had tried to convince her to put the baby in his carriage when they were led to their booth here, that he'd objected in the first place when she'd scooped the sleeping baby up after the ceremony and left him—her *husband*—to push the empty carriage behind her. All he said as he took the baby now, however, was, "Just look how nicely he is sleeping. Too bad he won't sleep so well as this at night, when we are sleeping too."

She forced out a smile. She hated it when he complained, or made a joke, about the baby's nighttime habit of waking and crying for her at two-hour intervals, not falling back to sleep until she'd held him, nursed him, rocked him, sung to him, and then walked him around and around the dark room, sometimes for as long as half an hour. This did not seem so terrible to her. That Alexander needed her attention (*her* attention; Bartha's would not do) so much that this need could awaken him from a sound sleep was rather thrilling to her. She had hinted at this once to Bartha—had mentioned, with a laugh, as if this time she were the one making jokes about it, that she did not find interrupted sleep so great a price to pay for being loved—but she saw from the look he gave her then that this was not a sentiment that he approved of. After that, she felt she had no choice but to feign sympathy with him when he complained about the way the baby slept (or didn't sleep), and she pretended now, smiling and nodding. But when she saw that he had begun to stand up, that he was about to put the baby in his carriage after all, she stopped smiling her false smile and said, sharply, "Please, *hold* him. For five minutes, hold him. Then I'll take him back."

"Esther, you cannot eat while holding him," he said.

She thought of telling him, "And why not? I've done it before, and will again." But did she *want* to argue with Bartha? She considered this. They had never argued. She could not imagine what an argument between them would be like.

Carefully, she said, "When the food comes, I promise you, I'll put him down."

"Fine," he said. "Good." And that was that, the end of it. Still, watching him resettle himself with the baby, she could feel her anger prickling at her as if it were something caught under her skin. *You are being foolish*, she told herself. Foolish and unreasonable. Why angry? Nothing had changed—everything was just the same as always.

So it was, she thought. Exactly.

Everything *was* just the same. She felt as if she had been tricked.

She watched Bartha as he began once again to read his menu. He held Alexander securely, with both hands, but Esther could see that he had already ceased to be aware of anything except the list of choices that lay on the table.

What if she were to snatch the menu away? But this was just the sort of childish thought she most despised herself for having. Somehow, even if she could prevent herself from doing childish things, she could not keep herself from thinking of them. It was as if there were a part of her that was determined to show her (and him? How lucky it was that he couldn't read her mind!) how much of a child she *was*, still. (But she wasn't, she told herself. How could she be, now?)

"Esther, have you come to a decision?"

She blinked at him. "A decision?"

He inclined his head. The waitress, in her costume— multicolored flowers stenciled on her tall white hat and on the square of apron over her short, stiff black skirt—stood beside the table.

"Oh—no." Esther felt herself blush. "No, I'm sorry." She glanced at the menu, but there were too many choices. She couldn't think of any reason to name one of them. "Maybe you could…" she began, but as she spoke, she looked up at him, saw the start of a frown—no, no, this wouldn't do—and she began again, taking a different tack. "Everything looks good. How can I decide?" She paused. "No, I can't. Please, won't you choose for me?"

He smiled. "Of course. I will order for us both then."

She paid no attention to what he chose for her. She set her menu down on the tiled tabletop (the tiles were flowered too, and she wondered if the hats and aprons had been made to order so they'd match the tables, or vice versa; or if everything had been planned from the restaurant's inception) and while he ordered she reflected on how fussy he was, how strict, really, about the *reason* she deferred to him. She knew that if she let him take charge when she wasn't interested in taking charge herself, because the issue at hand bored her or did not seem worth the trouble to her, he would be displeased. But it never failed to delight him when she asked him to take over because she knew he knew better. The distinction, she thought, was almost too subtle (she did not have to come out and *say* that he would make a wiser choice than she would—indeed, she had learned that it was better to imply this than to say it), so that it was easy for her to forget how much it mattered to him and make a mistake, as she nearly had just now. And yet it had mattered to him from the start. He had taken pains to tell her, early on, that he didn't want to make decisions for her, to treat her "like a father treats a child."

"That's all right," she had assured him. "I don't want you to. But there's no chance that I'll confuse you with *my* father. He assumes he knows best always, about everything."

"Yes, precisely," Bartha had said. "I shall not—we shall not—make such an assumption."

But it didn't seem to her so terrible if sometimes he did, especially once they'd left Brooklyn and come here and she had no one but him to depend on. And he did know better about most things. "He's read everything and he's been everywhere," she had told her two closest friends after she had met him for the first time. She'd called Kathleen and Leah one after another, right after her first lesson with him. Just as she had called them after every lesson after that— until she had to stop calling, stop telling them anything.

She had talked about him far too much at first, so that when she had to stop, afraid she would reveal her secret if she spoke of him at all, she was afraid her friends would notice something. It still seemed strange to her that they had not: she had believed that they knew her so well they'd see the change in her without her telling them—and it had confused her when it was clear that they saw nothing, for she had been unable to decide if she were disappointed or relieved.

In the beginning she had talked endlessly about him, about how brilliant he was, how interesting. "Interesting?" Kathleen had said doubtfully. "He's, like, as old as my grandfather"—though he probably wasn't, or not quite, and even if he were, the comparison was nonsensical. Kathleen's grandfather lived with Kathleen and her parents and told them stories no one was interested in, the same stories again and again, and when he wasn't telling stories to Kathleen's family or friends, he was with a bunch of other old men playing pinochle and sitting in the sun on folding chairs, complaining to each other about "the government."

Kathleen and Leah listened politely when Esther told them how many different foreign languages Bartha could speak, or talked about how elegant his manners were, or mentioned famous people he had met—and then they changed the subject without asking any questions, as if gossip about kids in school or the cute new math teacher, or comparing their complaints about their parents, or deciding what to do on Saturday night (the same boring things: a movie at the Oceana, bowling, listening to records at Leah's) were at least as worthy—more worthy—of their serious attention than "this old guy who gives Esther singing lessons" (which was what Kathleen had said when someone at school, overhearing Esther talking as they stood outside the building waiting for the bell to ring one morning, asked who she'd been talking about).

Esther told them how kind Bartha was, how he fed

the stray dogs and the alley cats and even the pigeons in the courtyard of his building—and how gently he spoke to them; she told them how honored she felt by the way he talked to *her*—as if she were his equal, she said, when she obviously wasn't ("Grandfathers always want to talk, though," Kathleen said. "I don't see what's so *honoring* about it"). They claimed to be baffled by how impressed she was by him. It didn't seem to mean anything to them when she told them that Bartha had had the most extraordinary life of anyone she'd ever known or even read or heard about—and when once, long ago, she told them that she'd "fallen absolutely and completely madly in love" with him, even though they didn't take it literally (well, she hadn't meant it literally—not then, not yet), they begged her not to say that. "Not even as a joke," Kathleen said. "It's just much too creepy." And Leah, with a theatrical shudder, said, "He's so *old*, Esther, it's too weird and awful when you think about it."

Neither of them understood anything. They remained unmoved when she said (lowering her voice, thrilled again each time she said this—thrilled each time she thought about it), "But of course you know he was a famous tenor in his time, in Europe."

This he had told her during her first lesson. He had not been bragging, she understood, but letting her know what she should have known already when she came to him that first time with the note of introduction from her music teacher at school. He mentioned it in passing—the way someone else might have said, "Oh yes, I sold vacuum cleaners once, a lot of them. I was pretty good at it." Without arrogance, and yet also without false humility, he spoke of a certain performance, a certain mezzo soprano with whom he had sung then for the first time. He was making a point about Esther's own voice, if she worked hard and did everything he said, if she stopped singing from her chest and from her throat and set aside the "very silly" show tunes she so loved, two of which she had just sung for him, or tried to sing for him—for he had interrupted the first one, saying, "Clambakes? Do not use this lovely voice to sing to me of clambakes!" and the second with a shout ("Corn and Kansas and blueberry pie? And what does a beautiful girl who has spent her entire life in New York City know about corn and Kansas and the making of pies and so on? No, no, no! This is a voice made for singing of tragic love, of longing"). She was flattered, naturally, but so dazzled by what he had just revealed about himself that she couldn't concentrate on being pleased. She was speechless as she watched him move about his studio that afternoon, his hands—small, pale, slim-fingered hands that shot out extravagantly, suddenly, from the cuffs of his suit jacket like little white birds newly freed—making eights and circles in the air as he explained his method, explained what she would have to unlearn to begin her studies with him.

She had never met—had never seen—anyone who was in any way like him. His hair was the longest, wildest hair she'd ever seen on somebody who wasn't young, and much longer than she'd ever seen on any boy or man of any age. The long white curls flopped and swung around his head as he paced, telling her what she must not do anymore and what she must begin *to* do. She saw that he was old, she *knew* that he was old—it was not as if she didn't notice it, or noticed it but didn't "understand" it (which was what Kathleen had said once—"It's like you don't even understand how old he is"—and also what her father had said, later, in a meaner, uglier way she still didn't want to think about, even after so much time had passed). Bartha was old but he was not "an old man," she tried to explain (to Kathleen—not her father; to her father that night she did not try to explain anything once he started yelling at her and pounding his fists on the door frame and the stove and the kitchen table, and she left home that same night, climbing out the window like a thief whose job was done, without having said another word to him).

Bartha didn't look or act or move like an old man—not like the old men she knew, not like Kathleen's grandfather or his friends or the other old men in the neighborhood, the ones who came into her parents' candy store. He was nothing like her own grandfathers—what she could remember of them. Both had died a long time ago. What she remembered was that both had been small, mostly quiet men, though one—Papa Jack, her father's father— had been given to sporadic fits of temper, during which he would yell, either at his wife (Grandma Leni, also long gone now) or at his only son, Esther's father, in a language Esther didn't understand and which her father never spoke although he must have understood, and which she knew was called Ladino. These outbursts sent shock waves through the family but seemed to leave Papa Jack himself unaffected, for within seconds after each of them, he was calm, he was speaking English again, and his voice was gentle, so unscary it was hard to imagine how it could have been so terrifying not even a minute before.

Her other grandfather had been Papa Shimon, who hardly spoke at all, but when he did it was in a mix of three languages—Yiddish, Russian, and English—so that Esther

17

had understood only a third of what he'd said. Not that it mattered, since she could not recall him ever speaking to her, only to her mother or, stiffly, to her father. His wife, Grandma Pesse, Esther had never even known. She had died when Esther's mother was still a child.

Both grandfathers had died before Esther was ten years old, but she remembered that they had both been nearly bald, a few strands of stiff gray hair slicked down flat across their shiny heads, and that both of them had spent all their time in chairs or in recliners—sitting, resting, lying down. That was what old men did.

Bartha didn't sit that first day, her first lesson, for more than a minute at a time. As he talked, he kept on pacing— confidently, grandly: around and around the piano and the chairs and the glass-shaded stand-up lamps behind them, around the little tables topped with stacks of books and papers, around the music stand and the green velvet sofa and Esther herself as she stood, hands clasped (clenched, in fact—and even so they trembled) in the center of the room. If he sat, briefly, on one of the upholstered chairs or on the piano bench, it was only because he had snatched a book from one of the piles and wanted to find a particular piece of music, to demonstrate a point—but then he was on his feet again, moving again.

More than two years had passed since that day, the day he had become her teacher, and for months now (three more months and it would be a year!) he had not *been* her teacher—and yet even after all these months that they had lived together, sometimes she would catch herself still thinking of him in that way. It happened when she came upon him unexpectedly: if she saw him on the street when she was out with Alexander and he had decided to come home a little early, or if she returned from a walk with the baby and found him already there, drinking a cup of tea and studying *The New York Times*. She would not think *János is home*, as it seemed to her she should by now. She would think *Here he is, the teacher*.

She never spoke of this to him, since she could not be sure how he would react. She never liked to tell him things if she could not prepare for his response first. What she told herself was that a lapse like this was natural, that after all he'd been her teacher for a long time before he had become her lover—and even then he had not ceased to be her teacher, for her twice-weekly lessons with him had continued right up to the day before they had had to run away together. She had not yet had the opportunity to grow accustomed to the change in their relations—that was what she told herself, and sometimes it eased her mind. But at other times it seemed to her that there had *been* no change in their relations—that, but for their lovemaking itself (on the green velvet sofa, folded out into a bed, after her lesson each Tuesday and Friday afternoon), nothing had changed between her first lesson and her last.

And in the months since? What had really changed, besides the plain fact that they now lived together? He continued to treat her just as he had when she had been his student, formally (though pleasantly, and almost always kindly), tolerantly (and some days *only* tolerantly, which both then and now disheartened and unsettled her), and sometimes with pride (then, when she had sung particularly well; now, when she behaved the way he wished her to—graciously, unchildishly, "as befits a gentlewoman." *Yentlevoman*, he would say).

The form of their relationship had certainly changed,

she thought. But had its contents?

This was such a coolly grown-up question that for an instant she was pleased, and praised herself for thinking of it. And all at once she was thinking of her English teacher, Mr. Inemer—her favorite teacher, the best one she'd had at Lincoln. He was the one who had taught her, junior year, to think about form and content—and now, as if it had been only last week that she'd sat in his classroom, she could hear Mr. Inemer saying *sound, direction, rhythm, predetermined limitations, technique, imagery, devices.* Wouldn't he be pleased, and proud of her?

But what could she be thinking of? This was her *life*, not a poem. And yet—*form, meaning structure, shape*—she could not only hear him, she could see him perched on the front edge of his desk, counting off each term on his fingers, just as he always did. *What do I mean by content? Anybody? Subject matter, theme, motif. Can anybody tell me what motif might be? Esther? I'm willing to bet that you can.*

And she could, too. She always could.

But this wasn't poetry or art or music, this was just her life, and Room 325—last row, first seat—was thirteen hundred miles away. Mr. Inemer was at this very minute saying the same things he'd said to her class to a group of kids she probably wouldn't even recognize.

And she was here, in the Bohemian Café, beside her husband and her son. Of course things had changed—just look at how they'd changed. It was her wedding day, and she was no one's student anymore.

Tears filled her eyes. Now? she thought. *Now* she was crying? She had been dry-eyed throughout the ceremony, though she had imagined she would cry, and she had even wondered whether or not she would hide her tears from

Bartha. She stole a sidelong glance at him but he was pondering the wine list, not looking at her. When he spoke her name—still not looking at her—she started at the sound. Before he could say anything else, she said, sharply, "I'm *fine*."

She held her tears back, blinking, as he turned to her. He looked at her quizzically but said only, "So, will you drink a little something? I have found a good wine." He took one hand off the baby, briefly setting it atop hers where it lay on the tiled tabletop before returning it to its place beneath Alexander's head. "Or…here is another which is very good." He closed his eyes, deliberating. "Perhaps we might try both."

"Both, yes!" Vilmos said. He slapped his menu down and rubbed his hands together like a character in a novel. "Two bottles of wine, why not?" And to the waitress, he said, "At this table we are celebrating!"

"The waitress isn't interested," said Clara. "Let her do her job."

"Did you hear this, Alexander?" Vilmos said, and Esther thought he was about to complain about his wife for once, even if only to the sleeping baby, but he said, "See, we are ordering some good wine so that we may drink a toast to your health. Your family is all around you, little one." He half stood and leaned over the table so that he could look down at the baby in his cousin's lap. "Still sleeping? Alexander, you are missing the whole party! Time to wake up, darling boy."

He said it quietly, certainly not loudly enough to wake the baby, but still Esther was about to protest, to warn him *not* to wake the baby, when, as if he'd heard and understood, Alexander did wake up—opening his eyes, yawning and smiling, reaching out with one hand toward Esther—and then suddenly he was asleep again, exhaling a great sigh, before Esther had had the chance to take him out of Bartha's lap. His right hand had fallen palm-up on his forehead. "Look at him," Vilmos said. "I think he is saying to us, 'All of this happiness is making me very tired. Please go ahead and have the party without me.' He is a very thoughtful baby, I think."

"Or else he's just bored," said Clara.

"Bored? This baby? Never!" Vilmos said. "The brilliant are never bored, and our Alexander is a brilliant baby."

"Oh, indeed," said Bartha, laughing. "The most brilliant of babies."

"Don't joke," Esther heard herself say, though she hadn't meant to speak. "He *is*," she told Vilmos, who as he sat back down reached for her hand.

"Of course he is, darling."

Bartha wasn't listening. He was busy with the waitress—telling her which wines he'd chosen, and which one of them to bring out first. As soon as he finished, as the waitress turned to leave, Vilmos called to her, "Excuse me, miss, but have you ever in your life seen such a baby? Tell the truth."

"A beautiful baby," said the waitress, without turning.

"Yes, that's right," Vilmos said. "A beautiful *and* brilliant baby. An excellent baby! What more could one hope for? My own little cousin! My own—oh, now you must tell me, Clara"—he winked at Esther—"tell me if I have this right. My own first cousin…three times removed?"

"No," Clara said. "Are you making a joke?"

"A joke? Naturally not. I am only—"

"I don't understand why this is so hard to remember."

"I don't understand either," Vilmos said sadly, "yet somehow I cannot." He took his wife's hand now and at the same time winked again at Esther. "Tell me once more, Clara, please."

"Only once more," Clara said, "and that's all." To Esther she said, "I've been through this with him half a dozen times. He just can't keep it in his head." She shrugged, and Esther shrugged too, looking down at Clara and Vilmos's linked hands. It always came as a surprise when Clara spoke to her. "Listen closely this time," Clara said. Then, in a singsong: "You and János are first cousins twice removed. Your grandfather was János's first cousin. Your great-grandfather, József, and János's father, Béla—"

"I remember him very well, my cousin László," Bartha interrupted her. "We were good friends, very close. But that was long ago. I saw him last before the war, in Budapest. His father, my Uncle József—you have an excellent memory for names, Clara, it is remarkable—he was quite something. Such a temper! László used to come—"

"—were *brothers*," Clara cut in, raising her voice, "and therefore you are twice removed as a first cousin to János, because you are two generations removed from his first cousin. But Alexander and your father are of the same generation"—here she cast a meaningful, angry-looking smile at all of them—"which means that they are second cousins, and *you*"—once more she flashed that chilly smile like a triumphant scowl—"are thus a second cousin once removed from Alexander."

Vilmos slapped his forehead. "Therefore? Thus? To me it's not so simple, not so obvious." He sighed. "János is right. You are remarkable."

"Don't be silly," Clara said. "It isn't difficult at all. It

23

follows simple rules."

"Yes, for a bookkeeper, it's simple. But for me...." Vilmos shook his head. "Esther, tell me. What do you think?" But before she could respond—*I'm no bookkeeper either*, she was going to say (and it was just as well she didn't have the opportunity, for Clara hated being called a bookkeeper, even though there was no other word for what she *was* in the insurance office where she worked part-time: she kept the accounts, and *thus*, Esther thought, with a smile she hoped nobody saw, she was a bookkeeper)— Vilmos said, "All right now, you must tell me once again. Just once more, and I promise I will never ask again."

"I don't think you really listen when I tell you," Clara said. "I don't know why I tell you anything, I really don't." And yet, surprising Esther, she began again: "József and Béla," she said, "were two brothers, out of five. The other three...."

Bored, Esther stopped listening. (It occurred to her to wonder if Vilmos was right: if she were brilliant, would she *not* be bored?) But she was not only bored, she was insulted, too, she recognized belatedly, by the way Clara had spoken of Vilmos's father and the baby as being of "the same generation." Between Alexander and Vilmos's father, another József—whom Esther had never met, and who lived in Fresno, California, the other city Bartha had considered settling them in when they'd first discussed the possibility of leaving Brooklyn—there was a good half century.

Esther didn't doubt that Clara had *meant* to insult her— to remind her of the "inappropriateness" of the match between her and Bartha. She had heard Clara use that word, speaking privately to Vilmos, not long after they had first arrived in Omaha. She hadn't meant to eavesdrop, but she'd heard a lot of things she wasn't meant to hear, living with Vilmos and Clara. Of course, she should not have been surprised by anything Clara had said to Vilmos (it had not been so unlike what Esther's father had said that last night in Brooklyn—although her father's language had not been coldly polite, like Clara's, but vicious and hateful). She should not have been surprised, but still she was. Bartha had told her they would be welcome here. He had implied that she and Clara would be friends, *good* friends, before long.

Clara was droning on still: first removed, twice removed, third cousins, grandfathers, great-uncles, even a stepbrother. Vilmos interrupted her repeatedly, encouraging her to name *all* the brothers if she mentioned one. Evidently Vilmos had taught Clara the names of all his relatives in Hungary, most of them long dead, and now he was showing off her memory to Bartha (who kept joining in, irrelevantly, interrupting both of them to reminisce about László and László's younger brother—yet another József—or his favorite uncle, Oszkár, or Oszkár's beloved only son, Károly). *Uncles, nephews, fathers, brothers.* Why were there no women in this recitation? Hadn't every one of these nephews and great-grandfathers had a mother?

She was angry again. It was astonishing to her as she paused to consider—to *appreciate*—how angry she was, for there had been so many times she had told herself she should be angry with Bartha and hadn't been. When he was short with her, when he spoke to her as if she were a small child, when he seemed to dismiss her—as if what she'd said was too foolish or trivial for him to think of taking seriously—or when he berated her for carrying the baby around "all day long" ("Put him down," he would say, "please, for half an hour, even. This cannot be good for him, to be held in your arms for every minute") or when he ignored her, lost in his own thoughts, so that she'd ask a question and he wouldn't even look at her, much less give her an answer. At such times she would feel sorry for herself, but she would not be angry—although she would often think about how someone else would certainly be angry. She would think of Leah and Kathleen, to whom she hadn't spoken in so long now, who would not have stood for being scolded, or for being lectured the way Bartha lectured her, or for being treated as if they could not be seen or heard—and inevitably she would think then of her mother, too, who would not have gotten angry but would have become depressed instead (infuriating Esther, who had always been able to see for herself when her mother should have become angry and had not). She would tell herself she had good reason to be angry, but it didn't matter because *angry* wasn't what she felt—she only felt unhappy. And because she'd started thinking of her mother, and of Leah and Kathleen, by then she would be feeling lonely, too. She was too sad and lonely to be angry. That was how it always seemed to her.

And so instead of being angry as she knew she should be, she would start to cry. And when she did, she would sometimes make an effort to keep this hidden from Bartha, while at other times she would make sure he saw—depending on her mood (what she thought of as *mood:* depending on whether or not she wanted him to ask her what was wrong, which in its turn depended both on whether or not she wanted to have to answer him, and whether or not she thought it would make her feel worse if he saw her crying and then didn't ask her what was wrong). If she wanted to be left alone to cry, she would lie down with the baby on the bed—Vilmos and Clara's fold-out sofa, which since Alexander's birth she had stopped bothering to close up in the morning—and, holding him tightly to her chest, his back to her, curl herself all around him, her knees almost to her forehead so that she came close to making a full circle with her body around his, and then silently she would begin to plan a letter to her family, which she would write hours later, after Bartha and the baby were asleep. Just thinking about what she would write made her feel better—although she had learned that if she didn't actually write the letter in the first hours after midnight before Alexander woke up crying for her, the effects of having planned it would wear off by morning. Like a magic spell, she thought, although she couldn't think of any fairy tales that had to do with writing.

Sitting at the little table Vilmos had moved down into the basement for them, the desk lamp she'd bought at a garage sale (a spindly red Tensor lamp just like the one she'd left behind at home) making a tiny spotlight for the piece of paper and her moving hand, she'd write page after page on stationery she kept hidden in the bottom of the diaper bag, stopping only when she had run out of things to say. Then she'd hide the letter in her purse, and in the morning, when she took her first walk of the day with Alexander, she would mail it.

She knew that no one would answer. None of the letters she had written had been answered, and while she had never counted them, she guessed that by now there had been at least ten, maybe fifteen of them. As far as she knew, nobody was even reading her letters—but as they were not returned to her unopened, someone *might* be (she thought *someone*—she couldn't, even as she wrote them, bring herself to think *Daddy, Mama, Sylvia)*, so it was not impossible that someone, sometime, would write back. *Who, though?* she wondered every time she caught herself thinking this way. Her father? Not a chance. Her mother? She'd have to defy her father, and it was impossible for Esther to believe she would do that. And Sylvia was only twelve—not even twelve yet when Esther had left—and they had never really liked each other in the first place. Chances were that Sylvia would not have answered letters from her even if she'd left home in a normal way. Chances were, anyway, that her parents didn't let Sylvia see the letters, even though they were addressed to The Savarises, and Esther headed every one of them *Dear Family*.

Either someone opened them and read them and then didn't answer (decided yet again that there would be no answer), or they were discarded each time without being opened. Or placed in a drawer, just as they were? In books she had read, this sometimes happened, but because she could not picture herself doing this, she couldn't picture anyone she knew doing this either. She could, however, easily—too easily—picture her father extracting an envelope he recognized as coming from her, separating it from the small pile of bills and advertisements, that week's *TV Guide*, and perhaps a more welcome letter from somebody else, and holding it between two fingers as he carried it out to the trash can in the alley.

Did it matter if nobody read them? She asked herself this sometimes, because when she wrote, she never thought about anyone reading what she'd written. When she was thinking of what she would say, she never asked herself, *What will they make of this?* She concentrated only on what she was saying—as if the letters weren't, in fact, being written to anyone—and she hadn't been surprised or even very disappointed when no one wrote back.

She couldn't say why she had written that first letter. She didn't know how it had happened. In her memory, the pen was in her hand already, she was sitting at the table, it was just past midnight after the long day that was supposed to have been her due date. How or why it had occurred to her to write, or what she'd imagined the result of it would be, she didn't know. As for why she had kept on after the first one—how could she account for that? It was a good thing, she had often thought, that there was nobody to whom she was obliged to give an explanation. She could not have said that she was comforted or calmed by her letter-writing (on the contrary, she would sometimes become so agitated as she wrote that the pen shook in her hand and she would have to stop for a while). The letters didn't make her feel less lonely or less full of pity for herself—they didn't make her feel less of anything bad that she was feeling. But somehow, although her writing didn't lessen her unhappiness, it loosened it from her. All it took was for her to start writing a new letter in her mind, and the bad feelings that had seemed so settled in her would begin to shift and stir, as if they were becoming restless, and then bit by bit, as she went on, she'd feel them pulling loose—coming unstuck. As she lay coiled around the baby, thinking and rethinking what she meant to say this time and how she would say it, it was as if she *saw* her own unhappiness: it hovered everywhere around her, near enough to touch. It wasn't until later, when she sat down at her little table with her stationery and her pen, that the bad feelings would begin at last to drift away—not out of sight but far enough away so that while she was still aware of them she couldn't have reached out for them if she had wanted to.

By morning they'd be gone. She would wake up feeling light, unbound, unburdened—almost weightless. Free. She would sing to Alexander and dance him around the room. *"All I want is a room somewhere,"* she'd sing, twirling until she was dizzy and the baby had begun to laugh. Sometimes she'd catch Bartha looking at her strangely. "What?" she'd say, as if she really couldn't guess what puzzled him, but she would blush, and flutter over to him for an instant, long enough to kiss his cheek or touch his hand, then fly away again before he could reach out for her or look at her too closely—as if he could see what she'd been doing while he was asleep. He would shake his head and mutter, "Moods, such moods, who has the strength for this?" and, "But what a terrible song this is which you are singing." But that was as much as he ever said. He never asked her any questions, and Esther supposed that he was pleased enough, or simply relieved enough, to see her happy once again so that he wasn't troubled by, or even interested in, how this new mood might have come to pass.

Like every other morning, after breakfast at the little table (tea and toast and jam for him, and for her—"to keep up your strength," he said each time she pleaded with him not to bother, she was not that hungry—oatmeal and a glass of milk as well), he kissed her and Alexander and left for his studio. If he'd asked, she told herself once he was gone, she would have told him. That he hadn't asked (that it seemed he would never ask) left her feeling grateful and sad at the same time. But only for the first few minutes after he had left. Then, once those few minutes passed, she would pick up the baby and resume her singing and her dancing. *"We got sunlight on the sand,"* she'd sing to Alexander. *"We got moonlight on the sea."* She'd spin him so fast he would shriek with pleasure.

"Ah, exactly what we are in need of right now," Vilmos said, confusing Esther. Then she saw the waitress in her dirndl skirt and peasant blouse proffering a bottle of wine for Bartha's inspection. "Yes, good," Bartha said, and as the waitress poured, Vilmos announced that he wanted to make a toast. "To you, Esther my dear," Vilmos said. "To your health and happiness and a long life that's full of love." Esther blushed.

"Clara, lift your water glass, please," he said. "Esther—you, too, lift your wine glass. Just this once it's all right." She picked up her glass and looked at Bartha—he was the one who had taught her that one mustn't drink a toast to oneself—but he smiled and gave her a slight nod as he held up one finger *(just this once, yes)*, so she brought the glass to her lips and in three long swallows she drank the contents of it.

"Slowly, Esther, slowly," Bartha said. But Vilmos was laughing and already reaching for the bottle to refill her glass. She waited for Bartha to tell Vilmos not to, but he didn't.

"And now let us drink to Alexander," Vilmos said. "To *his* health and happiness and long life."

Esther took a single swallow this time, with one eye on Bartha, who nodded before he took his own sip of wine.

Vilmos held his glass aloft again. "To János," he said.

"Who has had already a long life," said Bartha.

Vilmos smiled. "To his health and happiness, and to

the many more years he has still to come."

They smiled at each other fondly. Esther took another, longer swallow of her wine.

"Let us drink to you now, Vilmos," Bartha said. "Esther and I both are very grateful for all you have done for us. You have been a good friend."

"Let us drink to friendship, then," said Vilmos.

Esther drank to friendship, draining her glass. She felt her eyes fill as she set down the empty glass. Again her tears surprised her. No tears for her wedding, but she was crying now over—what? Lost friendship? When she had stopped missing Leah and Kathleen even before she had left home? It had been so long since she'd felt free to talk to them that by the time she'd left she had been almost glad she wouldn't have to see them anymore. She'd grown so used to *pretending* with them, to hiding the truest things about herself, behaving as if she cared about things she had no interest in, things she could not believe she had ever been interested in. By the time she left, there was no real friendship to lose. She never even thought of writing to them the way she wrote to her family. What would she say? She had never told them she was pregnant. She had never told them she and Bartha had begun a romance. How could she have told them? (Even now, after so much had happened, she couldn't think of how to tell them that, that first essential fact.) It was not her friends these tears were for, she thought, so much as it was the idea of friends.

It was true that Vilmos had been good to them. He *had* been a good friend to her and Bartha both, exactly as Bartha had said. But this was a different sort of friendship than what she thought of as friendship. In its way it took much more for granted. She never felt she had to worry about whether Vilmos would "still" like her, and she could not imagine Vilmos feeling otherwise himself—but it was not a *talking* friendship. And that was what she missed, really. Not friendship so much as conversation. She missed the conversations she'd had every day when she had lived at home, conversations not just with her closest friends but with the other people she had known at school, people she had never thought of then as friends but wondered about now. The girl—Alice? Alicia?—who had sat next to her in homeroom last year, whom she'd never talked to, never even saw, except for that brief period each day, when they had had hurried, intense conversations in a whisper, mainly about parents—and mainly Alicia's (Alice's? or was it Alison's?), who were probably about to get divorced. The girl in her gym class junior year who always hid with her, both of them shivering in their gym bloomers, in the stairwell behind the gymnasium when the class played dodgeball—she could not remember *what* they'd talked about, and it astonished her now that they had talked so often, for as long as half an hour each time. Oh, and a soft-spoken, skinny, small boy named Ramon whom she'd met her first week, and his, of high school, when they'd both auditioned for the Drama Society, and who used to talk to her so seriously, if only for ten or fifteen minutes, every week before the Drama meeting started, about art and music, poetry, the theater, love and death and even heaven, which he wanted to persuade her to believe in.

She even missed the conversations she'd had with the people in the candy store, where she helped out behind the counter most days after school and all her after-school activities, including her singing lessons and what came after that. People stopped in at the store for cigarettes or the

33

Post or a cup of coffee and started talking about anything: their own private troubles or an idea they'd just had about something—God or baseball or politics or science—or a funny thing, or something terrible, that had happened to them (a long time ago or yesterday or a "just this minute, just before I came in here today"). And they would always say, after a while, "So what do you think? What do you make of that?"

Until she had left home, she'd never noticed how much of her time, her life, was spent in conversation. She would never have imagined that she might look back someday and marvel over it, or think with longing (think at all!) about the people in her neighborhood who dropped in at her parents' store each day. Certainly she'd never thought of them—the "regulars"—as friends. She had known them her whole life: she'd been working in the store in exchange for her allowance since she'd started seventh grade—and before that, all through grade school, she'd sat at the counter doing homework every afternoon, nursing an egg cream or a cherry lime rickey for hours, eavesdropping on the teenagers who gathered there and hoping one of them would speak to her. The teenagers—fourteen- and fifteen-year-olds!—she had spied on and admired so much had grown up and with hardly an exception stayed around the neighborhood (some had gotten married right away and moved into their own apartments, some had gone to Brooklyn College, and some had commuted up to Hunter or to City; two or three had left for upstate colleges and then returned once they had graduated) and then joined the ranks of "regulars," chatting for a while with Esther after she had counted out their change. There was almost no one who came in whom Esther didn't know, by sight if not by name, and yet if she had been asked, back then, about someone who'd come into the store, she would have said, "He's just somebody from the neighborhood."

But all of those somebodies from the neighborhood, all those familiar almost-strangers, had *talked* to her. No one talked to her now, not that way. Not that way, and not the way the girl whose name had been something like Alice had talked to her or the way Ramon had talked to her. Who would ever talk to her that way, in any of those ways, again?

She had not expected—had not even hoped, she told herself—that she would ever find friends like Kathleen and Leah again, that she would ever talk to anyone as she had talked to them, *with* them, since the second grade or even earlier. She'd known them both since the year they were born. She could not remember when they had begun to talk so earnestly and urgently to one another for hours every day. They talked on the way to school, at lunch, on the way home, and on warm nights on Kathleen's stoop until her mother sent them home and told Kathleen to go to bed. On cold or rainy nights they took turns talking on the phone—Esther called Kathleen, Kathleen called Leah, and Leah called Esther.

But that had changed, Esther had to remind herself, before she had left home. She still didn't know if she had started making up excuses to avoid them out of fear she'd give away her secret if they talked, or if she had begun avoiding them *because* they hadn't guessed she had a secret from them and guessed what the secret was—or if they had been avoiding her because she had become so secretive and strange (what was the point of talking to her anymore, they might have thought, when everything she said was dull and cautious?).

At first she hadn't even missed talking to them. Their conversations had changed so much that there was nothing much to miss. Besides, she'd had Bartha to talk to then—though that was a different kind of talking, she saw now. She hadn't noticed at the time, during their early days together, that it wasn't really conversation they were having. He had told her stories, and she'd listened—she had loved to listen to his stories, and she'd heard some of them so many times she had learned them by heart, down to the particulars of dialogue. But it had been a long time now since he had told her any stories—it had been a long time since they'd talked at all beyond the pleasantries they exchanged without fail each day. *Good morning,* they said, and *How did you sleep?* And later on, *Good evening. How was your day?* And, at last, *Good night, sleep well.* He might, at dinner, speak of something he had read in that day's newspaper or mention a new student—he had started giving lessons again—or she might tell him something Alexander had done in his absence (managed to roll over, closed his hand around a rattle, uttered a new sound). As for *talk*, real talk, about ideas or feelings, there was none, not ever. Not with Bartha, not with anyone.

There had been a few occasions when she had tried, early on, to talk to Vilmos. But he'd looked at her as if she had just spoken in another language—a third language, neither his own nor the second one he'd learned as an adult. He looked so bewildered it seemed hard-hearted of her to persevere, and so she did not. But she still wondered over it, wondered sometimes if Vilmos and Clara talked when they were by themselves—if Vilmos simply couldn't talk to *her*, or if conversation, any conversation, seemed to him to be conducted in that other language he had never thought to learn.

With Clara, of course, Esther couldn't talk at all. How could you talk to someone who disliked you so? How wrong Bartha had been about her! Imagine them as friends! And yet still, sometimes, Esther would find herself thinking that if only Clara had not been determined to dislike her from the start, they might have become friendly if not truly friends. They might have shopped together, taken walks around the neighborhood or sat down for a Coke together, chatted—chatted, at least, even if they couldn't really talk—even if Clara would never understand her in the way that Leah and Kathleen had (in the way Esther had thought they had, she reminded herself). And maybe that would have been better than the nothing she had now.

There were limits to understanding, anyway, as she had already learned. If Leah and Kathleen hadn't understood her—hadn't known her, really, even with all of that talk between them—who would? Perhaps she was better off not talking, for this way she wouldn't, couldn't, be fooled into thinking she was understood. Perhaps she would never talk again! Perhaps she'd take a vow of silence.

It dawned on her then that she was getting drunk. It wasn't altogether a familiar feeling, although she had been drunk four times that she could name. Bartha had introduced her to wine shortly after they had become lovers (often, right after her lesson, they would drink some wine together before opening the velvet couch that folded out into a bed) and while he was careful not to let her drink too much, he didn't seem to know how little it took for her to get drunk.

She noticed that her glass was full—Vilmos must have refilled it—and now she saw the second bottle on the table. The waitress had already come and gone without her noticing. Vilmos had raised his glass again. "Just one more toast," he said. "The most important one. To Esther and János—to their marriage, to their love."

She picked up her glass and drained it quickly. Then she waited for Bartha to scold her. It was time for him to tell her that she'd had enough to drink, that it wasn't good either for her or for the baby for her to drink too much wine.

But he didn't say anything, and as she watched him for a moment, sipping his own wine and keeping silent, she saw that he wasn't going to. That he could surprise her was itself surprising. It was disagreeable—and yet didn't it confirm what she had just been thinking? That no one knew anyone, that we fooled ourselves into thinking we were truly known, fooled ourselves into thinking we truly knew others, even the people we loved. This was a reminder that one must be vigilant. It was too easy to be fooled.

It was too easy to be fooled in ways both large and small.

"More wine?" Vilmos said. He refilled her glass before she had a chance to answer. "One last toast. Just one, all right?" He spilled a little wine as he lifted his glass this time, and Esther realized that he must be getting drunk too—none of them had eaten yet today. "Let us drink to passion," he said. "To true, beautiful, life-altering, great passion."

Esther took a sip of wine. *To passion.* She peeked at Bartha, whose expression hadn't changed. Vilmos was definitely drunk. But drunk or not, this must be how he saw them, her and Bartha—as two people caught up in a passion. Was it true? she asked herself. Was that what had happened to them?

"When I first set eyes upon my wife, I knew—I could see it for myself already, at that instant. She had changed my life forever." Vilmos reached for Clara's hand and clasped it. "And now, after seven years, perhaps you wonder how I feel?" He addressed himself to Esther. "Yes? You want to know? Well, I will tell you." He removed his hand from Clara's and slapped it to his chest. "I feel just the same!"

Esther stared at him. Vilmos and Clara! She couldn't tell if he was serious. She couldn't tell if Clara took him seriously either. But why shouldn't he be serious? Why shouldn't he feel what he said he felt?

A strange thought came to her. Perhaps the trouble between friends was not a lack of understanding—perhaps it was not a question of one person fooling himself about how well he knew someone else, or of fooling oneself about how well one was known, so much as it was the inability to *be* anybody else. For what if Leah and Kathleen had considered the idea that for the first time in her life Esther might have a secret from them? They could not have guessed the truth—how could they have?—when she had done something, felt something, neither of them would have done or could have felt. What had happened between her and Bartha was, for them (she knew—she didn't have to hear it from them, she had heard enough from them *before* anything happened), unimaginable.

She had had the right idea, then, she thought. No one *could* know anyone, not really. There was always the chance that someone you thought you understood completely would do something that you could not understand— something that you could not picture yourself doing. *And what of finding* yourself *doing something unimaginable, something that you surely hadn't ever pictured yourself doing?*

She chased this thought away as if somebody else had asked the question of her, interrupting her. *Please, let me be, I'm talking about something else now.* Why, just think of Vilmos—whom she'd never even thought she knew so well, whom she never would have said she "understood." And yet how he had surprised her! And even though she had just heard him, with her own ears, declare how he felt about his wife, didn't she still doubt that what he'd said was true? But why should Vilmos not be in love with his wife? Because *she* found her so unlovable? Yes, that was why. And this just proved her point, she thought. She could not even pretend she understood him.

She had begun to cry—she felt tears sliding down her cheeks. "Too much wine, Esther," Bartha said. She set her wineglass down, too hard, too quickly. Bartha had to reach for it and right it before it could break or any wine spilled out. "Just wait a bit," he said. "When the food comes you may want then to drink a little more. For now, I think perhaps you've had enough." She nodded yes, and looked away. The tears were still slipping down. She couldn't understand why she was crying.

She felt Bartha's hand on her neck, under the thick, loose knot of hair that she'd twisted and pinned into place for this occasion—it was the way her mother always wore her own long hair on special days, and she had thought it would make her look festive as well as more like a wife (she wasn't certain it had worked—she hadn't been able to find a hand mirror this morning so that she could check the back of her head in the bathroom mirror).

Bartha stroked her neck. He touched the nest of hair, tentatively, and then he stroked her neck again. He didn't say anything. He hadn't said anything this morning when she'd emerged from the bathroom and spun around for him, although he must have noticed that her hair was different, since she always wore it loose—she never even put it in a ponytail, or braided it. With two fingers now he stroked her hair beneath the bun, where it pulled upward from her neck; with his whole hand he stroked the sides, above and underneath her ears. She remembered how he had stroked her hair and neck after he had made love to her for the first time. She had been crying then—she had not been able to stop crying for a long time. He had guessed that she was crying because she was sorry, that she was ashamed of what she had done, and when she swore she was not—"I don't care," she told him, "I don't care about that, about *shame*"—he asked if he had "hurt" her, if that was what was wrong, and when she shook her head, he gave up, he stopped asking. He stroked her hair and waited silently for her to finish.

She wished he would be silent now, but he had started murmuring, "All right? Yes? Better?" She didn't answer him. She was thinking of that afternoon when he had first made love to her. She could remember everything about it, still—every little thing: the way he had leaned over in the middle of a lesson—they were sitting alongside each other on the piano bench—and kissed her, holding her head in both of his hands as carefully as if it were one of the fragile things he kept around the studio perched dangerously on the cluttered tabletops, the thin colored glass bowls and the crystal vases she had never seen with flowers in them. The kiss lasted a long time, just like kisses in the movies, and she remembered telling herself that this was exactly what she had imagined kissing would be like. When finally she noticed that his lips were not quite closed, she opened her own mouth, just a little, just like his, and as she did she told herself, *Now everything changes*—and all the while that he was kissing her (for after that first kiss, he kissed her again, and then again) and stroking her arms, and after a time standing up and drawing her up too, and taking her hand and leading her to the green velvet sofa (which she learned only later—the next time—converted to a bed), she kept thinking, *Now I am no longer myself, I am someone else—I am* becoming *someone else.* And while he undressed her, then undressed himself, she thought, *Soon—soon I will no longer be myself.* She wasn't afraid. She wasn't even nervous. She assumed that she would feel some pain but she was not afraid of that—it seemed so small a toll for a new self, a whole new life—but she did not, or she did not especially, feel any pain; she was only uncomfortable, and only for a little while; and then it was over. She lay in his arms and waited, but she felt no different—she felt nothing much at all. It was then that she began to cry.

She wasn't crying now, not anymore, but Bartha was still murmuring, still petting her. He had one hand on Alexander and one hand on her. On his wife. *Wife,* she thought. *Wife! Wife and husband. Marriage.* Magic words—and here she sat again (again? *still!*) waiting for a transformation. Always waiting, she reflected. Always disappointed. Always thinking, *That's all? But how can that be?* When she first began her love affair with Bartha; when she found out she was pregnant; when she told her parents—and her father for the first time slapped her, and said things she couldn't bear to think of even now, and ended by saying that he never wanted to see her again, then burst into tears, which surprised and pained her far more than the slap had; when she left home for good that same night after everyone had gone to sleep, taking just one small suitcase, leaving most of what was hers behind—she had imagined, each time, that she was poised on the brink of some momentous change. And each time there had *been* momentous change—but not within her. Always, she felt that whatever happened hadn't *worked*, that her experience of what had happened—her experience of the experience—was smaller than it was supposed to be. Even during her first months in Omaha, lonely and restless (*fidgety*, her mother would have said), even when she felt the baby's own first restless movements (and caught herself thinking *fidgety*) inside her—even during childbirth, even when she first saw Alexander—what she felt was never what it seemed to her she should have felt. It was insufficient. It was never as momentous as she had imagined it would be, never momentous enough.

And you'd think, she told herself, that by now she would be used to this. She should be used to disappointment. Yet here she was again. *Still.* She'd convinced herself that this time, this great change, would be sufficient finally to change *her.* She had tricked herself—had tricked herself again— for, married or not married, she was still herself, the same person she had been this morning. She would always be the person she had been this morning—the same person she'd been yesterday, last month, last year.

Always, she thought. Now and ever after. *Forever.*

How was it that she'd never understood this before?

She seized Bartha's wrist. "Please," she said, lifting his hand from her neck. And then she added, politely, "Thank you."

He looked at her curiously.

"I'm all right. Really, I am."

It took him a minute to make up his mind not to say anything. Then he gave a little shrug and used the hand she'd freed to cup the baby's head again.

"No," she heard herself say. "Please—I want to hold him now." She held out her arms.

"Now? The food will be here in a moment."

"When it comes, I know, you'll put him in his carriage. I don't want him in his carriage." She was surprising herself. Her voice rose. "It's not fair. This is his celebration too."

"Of course it is," Bartha said. "But he can celebrate with us equally well from inside his carriage. And you cannot eat while holding him."

"I can eat with one hand just as well as you can drink with one hand."

There was silence then, and as she waited for him to say something she wondered if he might allow himself for once to argue with her. But when he spoke, it was only to say, "Fine. As you like."

As soon as she had Alexander in her arms she regretted that she had given him up at all. It was too easy to take for granted how much better she felt holding him, too easy to forget, once she'd been holding him for a long time, that she was always better off with him in her arms than without (and then, when she had him back again, and she remembered, she would ask herself why it was necessary, ever, for him to be anywhere *but* in her arms). She slipped one outstretched finger underneath the half curled fingers of his right hand, poised as if to play a miniature piano. Lifting the hand, she kissed it—kissed it first below the ridge of tiny knuckles, then turned it around, her index finger and her thumb making a circle (the smallest of bracelets, and yet still too loose for him) around his wrist, and kissed the open palm. His fingers curled reflexively into a fist, closed tight, and Esther kissed that too, then laughed quietly as it sprung open, like a locked box in a fairy tale.

She bent her head to kiss his cheek and then his forehead. She might wake him, she knew, but she told herself that he had slept so long already, it would probably be better if he did wake up, or else he wouldn't sleep at all tonight. She picked up his hand again and kissed each dangling finger, and when she was through she started over, at the thumb, and kept on kissing fingers until he began to blink and stretch. She could feel the milk already leaking from her as she watched him. Now came the little sounds he always made before he fully woke: desperate sounds, half gasps, half moans, as if he were in pain, or terrified—and maybe he *was*; maybe for him each waking moment was like being born, for how would he know how to tell the difference between not born yet and sleeping?

When he understood that he had woken up, she knew, he would begin to cry. In outrage? That was how it sounded. Or was it not fury but still greater fear—or fear confirmed? Or, as Bartha had once speculated, was it grief? "He cries so bitterly," Bartha had marveled in the first days of the baby's life, "you would think the world were coming to an end."

She intercepted him, this time, before the crying started—before, she hoped, the others even noticed that he was awake. She untucked her blouse from her skirt and whispered, "All right, it's all right, I promise you, I do," while she undid the last two buttons and drew him in toward her. No one was paying attention. They were all talking again.

She was glad, because she hated being watched. She didn't feel nearly as self-conscious about nursing as she had in the beginning, and by now she'd grown accustomed to having to nurse him sometimes when there were people around, but still she preferred privacy, even from Bartha, who could not resist making remarks that irritated her, as harmless as they were ("Ah, look how hungry he is!"), but especially from Clara, who stared openly and, it seemed to Esther, with hostility. Strangers, in a way, were now easier for her to deal with. They never said anything, and when they stared they tried to hide it, so that she could act as if they weren't staring if she wanted to, and she had taught herself to look up coolly at the ones who really bothered her, which nearly always made them turn away. But at first! At first she couldn't bring herself to nurse Alexander when there was anybody else around, and as a consequence, at first, she had been unable to go anywhere.

At *first*, of course—even before the first—she hadn't wanted to nurse at all. When Bartha had first brought it up, before Alexander was born, she had been appalled. She'd never heard of such a thing, she told him, not in normal life. "In what life, then?" he asked, amused, she knew, but she was serious—she meant she'd never known, or even known of, anyone who had breastfed a baby. "In books," she told him, and he said, "So then!" as if this proved his point. "Not in books written *now*," she said. "In old books, from a long time ago." Bartha laughed then, and she thought that was the end of it. But he brought it up again—and again—insisting that she try it, "only *try*, for two weeks, no more. Then if you don't like it, you can stop," until, worn out, she gave in, she told him she would try. "For two weeks only," she said grudgingly, without the

46

slightest doubt that she would hate it.

But she loved it—oh, how she loved it! How satisfying it was to know that her body—her own body that had always seemed a thing apart from *her*, her true self—was so useful! How happy it made her that it, that *she*, could provide her baby with the very thing he needed most! Bartha as he watched her feed the baby said, "You see? This is good, yes?" but she couldn't talk to him about it. She could hardly bear the thought that she had ever meant not to nurse her son.

When the food came, Alexander was still nursing. Esther freed one hand and picked up her fork, even though she wasn't hungry. Bartha always noticed if she wasn't eating, and she knew that if she didn't at least manage to look as if she were interested in the food on her plate, he'd insist she put the baby down and "concentrate on eating." *Concentrate on eating!* As if food were something to be studied, contemplated, memorized.

He and the others were concentrating very hard on their food, not only eating it but also yet again talking about it. As Esther poked her fork into a piece of chicken and stirred it into the noodles Bartha had made such a big to-do about, he was reminiscing about food he'd eaten long ago in Prague and claiming that the meal that they were having now, "while not bad—I don't say that it's bad," was only an "approximation" of the wonderful meals he remembered. "Oh, is that so?" said Clara. "The way you talk sometimes, you'd think your last good meal was in 1935."

"No, not at all. I have had many good meals in this country. Not so much in Omaha, perhaps—"

"Uh oh," Vilmos said. "Now here it begins again."

"I thought you liked this place," Clara said.

"Omaha?" said Vilmos. "Or America?"

"This restaurant," Clara said, as if she couldn't tell that he was making fun of her.

"Oh, but I do like it," Bartha said, and went on to explain that in spite of its shortcomings (which he then enumerated: the food itself, invariably overcooked as well as incorrectly spiced; the gaudy, inauthentic "Czech" decor; the costumes on the waitresses), it was "very nearly brilliant" in comparison with all the other restaurants in Omaha—"and in particular the steak houses for which, I am so often told, this city is so famous, and yet where one cannot find a steak so good as can be found in New York City." And he added, slyly, "Perhaps the trouble is that they send to New York all the best steaks of Nebraska? Or"— pausing, pretending to think—"perhaps the explanation is that there is not one person here who knows how to prepare properly a steak, so that no matter how excellent the meat, it is ruined in the preparation?"

Was it possible, Esther wondered—this had never occurred to her before—that he said such things just to tease Clara?

"You can't be saying that you believe there isn't one good chef in Omaha!" Clara said, as he must have known she would.

"Oh, yes," said Bartha. "Yes, indeed I am. If someone should learn such a skill, or discover in himself so great a gift, would he not upon that instant run away from here?" He said this as if he didn't know—as if he himself had not been the one to tell Esther—how proud Clara was of having come to Omaha to live. Vilmos had told Bartha, who'd told Esther, that Clara had "run away" as soon as she was old enough to leave her family behind in the small town (the name of it would not stay put in Esther's mind) in which she had grown up, somewhere in the middle of Nebraska. Vilmos had met her soon after, when he'd come here on a business trip, and Clara had (so Bartha joked—or Esther assumed it was a joke) "with feminine wiles arranged for him to stay forever."

Omaha, as far as Clara was concerned, was *the city*. Maybe not so differently from the way she herself had grown up thinking of Manhattan, Esther thought: the place she had aspired to escape to. And like herself (like the way she used to be, before she'd found herself in Omaha), she seemed not to be aware—or not to care—that there were other cities.

About anyplace but Omaha, Clara had no curiosity. She'd never asked Esther anything about New York, and when conversation turned to California, where Vilmos had lived in a series of cities—Northern, Southern, Central, coastal and non-coastal (he'd hold up his right hand and tick off the categories on his fingers, and a wave of homesickness would sweep through Esther—not for California, a place she'd never been, or even for her childhood self, who had enjoyed thinking of all the places she had not been to yet, places she might someday go, but for her English teacher junior year, Mr. Inemer, counting on his fingers *form and structure, voice, tone, meaning*)—Clara expressed only suspicion and disdain. Esther had asked her once if she had ever visited the state in which Vilmas had lived for so many years before he'd met her, and Clara said, "*California?*" in a way that Esther understood to mean, *Why would I?* And Esther, sorry that she'd asked, said, "I thought maybe you'd made the trip to see Vilmos's father." Clara snorted. "If he wanted to see us, he would come here, the

49

way my parents do." As if a trip from…whatever Clara's town was called—Long Something—was the same as a trip from Fresno, California.

Esther put down her fork and picked up her wineglass, wondering if Bartha would tell her again that she had had enough to drink. But he didn't say anything and she took three sips in quick succession before she set down the glass. She tried to think of what the town where Clara's parents lived, the town Clara was from, was called. *Long Island? That can't be right. And not Long Beach, either*—but it was something that reminded her of beaches. *Rockaway? Rock Island?* No, that was from a song. *The Rock Island line is a mighty fine line.* Absently she hummed it under her breath. No one noticed.

The baby's sucking had slowed down; his eyes were closed. Was he going back to sleep? She joggled him a little on her lap to perk him up and he began to nurse again in earnest. He was more like her than he was like Bartha: he too had to be reminded to "concentrate on eating." In solidarity, she stabbed a piece of chicken and made herself put it in her mouth. She *should* eat something. She didn't have to wait for Bartha to remind her.

Grand Island—it came to her unexpectedly. That was the name of Clara's town. She almost said it out loud, almost said, *An island in the middle of what?* And then when Clara didn't have an answer, she would say, *So tell me—please, I'm interested—in what way is it grand?*

These were the kinds of questions Clara would ask her, so why shouldn't she?

Leah used to tell her, *Don't even try to be sarcastic. It's not your style. Leave it to the people it comes naturally to.* And what was her style, then? she wanted to know. *Sincerity, Esther.*

You are all about sincerity. But Esther hadn't been able to tell if Leah meant this sarcastically.

"What a snob you are," Clara was saying to Bartha now. "Oh, yes," he said, laughing. "There is no doubt of that." And when Clara told him this was nothing to be proud of, he said, "Oh, you are absolutely right about this too." He was still laughing, and it dawned on Esther—and here was something else that she had never thought of before!—that arguing with Clara amused him. Perhaps it also amused Clara, who was now launching into a defense of restaurants she liked in Omaha—a list that even Esther could have reeled off by heart: Johnny's, which was near the stockyards, and the Black Angus, and King Fong's, downtown, where Bartha claimed he'd had the worst Chinese meal he had ever had, "in all my life, my long life, in any city, on any continent."

If they were not amused by this, why would they bother jumping into the same argument again and again?

"Alas, it is hopeless, my dear," Bartha said, sounding cheerful. "We will not agree, not ever."

"*You* are hopeless," Clara told him. "You are impossible to please."

"Not at all. To please me is quite simple."

"Oh, yes. As long as you're in New York. Or Prague or Budapest. Or Paris."

"Or Vienna," Vilmos put in. "Ah, my friends"— he brought both hands to his chest, and in an excellent imitation of his cousin, he cried, "the sausage, sausage such as I may never hope to see again. And such beautiful homemade sauerkraut! And the bread—I weep to recall it. And now?" He thumped the tabletop. "Now I am to be satisfied with the American red frankfurter with its curlicue of yellow mustard and eight skinny limp gray strings of tinned *kraut*—as your vendors so charmingly call it—on a white bread roll that tastes like…ah, like—"

"Like air," Bartha said obligingly. "Like emptiness."

Clara said, "Oh, yes, that's very funny. But the truth is you've been in America long enough to have grown accustomed—"

"To your 'hot dog' buns? A lifetime would not be long enough for this."

"They're not *my* hot dog buns," Clara said. "Besides, nobody really likes them. That's not the point of them."

Esther was tempted to speak up then, to ask Clara what the point was. Vilmos winked at her but she ignored him. What she really wanted to know was how it was possible to talk so much—to think so much, to care so much—about food. She could not understand how Bartha, who was so worldly, who unlike Clara had many more important things on his mind, could devote so much of his attention to what he ate and where he ate (and also when and how he ate—for he liked to have his dinner at six forty-five, with the table set correctly and with linen napkins, and he had to have his salad after, not before or with, the main course). Esther would just as soon have lived on sandwiches—tuna salad or cream cheese and grape jelly or bologna—and when she felt the need for something more substantial, with side dishes included, heated up a TV dinner. As for where and how and when, she'd be content to eat propped up in bed or sitting on the couch, with paper plates and napkins, plastic cutlery. She would be glad to give up restaurants forever if only Bartha ever took her anyplace besides a restaurant—if there were anyplace to *go* besides a restaurant to which the baby would also be welcome. If there were anyplace at all to go, baby or no baby.

But with "no baby," she thought, they would not be in Nebraska. They would still be in New York, and there would be a million places they could go.

But with "no baby," what would have come to pass between the two of them by now?

She swatted this thought away. It was a question she never asked herself.

Certainly she would never dare to ask *him*.

But then there were many things she did not dare to say to him. Even at this moment, she thought, what she would have *liked* to say was that she saw nothing wrong with hot dog buns—or at least nothing wrong enough to talk about—and also that, to her, King Fong's was no better or worse than the Chinese takeout she used to have at Leah's house on Brightwater Court.

But even if she'd dared, this would not be possible. There was no place to edge in even a single word between Bartha and Clara once they started down this road, not unless one shouted or pounded on the table, as Vilmos did when he was moved to interrupt them. And now Clara was speaking of a restaurant that Bartha hadn't been to yet, one that she claimed was "out of the ordinary— even you would see that." "Even I?" said Bartha. "Even I who have given up hope of having an extraordinary meal ever again? I have accepted my fate, dear Clara." And of course Clara took umbrage at what she declared was an insult to the city of Omaha itself, "which has been so welcoming to you," and Esther was silently astonished (in what way, welcoming?) but Bartha said only, "A city, like a gentleman, must not be insulted by an honest appraisal of its shortcomings." "Then you will not be insulted," Clara said, "if I tell you that you're being a bit of an ass." Bartha laughed. "I will try not to be."

Vilmos was laughing too, and looking from his cousin to his wife with such evident pleasure that just then Esther wondered if it might be for his amusement that these arguments were staged.

Everyone was amused but her, it seemed.

As Clara extolled the virtues of her adopted city—its friendliness, its "nice neighborhoods," its symphony and art museum (Bartha groaned and shook his head), Esther considered Vilmos, who never felt obliged to come to the defense of the city in which he had made his home because Clara had made it hers. Bartha was quite sure, he had told Esther, that his cousin would prefer to live elsewhere, but it didn't seem to her that he had any objection to living in Omaha. She'd never heard him say a word against it, or for that matter express any affection or nostalgia about any other place he'd lived. Certainly he didn't long for California the way Bartha longed for New York.

This thought was a surprise. Did Bartha long for New York? He was talking now, with what might be longing, about the restaurants he loved most there. Esther knew which ones he meant before he named them—they were little Hungarian restaurants run by families, and to get to them he had to change trains twice, then walk for what had seemed to her a long time on the one occasion she had gone with him to visit one of them.

Alexander had slowed down again, and Esther glanced at Bartha as she rearranged the baby in her arms so that he could switch to her other breast. She was still expecting him to observe that she had hardly touched her food and to tell her to put Alexander down—she was all set to say,

"I can't now. Look, he's nursing, can't you see?" (and, indeed, the baby had begun to nurse again with renewed interest)—but Bartha was telling Clara, in great detail, about the food served in those little restaurants. He made the food sound a great deal nicer than what Esther could recall from her one visit (a brown heap of meat for each of them, mounds of mushy vegetables, dumplings and gravy, noodles—again noodles!—and saucers of sour cream). She'd gone with him only once because it was so hard for her to get out in the evening. She had to tell her parents it was something to do with school, that it was *required* (the sacred word!). Between the lying, which she wasn't used to, and the hour-long subway ride and then the long walk at night from the subway station to a neighborhood she'd never even known existed, she was so unnerved by the time they reached the restaurant he'd chosen that it would not have been possible for her to have a pleasant evening. As it was, she had been miserable. Bartha hardly spoke to her, he was so busy chatting with the waitress and the cook, and exchanging greetings with some of the other people eating there. She'd never heard him speak in his own language before and it made her uneasy, despite (or else—but it was only later that she thought of this—*because* of) seeing what a pleasure it was for him: it made her wonder if the rest of the time, forced to use another language that was not his own with students and with friends and neighbors—with *her*—he was less than happy. And the food, which Bartha told her was "exactly" the food of his youth, was too heavy and too rich for her—she ate almost none of it.

But what made her most miserable was the lie she had told. She could not stop thinking about it; she could not stop worrying about getting caught in it. How would her father punish her if he worked out that she had been lying? Would he then find suspect everything she said? Surely he would watch her more closely. Oh, to have risked everything for this evening that had given her no pleasure!

Throughout the meal she worried, and throughout the long trip home. How was it, she marveled, that so many girls her age lied so assuredly and frequently—how was it that they behaved so recklessly, so *badly*? (What she overheard from girls she didn't know or hardly knew in school astounded her. How did they cause their parents so much grief and worry without ever worrying themselves? "It's just as if they were a different species," she'd said once to Leah, who'd said, "No. They're only silly. They're only stupid. They don't *think*.")

She was exhausted and close to tears when she let herself into the apartment, and so pale that her mother exclaimed, "You're getting sick!" and insisted on taking her temperature. (She would not have been surprised if she had *had* a fever.) She was relieved when after this one evening out with her, Bartha resumed his habit of so many years of going to these restaurants alone.

How was it that she had never thought before about how he must miss them? He used to go twice, three times a week. And she had never given any thought to all the other things he must miss, too—the opera and the Philharmonic and Carnegie Hall. The Metropolitan Museum, to which he had taken her on every one of the occasions (three) she had managed to slip away from her parents and the store *and* her friends without a lie—except perhaps a lie of omission—on a weekend afternoon. Oh, and also the Frick, where he had promised to take her but had never had the chance to, "to see the Vermeers, the best paintings in the world," he said. And the Museum of Modern Art, which she had never visited with him, although she'd been there on class trips, once almost every year. Bartha liked to "drop in, he told Esther, "once each season, at its start, to mark time's passage."

And how he must miss Sheepshead Bay, where he often walked, admiring the docked fishing boats! They made him feel as if he had slipped away to somewhere else, he would tell her ("but then it is so reassuring to find that one is still here after all"). Sometimes he would talk for a few minutes with the fishermen, whose Brooklyn accents were, he said, "so magnificently, so beautifully at odds" with the fishing stories they offered him.

Sheepshead Bay. And the boardwalk along Brighton Beach. And the pavilion *on* the boardwalk, where he used to sit on Sundays in good weather, looking at the ocean while he listened to the men who played accordions and fiddles there and told each other jokes in Yiddish. How he must miss a place to sit where there was anything to see, to hear.

As she used the back of her fork to nudge her vegetables up to the edge of her plate, she thought of how, when they'd first come to Omaha, Bartha had sat once for an hour on Vilmos and Clara's front porch, and afterwards told her that he had seen "a hundred cars fly down the street, and not one person walking." Why, he must miss walking in a place where other people walked. He must miss Brooklyn and Manhattan's streets, he must miss seeing crowds of people. He must miss subways, buses— everything, she thought, and that she'd never thought of this before filled her with shame.

Think how much he must miss his studio, she told

herself. Think how much he must miss his own belongings. There had been nothing in the apartment she'd grown up in that had felt to her as if it were importantly her own, that meant enough to her for her to think of taking when she left—and even so there were times when she missed some object—the round, blue plaster of Paris box with the doll's head (head, neck and shoulders, and cascading blond hair) that topped it, a gift from the first-grade teacher for whom she'd worked as a monitor when she was in the sixth grade; the tall lamp beside the loveseat in the living room that had three colored glass globes, red, blue, green, that could be lit separately or all together, that she used to read by, choosing lights in different combinations; the eight-inch-tall "grandfather clock," its face painted with the tiniest of flowers, that stood on the dresser in the room she shared with Sylvia; the small brass bowl on the bathroom shelf in which she'd kept her hair pins and barrettes—objects that she had looked at without feeling anything all her life. But Bartha had left behind things he'd collected, things he had chosen.

Even the things he hadn't left behind but had sent on from Brooklyn were not with him now but were in storage, for there was no room for them in Vilmos and Clara's basement. He had told her at the start that there was plenty of money, that she was not to worry (it had not, in fact, occurred to her to worry), that he had "investments and so on" and they would "manage nicely." Still, he'd told her, as calmly as if it were nothing to him, they would stay with Vilmos and he'd manage with a rented room nearby in which he would give lessons using an old upright piano he had rented while his own grand piano remained locked up in a warehouse, until such time as he had sufficient students once again to justify their renting a house of their own, part of which would be set aside as a studio.

Somehow he had made it sound as if this might occur at any moment, although the few students he had found so far (there were two of them; there had been three, but one had not returned after the second lesson) had come to him through Clara, who'd hung up flyers she had typed herself. NEW YORK SINGING TEACHER WILL GIVE LESSONS TO YOUR CHILDREN AT A REASONABLE PRICE! Bartha had also taken out an ad in the newspaper, but so far that had come to nothing. And yet he spoke as if he had no worries, no regrets. He acted—they both acted, Esther thought—as if it went without saying that she'd left behind much more than he had. The only time he'd spoken of how he felt about leaving was when they had first discussed the possibility of doing it, and what he'd said then was that leaving New York would be "nothing" to him, that it would not trouble him at all, that he was worried only about her—about her leaving school, her family and friends, the only place, the only people, she had ever known.

He had been lying. She had not even considered this as she sat across from him in a luncheonette on Coney Island Avenue, one neither of them had ever been in before, in a back corner booth. By then they had been sitting, talking (*she* had been talking; for once he was not telling stories) for a good two hours. He was asking her questions, so many questions about her life it was as if he had prepared a list, and by the time she asked him, over the litter of two hours of coffee refills—torn-up sugar packets and empty cream pitchers, balled-up napkins, dirty spoons—if it might be better "just to go away" if her parents responded to the news she had for them as she feared they would, and he

59

had answered without hesitating. *Yes, of course. I have some family, I'll write to them,* she was only grateful that the path was clear, that everything had been decided.

In the beginning, he'd asked her nearly every day if she'd begun yet to regret what she had done, and she'd said no and meant it. And yet he would ask again and again. (Because he thought that *she* was lying? Or did he think she might have changed her mind, from one day to the next?) And then he had stopped asking—she could not remember when. Did he believe her, finally? Or had he stopped wondering? Or—could it be?—had he just grown tired of asking her what he was waiting for her to ask him?

She felt her eyes fill with tears again. Dry-eyed throughout the ceremony, and so many tears since! And why was she crying now? Out of sadness for Bartha? Because despite what he had said that day over all those cups of coffee in the Cozy Corner, he must have felt he was too old to have to start all over somewhere else? Or perhaps what she felt now was remorse, because she'd never *asked* him how he felt, she'd never pressed him for the truth. She had taken him at his word. His lack of words.

She tried to imagine now what he must have been feeling as he contemplated making such a change more than two decades after he had settled himself for what he must have thought would be the rest of his life. But of course she could not imagine it—how could she? Even now, even after everything that had come to pass since then, even after living with him for so many months in Vilmos and Clara's yellow shag-carpeted and mock-wood-paneled basement under three strips of fluorescent light, she had no idea how he felt or what he thought.

No idea at all. She put down her fork, which she'd been

using to push her vegetables around as if she were a child, so that it would look as though she'd eaten something. She put the fork down carefully, as if the way she did it mattered, lining it up precisely alongside the knife she hadn't touched and making sure it didn't make a sound against the tile.

He was a stranger to her. Her husband, and a stranger.

He never told her what was in his heart. He didn't volunteer it and she never asked—she could not even picture herself asking. He had never even told her that he loved her, and how could she ask him that? She had told herself he must, for otherwise how could things have turned out the way they had? If she allowed herself to wonder why he had become involved with her in the first place, she became frightened, as if that question were a door behind which lay in wait the vastness of everything she didn't know or didn't understand, and if she opened it more than a crack she might be pulled in, pulled deep into that blackness.

What would happen to her then?

What would happen to her *now?*

The question shocked her. She wasn't even sure what she had meant by it. *Now* she was married. The question of "what would happen" had been settled.

Why, then, did she still feel so *un*settled?

She looked at Bartha, as if he could tell her. He was talking to Vilmos and Clara. About what, she couldn't guess—she'd long ago lost the thread of their conversation—but he caught her eye and smiled at her reassuringly. Reassuring her of what? To be *re*assured, she'd have to have been sure of something to begin with, and it seemed to her at this moment that she had been, from the beginning, sure of nothing.

She thought suddenly of the stories he used to tell her about himself—about his singing career, his travels, all the things he had done during the war (*that* war—his war, as she thought of it—a war that was part of History, not of ordinary time). She used to lie beside him on the sofa bed's thin mattress, in the curtained darkness of his studio after he had made love to her, and listen as he told her stories. It was like going to the movies—the daylight shut out, another world opened up. She already knew most of the stories he told her by heart, but that never bothered her. In fact, it added to the pleasure, the same way the second or third time she saw a movie was more satisfying to her than the first, for everything that was lost in surprise was made up for by the strange, thrilling sense that everything that happened was inevitable. She had gone to see "The World of Henry Orient" three times—once with Leah and Kathleen, and then once alone with each of them—and it got better every time; they'd all gone together twice to see "To Kill A Mockingbird," and she'd seen "Charade" twice, too, once with both of her friends, who didn't like it, and once by herself, which she'd never done before but enjoyed so much that when one of her favorite movies, "West Side Story," which she had first seen when she was in ninth grade, came back to the Oceana for two weeks, she went by herself three times after she wore out Leah and Kathleen, who went with her on the day it opened and then went back with her once apiece, which they said was enough. She'd have gone more than six times if her father hadn't put his foot down. By the fourth time—the fifth time, if she counted the first time she'd seen it, years earlier—she had started crying during "Something's Coming." By the sixth time she had felt her sorrow starting while she waited in the dark before the movie even came on to the screen.

When she left Bartha's studio, it was a lot like when she left a movie theater, too. She would stand for a moment, dazed, on the sidewalk before she started walking home, still blinking in what was left of daylight. Every Tuesday and Friday afternoon she would just stand there for a little while outside his building, letting the stories and the lovemaking, all mixed together in her mind, begin to melt away before she started her walk through the neighborhood. If she stood there long enough she might see Mrs. Pullman (Tuesdays), who taught second grade at P.S. 209 but loved to sing, or Milton Hagan (Fridays), who was a theater major at Brooklyn College and was as handsome and as casually charming as a movie star. If she stood there long enough, and Bartha had the window open, she might hear them singing scales for him. It wasn't a bad feeling, being outside while he gave a lesson. It wasn't bad to have a secret, and to be reminded that as other people went about their normal business you knew something they knew absolutely nothing about. And it was good, too, to be reminded that ordinary life was still going on. It helped her make the transition, back into her life at home from her secret life with Bartha and the things she knew about him.

There were a dozen stories he'd told her a dozen times or more as she lay next to him, her eyes closed, a thin wool lap blanket over her, its fringes brushing her bare ankles. Stories that concerned adventures he had had in Paris, London, Prague, Vienna. In his stories, he was always traveling. Even during the war, when most travel, for most people, had been banned, he had continued traveling to give performances. "I was very popular," he explained, "and the Nazis, I suppose, said to themselves,

'Ah, this is good publicity for us. Why not let him go about freely?'" Thus it had seemed "only natural," he said, "given the circumstances," for him to become a sort of spy, and soon he began to carry secrets for the Allies out of Budapest. What sort of secrets, and how he acquired them, he had never told her. Perhaps he'd thought these details would not have been interesting to her, and perhaps they wouldn't have been—for she hadn't wondered *then*. It was only looking back, thinking of all the things she didn't know, that she found herself wishing for more facts, more information. His wartime stories in particular were full of missing pieces, mysteries, and contradictions. They were full of characters he'd never named or told her quite enough about.

There were stories about secret meetings with spies who had been apprised of his arrival only by the broadsides that had advertised it—stories in which passwords, whispered conversations at stage doors, and dark corners of cafés figured largely. There was a story about how, when the Hungarian government tried to shift away from its position of sympathy toward the Nazis, and the Nazis responded by taking over Hungary by force, he was abruptly told he would no longer be allowed to travel. This was how he came to know that he'd become the object of suspicion ("like so many who had been in the former government's good graces"). He went into hiding then. He hid in the cellar of a house belonging to a woman who admired him, the mistress of a high-ranking member of the new pro-Nazi government. "Therefore, you see, no search was ever made," he said at this story's end, and Esther nodded gravely, as if nothing about what he had just told her puzzled her. But she wondered if the woman who had hidden him had been *his* mistress too—for why would she have taken such a risk on his behalf if she were not? And yet, why would he have had such a mistress? But she could not ask him, no more than she could have asked him why he'd never married, why none of the women in his stories had names or were identified beyond a single, straightforward, descriptive sentence—"the daughter of an old school friend," "the young wife of an excellent composer I used to sometimes have a drink with"—or if he'd been in love with any of them or with anyone else, ever.

She would murmur, "Ah, yes," or, "I see," or even, "Goodness," when it seemed that it was necessary to say something, but she never asked him anything about his stories, not even when he told the grandest and most complicated, and most puzzling, of them, the story of how he had escaped from Hungary after the many months he'd spent in hiding. With his savings from what had already been a long and lucrative career, savings he had had the foresight to convert into gold well before the Nazi's mistress had taken him in, he bribed the conductor of a train bound elsewhere to take him—him, the train, and all its passengers—from Budapest to Istanbul, where he had British contacts he was certain would arrange safe passage for him to America. Which they did. In America, he was granted instant citizenship by Presidential decree.

To make sense of such a story, Esther thought, she would have to know more history than she did, and history had not been among her best subjects, not like English or music or art. Once, when they were still in Brooklyn, she had gone to the library and found a simple history book in which there was a chapter titled "Hungary During the

Second World War." She read it carefully from start to finish, but when she was done she felt she hadn't learned much, or at any rate not much that helped her understand what Bartha had lived through. As it turned out, her having read what was only a dry recitation of dates and events made matters worse, for the insistent, unembellished emphasis on what had happened when forced her to contemplate directly what she never thought about—that when Bartha was carrying his secrets out of Budapest into Istanbul, meeting British agents on street corners and in dimly lit hotel lobbies between performances of *Lucia di Lammermoor*, she had not yet existed: Dr. Azogue had not yet helped her to escape from her mother ("for the first time," as she had said to Bartha nearly ten months ago as they rode the train to Omaha—trying to be witty to prove that she was not sorry or afraid, and choosing her words carefully to let him know that she considered this too an escape and not a banishment).

After that, she didn't look for books to help her understand the stories he had told her. The truth was, she had never minded very much—not then, at least—not really understanding. She never thought of interrupting him to ask a question, even when he mentioned without explanation something she had never heard of, or hinted at things she might have liked to have known a little more about—no more than she would have thought of asking the projectionist to halt the showing of "West Side Story" while she interrogated Tony and Maria about what their lives had been like in the years before the overture.

She'd acted, she supposed, as if his stories—as if his whole life—*were* on a movie screen in front of her. Or as if the things he told her were parts of a novel (a difficult, beautiful novel, perhaps a novel she was reading in translation) or an opera. She didn't have to understand it, then, or not completely. She could just be in its world for a while. "Don't work so hard," she used to tell Kathleen and Leah when she got them to listen to *Madama Butterfly* or *La Bohème* with her, when they complained that they could not make heads or tails of what was happening. "Just let it come over you," she'd tell them. "Understanding isn't necessarily the most important thing."

And yet, once she and Bartha came to Omaha, she found that she was thinking of his stories in a new way—that she was, indeed, *thinking* about them. There was very little else for her to do. She could read or listen to the little radio Vilmos had given them, since Bartha's stereo and all his records were in storage, or take solitary walks without a destination (which left her feeling restless—more restless than before she had set out—and a little stupid, too; in Brooklyn, it would never have occurred to her to set foot on the street unless she had somewhere to go—but here there *was* nowhere to go, and she could not stay locked up in Vilmos and Clara's basement all day long, day after day). She did go to the library—in the beginning, with a shopping bag that she would fill with novels once a week, and later, when it was all she could do to steer her own weight through the half mile trip each way, she made two or three separate trips each week, two novels at a time—and also to the Hinky Dinky, where she would shop for groceries among the worn-out, weary-looking women three times her own age (which left her feeling worn out, too, and gloomy; she would always take a long nap afterwards).

With so much time on her hands, she passed entire afternoons telling herself the stories Bartha had told her.

She took them apart, isolating details and considering them in as many different lights as she could think of. She was trying to get at his stories as she'd never even thought of doing when he was still telling them to her. She started, too, then, to wait for him to resume his storytelling, and the way that she was waiting, trying to prepare herself for what might come next, reminded her of how she'd studied math last year—how hard she'd had to work at trying to make sense of what she had already learned by rote before the teacher went on to something more difficult that she knew would require her to understand and not just *know* what she had learned before. It reminded her of how often she'd failed at this. The class had been called "fusion"— trigonometry and advanced algebra, combined. Math had not been one of her best subjects either.

When the baby came, she was much busier, but she had started something and at first she couldn't stop. While she sat on the bed and nursed Alexander, or rocked him in the rocking chair Bartha had found for her at a garage sale on his way home from the studio one afternoon; while she walked him around the same small circle again and again in their basement room, or wheeled the carriage slowly, aimlessly, along Saddle Creek Road—whatever she was doing, for the first few weeks after his birth—she kept turning Bartha's stories over in her mind, and sometimes she even murmured one of them to Alexander, saying "I" as Bartha had, pretending that the story was her own to see what feelings it produced in her; but she could never manage it—she never really fooled herself, so she never felt anything. She told herself that this was not her fault, that there was too much background missing for the exercise to work, but still her failure left her feeling stupid, just as fusion had.

Alexander whimpered now and Esther bent to brush her lips to the top of his head. "Hush," she whispered. "It's okay." He stared up at her, his mouth in a worried shape. Sometimes she could swear he knew what she was thinking or feeling—not that he could understand it, of course, but that he could sense it. And yet so often it was hard for her to figure out what *he* was feeling. He would cry and she would try to nurse him and it would turn out he wasn't hungry, that something else was wrong, but she didn't know what. Then she would start trying things, asking herself: Was he tired? Bored? Cold? Hot? Dirty or wet? Was the light too bright? Did something hurt him—his stomach? His bottom? His head? (Did babies get headaches?) She would put him in his crib and pat his back, and when that didn't help, she'd take him out and rock him in her arms and sing to him, she would put him on the floor with all his rattles and stuffed animals and play with him, she'd add clothes and remove clothes, change his diaper, turn the light out, rub his belly—she'd try everything, and sometimes nothing worked, he just kept crying, and she would still be fretting, making guesses, when he fell asleep, spent from his efforts to communicate his troubles to her.

This was backwards, she knew. She was supposed to understand him better than he understood her. But when she was feeling anxious or afraid and he looked at her solemnly, so steadily—as if he were trying to say, "Don't be frightened, everything will be all right"—or when she felt good and he gave her one of his goofy, toothless smiles, how could she help thinking that he knew her well enough to read her mind? It seemed to her that half the work of taking care of him was trying to stay even the slightest bit ahead of him.

She wasn't sure exactly when she had stopped thinking about Bartha's stories, but she knew that it had to do with this, the effort to keep up with Alexander. Her days were so full of him (what he needed, what he might need soon, what he had needed that she hadn't figured out an hour ago but was still trying to work out as he slept it off) that it had been weeks, months, since she'd given any thought to Bartha. It was as if she had said to herself, as she used to when she took a test and there was only so much time left and one too many questions still to answer, *Which of these problems do I stand a chance of solving? All right, then— concentrate on that one and forget about the other.*

But even though she had set it aside, she'd kept expecting that the answer to the other question would come to her somehow—that the stories Bartha had already told her would begin to fit together, and that as new stories came she'd have only to slip the bits of information that had come embedded in them into the blank spaces she had held for them in her mind; until there occurred a moment of pure comprehension—when she'd see, at last, the meaning of the bits and pieces (of his life—of him) that she had been collecting for so long. She had imagined something like the moment when she'd finished up the central part of one of the big jigsaw puzzles that her mother used to buy her when she was sick with strep throat or the flu and stuck at home, that sense of triumph, even joy, when she realized that she had put together enough of the part that mattered to see what she was supposed to see (and she would put the puzzle away then and never take it out again, for she never had the patience to go on with it, nor saw the point of starting it anew, once she had mastered the most crucial part).

But what she'd been expecting all this time had never happened. It was as if, with Bartha, there were no central, most important part—or, if there were, there might as well not be, since too many of the pieces needed to complete it (or even to complete enough of it so that she could *begin* to see it—enough to form at least a partial, blurry outline of something she could recognize and name) were missing, and Bartha seemed to have no interest in supplying any more of them.

Or perhaps there weren't any more of them.

This thought stopped her. It could not be possible—could it?—that he had already told her everything that he would ever tell her, that what she already knew about him was all she would ever know.

But how could that be, when she knew so little, when what she knew amounted to a jumble of isolated, if astonishing, facts—and what she understood amounted to so much less than that?

She looked at him now in wonder. Was she really meant to make do with no more than this? With these assorted, too-few scraps, these odds and ends? She stared hard at him, daring him to read her mind as Alexander could, and to respond, to tell her, "Of course not. Just wait and have patience." But he only smiled and patted her arm without pausing in his conversation. He was talking about his much-admired cousin László again, about *his* wedding day, and as he spoke of "the charming, marvelously beautiful young woman" László had married ("who, as you well know, Vilmos, was destined to become your grandmother"), Esther felt herself shrink from his hand and from his absentminded smile—from *him*.

He had tossed her handfuls of his life, she thought, the way he'd fed his table scraps to the stray cats and dogs in his courtyard in Brooklyn. A little here, a little there—nothing to count on. Casually, when it happened to occur to him, he'd hand out food to them—rich food, exotic food. And just like those lost (or more likely abandoned, Bartha always had said, and she'd clap her hands to her ears and pretend that her refusal to hear this was only playful), half starved cats and dogs, she'd been excited beyond reason every time. She had never (no more than they had) considered how these treats might be affecting her, and Bartha hadn't either (no more, she supposed, than he had thought about how cabbage cooked in vinegar and sour cream or Black Forest ham or brie or jam-filled pastries would affect the strays).

How could she not have seen that there would come a time when she'd require something more substantial? She hadn't the excuse the poor strays had. As far as they knew, crumbs and too-rich leftovers were all there ever was and all there ever would be. But how could *she* have taken what he offered without asking any questions? How could she not have known that Bartha's offerings would someday, suddenly, come to an end?

But she knew how. She could remember very well how thrilling she had found the stories he had told her. She had been unable to think reasonably; she could not have thought ahead. It had seemed to her sometimes that it had been *them*, the stories he had told her—his stories, along with all the operas he'd performed in, and his voice itself—which was still beautiful, and which had made her heart constrict with what she'd had to guess was love (real love, this time) when, after she had studied with him for a year, she had at last persuaded him to sing for her—that had drawn her into his bed.

Indeed, it had come into her mind more than once during her pregnancy that what had impregnated her had *been* the stories he had told her of his brilliant long-ago career, his wartime life, his youth in Europe; the operas she had listened to on record albums borrowed from him, one each week; and the aria *Vesti la giubba*, which he had sung for her the afternoon he had first taken her to bed. As she drifted through the second, then the third, trimester in Vilmos and Clara's basement, moving from the couch to first one kitchen chair and then the other, then to the shag carpeting—where she tried sitting cross-legged, then on her knees with her rear end against her upturned heels, and finally with her legs stuck straight out in front of her, before she gave up sitting altogether and lay down (on her left side, as recommended), trying vainly to get comfortable— she had let herself daydream that what she was carrying inside her was a bellyful of intrigue, the great vanished world of Bartha's Europe, *Cavalleria Rusticana* and *Pagliacci*, and a voice which grew bigger and more marvelous each day. Not a baby—or, as she had said to herself then, "not just a baby"—after all.

And yet of course (of course!) it had been a baby. She'd been playing, trying to amuse herself—telling *herself* a sort of story. And telling *him*, she thought now. Telling the baby. She had been telling him the story, too—telling him the story of himself, of his beginnings. *This is who you are. This is what you are made of, where you come from.*

Just then the baby let out one shrill, angry-sounding cry. But before she could do anything to comfort him, he'd stopped. One cry and he was done. He had raised both of his hands when he'd cried out, then dropped them, fingers curled but not quite fisted, near his ears. His elbows stuck straight up. He was frowning. Esther smiled—she couldn't help it. He looked so serious and comical at the same time. He was a little opera in himself.

As if to demonstrate the truth of this—as if those daydreams she'd allowed herself while she was pregnant had affected him (and why not, when he had lived with them, within them, all the while he was becoming himself?)—he struck his forehead with the back of one hand, closed his eyes, and turned his head away. When he turned toward her again—gravely, expectantly, his half closed hand still resting palm-up over one faint, tiny eyebrow—she felt as if she should applaud.

This was far from the first time she'd had the feeling that he was performing for her—this had happened often, beginning when he was only a few days old—and there were other times she hoped he was, for how could he endure it if he actually felt all the things that he appeared to feel, when sometimes his emotions seemed to change so rapidly and drastically that she was at a loss to figure out which feeling to respond to? How quickly he could move from one thing to another! He was so calm and watchful now that it was hard for her, just these few seconds later, to imagine that the wail of protest (protesting her explanation of his origins? Or her having troubled him—plagued him?—with it at such a delicate, portentous time?) she'd heard had been his cry and not someone else's—or even that she'd heard a cry at all.

No one but she, it seemed, had heard it. Clara was attending to her food, Vilmos was laughing at an anecdote Bartha was telling—either about Vilmos's father or one of the other Józsefs—and Bartha was concentrating on the telling of it, or so Esther assumed. She was startled, then, when he turned to her and said, "Do you see how hard he is thinking? And just look how sorrowful he is."

Confused, Esther said, "He hides it very well then, doesn't he?"

Bartha laughed. He set his hand down gently upon hers where it lay across Alexander's knees. "Look." He tapped her hand. "Not at my cousin," he said. "At my son. You see? He is thinking of the many people of his past whom he will never know. This is why he cried just now—thinking of the great-uncles and great-grandfathers he cannot see, only hear about. So many people he cannot see. His own grandfather, grandmother—"

He stopped himself, and Esther knew he was ashamed. He had not meant to remind her that their child would never know her parents, either, by their own choice. He took great care not to speak of things that might remind her of her family—as if he thought that if he didn't mention them she wouldn't think about them. And it seemed best to act as if she *didn't* think about her family, if that was what he thought was the best thing for her.

She never even spoke of them to Alexander. She'd told herself that even if she hadn't already grown used to keeping silent about them, it would be too confusing if she talked about them to him now, then had to stop before he became old enough to ask her questions. She would hear Bartha speaking quietly sometimes to him about his own parents—long dead, in Hungary, of course—saying, "How my mother would have loved you," or, "Here is a song my own papa used to sing to me," before he sang a certain lullaby. But if sometimes she caught herself singing a song to Alexander that she faintly recalled someone (her mother? Who else could it have been?) singing to her, she didn't speak of this to Alexander.

He would probably ask questions anyway, once he was old enough to know that other children had grandparents. She was already worried about how she'd answer him. But there was time for that, she would remind herself whenever she began to worry. And it was still possible, she felt, that if she kept writing to her family somebody would write back before the time came to tell Alexander anything. And this was perhaps why she kept writing to them. If she did not believe that it was still possible that someone, someday, would answer her, surely she would not still be writing to them, would she?

Suddenly, as she asked herself this question, she understood something. She understood that if Bartha were to find out that she had been writing to her parents, he would not be angry. He would feel sorry for her, that was all, and he might think her foolish. Well, she *was* foolish, she knew that. She knew that writing letters no one answered was—a phrase of her father's came to her now; it was what he'd said when he forbade her to see "West Side Story" again, what he said about going out with boys—"not making good use" of her time. But what was she to do? She pictured herself saying this to Bartha— her arms folded over her chest, speaking calmly, without tears—"What is it I should do, then? Tell me, please. *Not* be foolish? And be what instead? Be 'sensible'? Accept that I have lost my family?"

Accept that I have nothing now but you?

Esther shivered.

"Esther." Bartha spoke her name directly into her ear.

"Esther, I am very sorry." He squeezed her hand, certain that whatever she was feeling now was his fault. The arrogance of this was almost enough to make her angry—and she waited, hoping, for her anger to lift her from the sorrow that was settling in her. Did he truly believe that if *he* said something that might make her think of her family, she would begin immediately, as if by command, to grieve for them?

But the anger wouldn't come. She *was* grieving, wasn't she? Did it make any difference that he could have predicted it, that he knew how easy it was for sorrow to descend on her? And even if it made a difference—even if sometimes she wished he were less sure he understood her, without ever asking her what she was feeling—she could not afford to be too angry. Anger was a luxury. Anger—she had never thought of this before, and the idea brought with it a flash of comprehension of her mother's weeping (which had always so infuriated her) or mute, stricken-looking acquiescence at just those times when she should have been most angry, when Esther's father had unleashed the brunt of his rage upon her (the times Esther meant when she described her mother to her friends as "someone who can take it but can't dish it out")—was for people who had choices. And she had already made all her choices.

Was it grief, she wondered then, that she was feeling? Or was it something else? Bewilderment? Fear? Or—finally—what Bartha had for so long been expecting her to feel: regret?

No—she refused to feel regret. She'd made her choices. They had been *her* choices. She had known what she was doing when she'd run away with him. She had chosen him—him, and Alexander. This was her family now. That was what she would tell him if he ever asked again if she regretted what she'd done. It was what he would tell *her* if she told him about the letters to her family. "Your family is here," he would say. He would spread his hands. "Here we are, Esther. *We* are your family." She knew that, she would tell him, just as she told it to herself now. She did not need to be reminded. And yet it was only now that she felt—felt, and not just knew—what this meant. That she truly had nothing, no one, else.

This is my life now, she thought, and with her eyes still closed, she made a private, silent promise, one that felt real to her in a way that today's public vows had not.

This is my life and I will be true to it.

But this did not seem to be enough.

I will be a good wife. She waited to see what it felt like to make such a promise.

The trouble was, she had no idea what this would entail. Still, she felt somber and grown up as she repeated this silently, *I will be a good wife.*

Faithful. She could be certain of that much.

Kind.

Kind perhaps could go without saying.

I will be a good wife, she tried again. *Faithful*—she paused—*and devoted. Sympathetic. Steadfast.*

She decided to put *kind* back in. Surely it couldn't hurt to promise even what went without saying.

This is my life now, and I will be true to it.

I will be a good wife—faithful, devoted, sympathetic, steadfast, and kind…for as long as we both shall live.

And she could keep this promise, couldn't she? It would not be so difficult.

Bartha would not live forever.

Oh—but she had not meant to think *that*.

She had not even known she could have such a thought, or she would have promised herself not to think it.

She put one hand over her heart, which had begun to jump. She was afraid it could be seen throwing itself against her chest—seen through her skin and the fabric of her blouse, just as Alexander had so often made himself visible when he had lived inside her body.

What a terrible thought. How could she have had such a thought?

She glanced at Bartha. If he could read her mind, as he sometimes seemed to—or if he assumed, wrongly, that she had been thinking of this all along…or if he had just been waiting for it to occur to her—then she wanted to tell him she was sorry, it wasn't true.

But: "What isn't true?" he would ask her gently.

He knew how old he was.

She knew how old he was.

She was only *facing facts*, she told herself. Was that the same thing as being cynical, or cruel? Bartha had turned seventy last April—*a fact*.

But that was not the point, was it? It was not the point because while a fact such as this was bracing—or brutal—thinking of it had not been. Thinking of it had been comforting.

And even as she told herself that this was not what counted—that what counted wasn't that a stray, unbidden thought had snuck up on her and provided her with comfort at a time when she had every reason to be (hadn't she? who would not be?) apprehensive, that what counted was that she had made a choice, she'd chosen *him*, and she'd made promises she meant to keep; even as she took her right hand from where she had laid it over her wildly beating heart and buttoned up the bottom of her blouse; even as she pried Alexander's hand loose from the fistful of silky fabric he was clutching and moved him to her shoulder and began mechanically to pat his back—she found that what she was thinking was *It won't last long. Hush. It's all right. It won't last forever.*

two

And of course it didn't. Nothing does.

On the day of her husband's death, after nearly three decades of marriage—which, she allowed, might just as well have been forever to the girl she had been when she married him—Esther Bartha stood alone in her kitchen and thought about time: about the way it collapses, about the way it had, for her, doubled over and folded almost exactly in half.

She was forty-five years old. Her husband had just—*just*, only yesterday—turned ninety-eight.

When they had married, he had been almost four times her age. And now? Now he wasn't so much more than twice her age.

Not *now*, Esther thought. *Now*—nothing.

It seemed like a puzzle. Four times becomes twice. Or, almost four becomes not quite two. Or, one quarter turns into one half.

And finally, each of these turns into—nothing.

Everything becomes nothing.

Gone.

She had said good night to him. As always, he went to bed long before she did. Later, when she slipped in beside him, he was asleep and snoring loudly, and so she said, as she almost always said, "Hush now," which sometimes worked but last night hadn't, and so she slipped one hand under his back and pressed it upwards until, groaning, protesting in his sleep, he rolled over onto his left side. She knew he'd roll back soon enough, and then he'd start to snore again, but all she needed was ten minutes of silence and then she'd be asleep herself—and then she was, and she didn't wake up until morning. And when she woke up—

Time folded in two. Her life bent double.

But *she* was not bent double. She stood perfectly straight, looking out the window in her kitchen. Still in coat and hat, gloves and scarf—all of which she had methodically put on before following the young men and the stretcher on which they carried Bartha out of the house, and which she had kept on all the while she was at the hospital. Standing in her kitchen, in her pale gray coat with its big black buttons, her purple hat, black leather gloves, striped purple-and-black scarf, looking out the window at her garden.

Nothing was in bloom now but narcissus, but there were hundreds of them, and so even this early in the spring—a cold gray day, the sky a silvery lavender—the garden was still bright, still pretty. The narcissus lined a path that wound and wound throughout the garden, a path she'd made herself—dug out and graveled and outlined not only with hundreds of pink-and-white narcissus but with white and violet and yellow crocuses, and a thick blanket of primroses.

The crocuses had bloomed and died already, but the primroses were coming soon—and the tulips, her favorites. She planted tulips in drifts of twenty-five, thirty, forty, all the different types mixed up together, so that within each group they would begin to come up at different times. Now their stems stood at varying heights, and the shapes of their leaves were distinct, too—some of them narrow, delicately pointed, wrapped around themselves as tightly as crossed fingers; some of them, on short, fat stems, flaring from the ground like candle flames. There were tall, sturdy-looking stems that were still only half grown, with their broad, glossy leaves thickly creased and furled; there were slender, slight ones, already as tall as they would ever be, and on the stems that rose above their peeled-back leaves, the very first of the flowers were sealed in smooth pea-green skin, like tiny eggs.

You would never know, to look at them now, how beautiful they would all be later.

By the end of the month or early next month, the garden would be as she loved it most. There were many flowers in her garden that were showier, more obviously beautiful than her tulips (the peonies, so blowsy and theatrical, with their big, indulgent, gorgeous heads bowed, and the roses—she had all kinds of roses, and she admired them and attended to them faithfully—and the dramatic, glamorous Asiatic lilies on their tall spindly stems—not to mention all the annuals she put in in the spring, which were lovely enough to be worth the trouble for a single season's performance), but the tulips were the ones she loved most. They were not *only* beautiful. It was with her tulips—the forebears of these tulips—that she had begun her garden, had begun *to* garden, after a catalogue had arrived unsolicited one September not long after she and Bartha had bought this house. *Easy to plant, easy to grow,* Esther read aloud to Alexander, all those years ago. *No-care, no-fail flowers.*

What she'd had in mind, as she filled out the order form, was that planting the bulbs would be an afternoon's work for herself and her son. In those days she was always on the lookout for projects they could undertake together, and she'd also had the idea that gardening would be educational for him. She remembered that she'd told him this and he had nodded solemnly—no more than six years old, and already so serious. (When the carton of bulbs, twenty-four of the most ordinary Darwin tulips, finally arrived and she read out loud to him from the slip of paper that came with them—*"Time-tested tulips you know you can count on"*—he'd said, earnestly, "That's what we need *exactly.*")

The two of them had knelt together in the backyard digging holes and trying to tell top from bottom as they dropped in those first bulbs, and both of them had been elated (and amazed, they had confessed to each other, since neither, it emerged, had been certain it would happen) when, just over a half year later, flowers in bright kindergarten-paintbox colors sprung out of the little green shells they had been peeking at on hands and knees since they had first appeared, tucked within a twist of leaves on shoots that had thrust out of the ground weeks before. Perfect fire-truck-red and schoolbus-yellow flowers, cup-shaped, with square bottoms, waxy and smooth. They'd grinned at each other, shaken hands, congratulated themselves. "Nature," Esther had said proudly, as if she'd invented it, and Alexander had asked if he might take one red and one yellow tulip to school with him the next day for show and tell.

She owed her garden to those first two-dozen cheerful, ordinary tulips, and she knew this had something, and possibly everything, to do with how she felt about the tulips she'd grown since then—the Angelique and Palestrina, Queen of the Night, Burgundy Lace, White Triumphator, Negrita. It had something, or everything, to do with the way she mourned the passing of her tulips each year even as she sowed verbena, zinnia, and silene, even as she watched the columbine and bleeding heart come into bloom again, even as she dug holes to replant the pompon dahlias, the cannas, the callas she had lifted from the garden in the fall, and put in seedlings she had started indoors of pink salvia and dark purple petunia.

Her narcissus never troubled her this way, not even when they had to be replaced, when she had noticed that they had begun to come up smaller and the color had drained out of them. She dug up the aging bulbs and put in fresh new ones without a moment's thought. And when her crocuses gave out, she often didn't notice until days or weeks had passed. They gave her pleasure on the morning they first opened every year—and after that she didn't think about them.

But even on the hottest days of early summer, when all of her tulips were long gone and the antique roses were in full bloom and so fragrant that when she worked in the vegetable patch, in the garden's southeast corner, the scent riding on a wave of heat sometimes made her dizzy enough to have to stop and rest her head on her knees— even then she was not finished grieving for the flowers she loved most.

Bartha used to say that watching her as the last of her tulips faded and began to drop their petals every year was like watching her surrender Alexander to the bus on the first day of school each fall. "You would think, from all the sorrow, that this was good-bye for the last time," he'd said, year after year, when she returned to the house in tears. "Take hold of yourself, Esther. He will be home again this afternoon."

Until the year came when her son left home for good, and Bartha had grown so used to her sorrows he had stopped remarking on them.

Esther closed her eyes. If she concentrated, with her eyes closed she could summon up the backyard as it had been all those years ago, with those two dozen red and yellow tulips poking out of the tall grass here and there over the whole yard—one by the gate, one under the catalpa tree, one where for the last ten years she'd put in vegetables for Bartha, who had never been able to get over the fact that here in the middle west, with farms everywhere around the little brown-and-gray city in which they had made their home, it was so difficult to procure food that tasted fresh. She hadn't even known enough to clear away a bit of sod when she had planted those first bulbs: she'd only dug holes in the grass and dropped them in, and closed the holes right up again. So they hadn't been able to mow the yard that year until late in the spring, which had delighted Alexander, who'd asked if they could keep the yard this way forever—and she'd thought about it, too, because the tall soft grass was so nice, "like a jungle," Alexander said, but then she started thinking about how, come fall, she might put in more bulbs, "maybe a lot more bulbs," she told him, shyly, and instead of letting the yard turn into a jungle, she began to dig the sod out altogether all around the fence and in a circle around the catalpa tree, and on both sides of the back door, twin rectangles she filled that fall with parrot tulips and Emperor and Empress daffodils.

Alexander's interest in growing flowers had already waned by the next spring. He was becoming busier by then, old enough for projects of his own devising, only a few of which required her participation, and all at once he had friends in the neighborhood who would turn up at the house asking if he could come out to play. This was only as it should be, Esther knew, but still it was unsettling, and she would have been at loose ends if she had not bought her first bedding plants that May and put them in amidst the Golden Melody and Boccherini tulips, where they flourished.

She could see those first annuals in her mind, too, if

she tried: marigolds, impatiens, pansies, asters, lisianthus. On a whim, she'd bought a packet of mixed wildflower seeds, and one of forget-me-nots, at Hinky Dinky; she'd sprinkled them in, too. And when she took Alexander to the library that spring and summer, sometimes she would look for gardening books to check out for herself along with the novels she still brought home every week.

That was how it had begun—how she had become a gardener, the sort of person who sat up late on midwinter nights with a lapful of catalogues and a pad and a box of markers, drawing and redrawing plans for making changes in her garden. The sort of person who had pondered catalogues for two years before ordering the English roses she'd been eyeing, sketching, moving here and there in her various drawings. The sort of person who, at summer's end each year, would scrutinize the photographs of all the newest tulips, her heart aching even as she made her choices, knowing that the best of them, the most delicate and interesting ones, would give out the fastest, that they might come up again twice after the first time, and never quite as splendidly as that first year, before they vanished (unlike those first tulips bulbs that she'd put in with Alexander, which had come back undiminished for too many years to count, like the children of her neighbors who came home dutifully, unthrillingly, each year for holidays). She would turn down the corners of the pages featuring the most exotic, fragile tulips—pinks so pale, so nearly white and so translucent that the flowers seemed to glow; purple petals so dark and silky they looked not just black but as if they were made of liquid—to replace the bulbs that had begun to give out, and she was already thinking of the spring they would fail to return. Before she'd even dug the holes to plant them in (before she'd even ordered them—before she'd even made her final choices about which ones she would order), she was already grieving for them.

She opened her eyes. She needed to see the garden as it really was, not as it would be at spring's end in this or any other year, or in her memory of long ago (or as it would be in mid-May or in late June or at the end of August, when the drawings she had made all winter came to life, successively), but here, now, poised for spring, *true* spring, when the narcissus faded and the first of the early tulips opened, accompanied—like a great star's entourage, she thought—by the deep pink primroses with their little flame of yellow at each flower's heart. This happened at a slightly different time each year, and not just because the weather never caught up to the calendar at the same time from year to year, but also because it depended on which types of early tulips she'd put in that fall, or which ones would return from last year's planting or the year's before. Sometimes the entourage came first; sometimes it trailed. But it was with the entrance of that year's first tulips that she would announce to Bartha, "Winter's over, finally." And he would always say, "Thank God." Each year, each spring, they had this conversation, if it could be called a conversation. This exchange, this ritual.

So much of what had served as conversation between them had been like this, nothing more than ritual—that brief and that predictable, that circumscribed. "Don't stay up too late," he told her every night, before he went to bed. "I won't," she'd say, and add, "Sleep well."

She never knew if he knew that she stayed up— reading, drawing, listening to music—until two or three, sometimes as late as four. She chose to assume that he didn't know. He never asked, and he was asleep when she slipped into bed beside him. In the morning, when she woke, he would already be gone.

"Everything is all right?" he would ask her later, when he looked in on her from his studio. "Perfect," she'd say, sitting at the kitchen table, drinking tea, eating her breakfast. In early spring, there would be a jar with two or three fresh-cut tulips; when the tulips were gone, there would be peonies. "Very pretty," he would say.

And each summer, when she handed him the first ripe tomato of the season, he would say, "Who would have guessed that you would turn into such a gardener?" and she would shrug, she would smile, and year after year she would say, "Nobody. Nobody could have guessed. Certainly not I." And it was true. She had never given any thought to gardening. She had never even known anyone who gardened, never known anyone who had a yard in which *to* garden.

Each year, Bartha would take his first bite of the tomato she had handed him—biting into it whole, the way one bit into a peach—and say, "Esther, this is the best tomato I have ever in my life tasted. Thank you."

"Better even than last year's?" she would say.

"Always better," he told her.

This was either a good thing or a bad thing, this ritual, this predictability.

And thus: she had either missed out on something essential, or she had been lucky.

Her eyes were on the garden as it really was right now: all the tiny wrinkled heads of crocuses crowded on both sides of the path, along with the drooping, ballet-pretty, pink-and-white narcissus and the flat spread of not-yet flowering primroses; the many hundreds of still shut-tight tulips huddled in groups as if they were conferring with one another, waiting for something to happen; the large circular patch she had set aside for growing vegetables for Bartha showing no evidence that anything had ever been there but wet fallen leaves and mud and weathered mulch. *Who would have guessed? Nobody could have guessed.*

But things happened sometimes, Esther thought—and wished she'd thought before now (thought and *said*, just once, to Bartha, when he murmured his question each year)—things happened without anybody planning them, without anybody's being able to predict or direct or even pretend to take charge of them. In fact, it seemed to her at this moment, nearly *everything* happened that way, and maybe this explained, as well as anything could, why she had taken to the garden as she had. For in the garden she *could* plan, she could choose and predict. And if something went awry, or didn't turn out just as she'd imagined— why, then, she could fix it. Everything that went wrong in the garden could be righted somehow if she put her mind to it. Plants could be dug up and moved, separated from each other. They could be discarded altogether— pulled up and replaced. And the truth was that whether or not things came out exactly as she'd planned them in the garden mattered less to her than knowing that it was all hers, that nothing went into her garden that she hadn't thought about and chosen, that nothing went in anywhere except where she had made the choice to put it. It was all of her own making: every one of its effects, all of its charms. Everything that went wrong, too. It was because of something she had done—which she could then undo.

She turned from the window. How she had wished, all morning, to be at home and by herself. Now that she was here, she couldn't think of why she'd wanted to be.

Well, she had only wanted to be free of the hospital, to which she hadn't wanted Bartha to be taken in the first place. "Why the hospital?" she'd asked the driver of the ambulance. "What sense does that make?" "Where else should I take him, ma'am?" he'd asked her—patiently, it seemed to her, but she might have been wrong; it might just as easily have been insolence she was hearing, and not recognizing. It was always hard for her to recognize the difference, to distinguish mockery from kindness. Alexander used to point it out to her, telling her when salespeople or waitresses were being sarcastic—not helpful, as she'd thought—saying, "Do you need anything *else?*" when they had been wandering the aisles of Younkers for too many hours, "window-shopping from the inside," as the two of them called it, or lingering for too long over one hot chocolate and one tea with lemon in a luncheonette that was too big and brightly lit to remind her of her own childhood, that was not called a "luncheonette" in any case, on the way home from school when Alexander was in second or third grade, when she still picked him up and walked him home each day.

She wondered how long she had been at the hospital. She had no idea how long it had been since she had left the house—no idea how long it had been since she had woken up and found him. And even when she looked at the oven clock, when she could see that it was now eleven minutes after noon, she couldn't make the simple calculation: the time now, minus the time she had awakened and found Bartha in the bed beside her. *Gone*, and still beside her.

She began to cry. It was the first time she had cried since she had found him.

Found him gone.

It was the first time she had cried in years. It had in fact been so long since she had last cried, she could not even remember when it had been, or over what.

She had cured herself of crying long ago. But if he were here to see her cry now, she would tell him, *This is an occasion for tears. There are certain occasions on which tears are appropriate.*

She sat down at the table, not in her own chair, from which she'd still have been able to look out the window to her garden, but in Bartha's. She was exhausted. She hadn't known this until she sat down. It was all she could do not to lay her head on her arms on the table, all she could do not to go to sleep right there. All morning she had been obliged to hold her head up, to nod and seem calm, unhurried, interested in everything the doctor had to say. She had listened, she had answered questions. No, she didn't need a sedative. Yes, she would be fine at home alone.

The doctor had been kind, or had tried to be. She was almost sure of that. He had seemed to be working so hard at kindness that it had crossed her mind (he'd been young enough, awkward enough) that she might be his first new widow. She had told him—perhaps she had told him more than once—that it had been such a great surprise, so shocking, so bewildering, to wake and find her husband gone. "How could it be?" she had said to him. "And I was asleep! How can that be?" And the young doctor said, "I understand. But there was nothing that you could have done. It's important that you know that. Even if you'd been awake, there wasn't anything you could have done. You mustn't blame yourself."

He had misunderstood her. But he must not have been able to imagine that what she had said was true—that it could have been such a shock to her to find him gone. That she could have been so unprepared. "His heart simply gave out," he said. "It was his time. There was nothing you or anyone else could have done."

It was as if she had forgotten that this could, that it *would*, ever happen. He was old, yes. But he had been old since she'd first met him. He had been old for much, much longer than he had been young. He had been old for much, much longer than he had been middle aged—old for so much longer than he had been anything else, except himself.

Still, she thought. Still. What had she imagined? Had she expected him to live forever?

And as she sat in the chair Bartha would have been in at this very moment—eating, at this very moment, the lunch she would have made for him once she had finished her breakfast and left on a plate, wrapped in Saran Wrap, on the second shelf of the refrigerator—she remembered, for the first time in many years, the thought that had both consoled and shamed her on her wedding day.

So I was right. I was right after all.

She had only forgotten.

And yet think how lucky it was, she told herself, that she hadn't been able to see into the future on that day.

If she had known, her courage might have failed her. She might have grabbed the baby Alexander and run off.

Or perhaps it wasn't lucky. Even now, even after all these years, she wasn't sure.

That's enough.

She spoke to herself calmly, though her heart was racing—spoke to herself the way she'd once heard a girl speak to her dog, long ago on Brighton Beach Avenue. The dog had turned on its owner and Esther had watched them helplessly—the dog snarling and snapping, the girl neither dropping the leash she held and running away nor kicking it when it reared up on its hind legs and barked angrily at her. The girl only continued to say softly, soothingly, *That's enough now. Shh now. It's all right. Everything's all right.* And finally the dog calmed. Esther watched the two of them walk away together—turning down Brighton Fifth Street, disappearing.

In her mind Esther held out one hand and kept her voice soft. *All right now. Shh. That's enough.*

But it was as if a part of her really had gone wild. She—*it*—would not be calmed. *Enough?* she answered herself. *Enough for* what? Trembling, furious. *Oh, yes, do think of how lucky you've been. Think of all the girls your age who had their own adventures and moved on. Poor unlucky girls who moved on without hesitation from one thing to the next! And what became of them—of Kathleen and Leah and all the others whose names you can't recall—while you spent your whole life on what they would have chalked up to a first adventure? A first misstep, a mistake?*

Spent your whole life.

Spent, as in used up.

Stop. She had gone too far—either that, or she had only faltered because the truth was that she knew nothing about what those other girls had done. She knew nothing about how anyone else lived.

She was both ashamed and wounded. She stopped, and then she thought: *Can't take it* and *can't dish it out.*

This almost made her laugh, although she was still frightened—she was panting (she thought again of that long-ago dog, the girl her own age at the other end of its leash, refusing to run away, to scream, even to scold); her heart was still pounding. *Can't take it* and *can't dish it out*—this was something Alexander had said once to her about them both. He'd been comparing himself and her to Bartha, who was "strong both ways," he said. "He always gives as good as he gets." She could not recall now if he had meant this admiringly or derisively. Alexander had said, "You and I, we're the sensitive flowers in the family. Very delicate types. Dad's the indomitable one."

This must have been while he was in college, during one of his twice-yearly visits home—one of the early visits, his freshman or sophomore year, when each time he'd come home he had been full of insights and pronouncements about all of them, although he never spoke of them to Bartha, nor did she report them to him afterwards. She was certain Bartha would laugh and shrug them off, dismissing everything his son had said as "typical of Alexander, fanciful nonsense, phrased not half badly," as he said of Alexander's letters, and which she knew would hurt her not only on her son's behalf but also on her own, since she took everything that Alexander said seriously. What did it suggest about her, she sometimes wondered, if she took "fanciful nonsense" to heart? Of course, Alexander had once also told her—and she didn't know if this had been meant, either, as an insult or a compliment—that she took *everything* to heart. "It's always life-and-death with you, Mom," he'd said. "Everything is everything, or else it's nothing."

And now she remembered something she should not, she thought, have let herself forget—not even in the service of self-mockery or wryness (or to test herself, pitting her meanness against her capacity to suffer it—a contest both sides had lost, after all), she remembered that she'd *always* taken things so seriously that the girl she had been then would not have "grabbed the baby Alexander and run off." She *would* have stayed forever. It would not have mattered to her how long that turned out to be. She would have steeled herself, she would have stayed.

Would have? she thought. *Had.* Had, if what *forever*

meant was *up until the end.* And that was indeed what it meant—it meant *from the beginning to the end.*

For him, then, it had been forever. And for her—for her, it was so difficult to think about what had come before him, *forever* might just as well have started with him. And the part of forever that had ended sometime before she woke up this morning, when his heart stopped beating as he lay beside her, seemed as if it were a lifetime.

Seemed, she thought, because it was. And now she thought of what she was supposed to do, what she should have done already—from the hospital or even before that, before (instead of!)   calling 911 this morning—and she stood up, only a little bit unsteadily, and went to the phone to call her son, whose lifetime it was, and tell him to come home.

Nothing lasts forever was what she was thinking as she dialed.

Thirteen hundred miles away, Alexander had exactly the same thought, though not at exactly the same time. He had seated himself on the tall stool at his worktable as he'd reached for the phone, and now, while he listened to his mother, he looked beyond the clutter on the table and out the window, where he could see the gray-brown ribbon of the river. He couldn't see much of it, just a short section between buildings. Just enough, he'd always thought. He watched part of a ship—then more parts of it, piece by piece—move southward. The last fragment of the ship had been swallowed by the buildings to the left when he heard the click of a metal page flipping down on the clock that was buried somewhere on the table. It was a primitive digital clock he'd had since he was a child, when such clocks were still a novelty as well as "an advance over old-fashioned ordinary ones" (so he'd told his parents gravely—as was his style at the age of seven, when he'd asked for it for Christmas). He searched for the clock amidst the stacked-up notebooks, scraps of paper, hand tools, grease pencils and Sharpies, pencil stubs, slides of his work that should be labeled and put away, photographs and contact sheets and glassine envelopes of negatives, unopened mail, mail he had opened and meant to discard, a few letters that he'd read and meant to keep, *Art in America*, empty soup and coffee cans, and soup and coffee cans full of assorted things—chisels and files and screw-drivers, unsharpened pencils, drinking straws and chopsticks in the paper wrappers they arrived in when they came with food he ordered in from restaurants—until he spotted it behind a peculiarly neat lineup of coffee mugs (three in a row, each with its handle pointing to the right—each with a quarter-inch of hardened, ancient, light/sweet coffee at the bottom). 1:21. *1:21 here* was what he thought.

A decade in New York City, and still he thought *here*, as opposed to *there*.

She had been afraid he wouldn't answer. The phone had rung fifteen, twenty times before he'd picked it up. But then it always did (she simply could not get used to it). For years she had imagined that his loft must be cavernously huge, that he must have to walk a city block's length—and perhaps up and down halls, too, and turning corners, going in and out of rooms through doorway after doorway—to get to his phone, but when finally she told him that, he laughed. "In New York? Think about it, Mom. Nobody's place is that big. Remember?" She'd laughed too but hadn't risen to the bait of "think about it" or "remember?"—and in any case the New York she had known seemed to have no relation to the New York he lived in, a place made up of neighborhoods she had never even heard of when she was a girl.

The phone, it seemed, was never very far away from him. Instead, he had explained, it was "a matter of the principle of self-selection." No one hung on long enough to speak to him except the people who already knew him well enough to know they *had* to hang on—the only people he was likely to be pleased to hear from anyway. "Persistence is its own reward," he said.

Still, each time she called him she began to despair by the tenth ring. He wasn't there. Or he was there but he'd decided not to answer. She could not teach herself *not* to believe the phone would go on ringing, ringing. He had never had an answering machine; he despised answering machines, he said. "If someone wants to talk to me, he'll call back if I don't answer the first time. Or the fifth time. Whatever."

She could not prepare herself sufficiently for the long wait before he would answer. Nor could she prepare herself for the shock she experienced each time he did answer—could not prepare herself for the sound of his voice, the "hello" when at last it came, which was precisely his father's. And why was it his father's? Why only this one word accented in precisely Bartha's accent? And why did he *sing* his hello, just as Bartha had, with its exaggerated pause and the diminished third between the syllables, when Alexander didn't (couldn't) sing?

She had never been able to prepare herself, and this

time the sound of her son's voice after so many rings, after she had begun to despair, the *hello* of his father, left her stricken. She couldn't speak.

"Bad news," Alexander said into the silence. "Mom? It's you, yes?" And Esther nodded—she nodded twice—as if he could see her.

Alexander was accustomed to this, his mother's silence at critical moments. Just as he was accustomed to the way she would talk sometimes for no other reason than to *fill* a silence. He was used to listening to nothing—to nothing of one kind or another—when he talked to her, and to guessing what was on her mind when nothing seemed to be, or when her mind seemed to be on something else. Or when she hesitated. Or when, as now, she couldn't bring herself to speak at all.

But he didn't want to guess this time. He waited.

And after a long wait she said, "Dad." And then there was another silence before she said, "Oh, sweetheart, I'm so sorry."

In the silence after that he could have sworn he could hear her heart beating, but that couldn't be—not unless she'd taken the receiver from her ear and pressed it to her chest.

Which was possible, he thought. This was his mother, after all.

"Gone," she said finally. "Your father's gone."

For just an instant he thought she meant his father had taken off—packed a suitcase, left a note, and run away. Even in that instant, there was time for him to think, *He wouldn't leave her penniless, he'd take just half the savings, wouldn't he?*—and to conjure up a girl, a student, at the old man's side, a girl with long, straight, blond Midwestern hair and flat Midwestern features, broad hips and broad shoulders.

And then when he understood both how preposterous this was—his nearly hundred-year-old father running where, with what broad-shouldered pretty girl? (It had been years since the old man had last had any students—and why, anyway, would such a girl run off with him? For that matter, what on earth would possess *him* to run off now?)— and also what it was his mother meant to tell him, he thought, *But that's impossible.*

And why impossible? He was furious then—but at whom? He couldn't tell. At his mother? At himself? At his father—*gone*?

At all of them. As if they all had thought that the old man had lived so long already, he had outlived, *skipped*, the possibility of his own death.

Nothing lasts forever, Alexander told himself.

As if this were news.

He wanted to say it out loud, too—to break the news to *her*—but he did not allow himself to speak. He stayed silent. He waited for her to tell him the rest.

And once she began to, she couldn't stop. She just kept talking, and Alexander nodded as if she could see him—both of them, always, seemed to imagine that the other could see everything—and listened, or half listened, as she went on. There were no pauses during which he could have said anything even if he'd chosen to.

After a while he picked up a Sharpie and began to doodle on the back of an unopened Con Ed bill. His mother's voice—*Doctor. Earnest. Like you, in a way*—was like the background music he always kept on when he was working. *Morning*, she said. *Hospital.* And *late. Till late. Too late.*

While his mother talked, he drew a clock—an ordinary round-faced one with arrow hands and a big round alarm bell tipped to one side on its head. He gave it arms and legs, a suitcase bulging at its feet, a thumb stuck out: a hitchhiking alarm clock.

1:29. Here.

He hardly ever even noticed that he did this—*here* versus *there*—but when he did notice, it bothered him, not least because it made him wonder about all the times he hadn't caught himself. It made no sense. It was not as if he still thought of Omaha as home—it was not as if he had *ever* thought of Omaha as home. Even when he was still living there (even when he was a child) he'd been disdainful of the place, just as his father was. The old man had never passed a day in Omaha without complaining about it, though always in such a way—amused, resigned, self-mockingly regretful—that made it impossible to ask, "Well, why don't we move, then?"

It was a sort of joke—a permanent joke—that they lived in Omaha. A joke between him and his father. What his mother thought about their being there, Alexander couldn't guess. She had never volunteered an opinion, never argued with his father—or with Alexander either, once he grew old enough to voice his own complaints. But then she never talked about New York, the place he did think of as home, either. She didn't talk about it now and she hadn't talked about it then, but since it was where she was from, it was *her* home, too, if she chose to think of it that way. He thought sometimes that she just didn't think, or care, about *place* the way he did. The way his father did.

He had already capped the marking pen and put it down, but now he picked it up again and gave the clock a mouth—a slantwise slash above the six—and, dangling from it, at the lower end, a cigarette butt trailing smoke. What with the cigarette, and the bell and clapper at that jaunty angle, the clock now looked like a cartoon struggling-artist. A struggling-artist-circa-1950s clock. A beat clock. No—just a clock trying to *look* beat. Not an artist-clock, but an *artistic* clock. A clock with pretensions.

He could not remember why he had taken his old clock with him when he'd moved out of his parents' house. It was one of the few things besides his clothes that he *had* taken. He had even left his reading lamp and his portable stereo. He'd left his cassette tapes; he'd left all of the books he'd read and reread as a child and as a teenager, all mixed up together on the shelves—*Call of the Wild* alongside *Catcher in the Rye, Catch 22* sandwiched between *Johnny Tremain* and *The Phantom Tollbooth*—where to this day they remained. In fact, the room in all respects remained as it had been the day he'd left it: the books on the bookshelves, even the copy of *The Good Master* (set in long-ago Hungary, he knew, although he'd never cracked it; his mother had bought it for him when he was in the fourth or fifth grade, making a big deal about it, and so he'd felt honor-bound, somehow, to resist reading it—the only book he'd owned in his whole childhood that he hadn't read) still lying on its side atop the row of *We Were There* books (*We Were There with the Pony Express, ...with Lincoln in the White House, ... with Lewis and Clark, ...at the Klondike Gold Rush, ...at the Normandy Invasion*), the cassettes in shoeboxes stacked up by the dresser, the rock posters (Pere Ubu, Devo, the Cars) and carefully clipped pages from the art magazines he'd begun to read in high school—reproductions of paintings by Rainer Fetting and Sandro Chia, a photo of a Barry Flanagan bronze sculpture, one of a Glynn Williams—on the walls, and the postcards of Quattrocento paintings and Cyprian statuettes stuck all around the wood frame of the big square mirror. But for the clock, which had been on his nightstand, and the hardcovered dictionary and thesaurus he'd kept on his desk (which now lay somewhere under the mess on his worktable), the room looked just as it had when he had lived there. Unless you opened up the dresser drawers or looked into the closet.

He had offered several times while visiting to help his mother go through what he'd left and throw away whatever wasn't worth still keeping and pack up in boxes and put in the basement everything that was, so that she could use the room for something else. She always insisted that she didn't need "his" room for anything other than what it was. "I have a study," she would say, "and Dad has a studio. What do we need it for? This way it's here for you whenever you come home." And so twice each year he'd come back to Omaha to walk into what he had come to think of as a Cornell box filled with the detritus of his life up to the age of eighteen. The Room that Time Forgot, he called it. "Exactly right," his mother said. "And that's the way I like it." She said this to him every time—not ironically, but sweetly.

Would she keep his father's studio just as it had been, too? This was what he was thinking when he noticed that she had stopped talking and he set his pen down and asked how she was, and she said that she would be fine, that he shouldn't worry about her, and he lied and said he knew she would, of course he wouldn't worry. But he didn't know; he was already worrying. She had never lived alone. She'd never even spent a night in the house by herself. How *would* she manage, he thought, except by pretending that nothing had changed?

His mother had stopped talking. His little clock released another minute into the silence.

"Mom?" he said.

"Alexander?" she said. Was she making fun of him? Surely not. Not today.

"Are you really all right?"

"All right?" She paused. She seemed to be seriously thinking it over. "Well, no, I guess I'm not," she said. "Should I be?" But she didn't wait for him to answer. "No, of course not. Why should I be?" She did this all the time—carried on whole conversations with herself. "I shouldn't be. But later—sure. I'll be fine."

He could see her shrug when she said *fine*. He could see it as clearly as if she were standing right beside him, the receiver of the kitchen phone, a white Trimline which must date back to the same era as his clock, pressed tightly to her left ear—she always clutched the phone as if there might be thieves around who'd want to snatch it—and her right hand curled and tucking a long strand of hair behind her ear and then retucking it (not *it*, then, but the memory of it) again and then again, until she noticed she was doing it and stopped, and switched to raking her hand through her hair instead—or tugging on a handful of it, or else twisting it around her middle finger. Whenever she was nervous or upset or sad, her hands would become busy with her hair, which, except for the few minutes twice a day when she kept it pulled back so she could wash her face and brush her teeth, he had never in his life seen her wear any way but loose.

"Sure, Mom," he said. He shrugged, too. "Of course you will. I know that." But he didn't.

"You don't sound very sure," his mother said.

"You don't, either."

Now she laughed. (How could she laugh?) "It seems like you've been gone a long time."

"Just a day, Mom."

"That's not what I mean," she said. He was surprised by how sharply she said it.

"Mom. Seriously. You know that I just got back, right?"

"I don't mean since you *visited*. I'm not losing my mind. I know you were just here for Dad's birthday. I mean, it seems like it's been a very long time since you left home for good."

"Ah. Well, it has been. It's been over ten years since I left for college."

"I didn't know you were leaving home for good then. Did you?"

He didn't know how to answer her. He'd been in New York since September 1983. He'd earned the right to think of *that* as his home. Just as she'd earned the right to call Omaha home, if that was what she wanted to do. But he didn't say that now. He'd said it a hundred times, anyway, and it had never made any difference. She would just go on as if he hadn't said anything at all.

"Nothing lasts," his mother said then, and it startled him, because it was so like what he'd been thinking.

"I suppose not," he said. And then he said, "I'll be there as soon as I can," and realized as he said this that it was what he should have said immediately. "All right, Mom?"

"Yes," she said. "That would be good."

Now both of them were silent. Alexander studied the solidified coffee in one of the three unwashed mugs behind which he'd found his clock. Then he looked at the mug itself, turning it so that he could see what was written on it. He didn't have a single coffee mug without some sort of writing on it—evidently owing to the single mug he'd had when he'd moved to New York, a mug with his parents' phone number printed on it, and in parentheses, beneath that, CALL HOME (a gift, of course, from his mother, who'd had it made up for him at a novelty shop just before he left for college). Every girlfriend he had had since then had felt the impulse to add a new mug to his "collection." This one, from the ex-girlfriend who'd worked in sales at a news radio station, had a picture of a small globe on it and was inscribed, *You give us twenty-two minutes, we'll give you the world.*

"I'll be there tonight," he told her. "I haven't even unpacked yet, so it won't take me long to get out of here. All I have to do is throw in one more clean shirt and a pair of socks and put my bag back on my shoulder."

"Well, do what you can," she said. "Tonight, tomorrow. I'll be glad to see you whenever you can get here."

"I'm sorry I'm not there already. If I'd listened to you and stayed the extra night, I would be, wouldn't I?"

"Did I ask you to do that?"

"You always do." She laughed. "Mom, you're laughing?"

"That's terrible, isn't it?"

"I don't know. I don't know what you're supposed to do."

"We weren't prepared."

"We weren't. I don't know why not."

"That's what the doctor said. Implied."

He sighed. "Just let me call the airline and find out when the next flight out is, and I'll call you back, all right?"

He was about to hang up when she said, "I want you to know how glad I am that you came home to celebrate his birthday. I know you weren't crazy about the idea, but it turned out to be a good thing, didn't it?"

"Yes," he said. "It did. I'm glad too."

"And you know what, Alex?" she said—and although she said it softly, it was as if she had grabbed his shoulders

106

hard and shaken him. How many years had it been since she had last called him Alex? Twenty? More than twenty. Before he'd even started kindergarten. His father hadn't liked it, he remembered that. There'd been some discussion about how she must stop before he began to go to school, where if he called himself by that name it would catch on with the other children.

"No," he said. "What?" But before she could answer, he said, "Mom, you called me *Alex*."

"Did I?" she said. "That's odd, isn't it?"

"Yes," he said. "It's very odd. You haven't called me Alex since at least 1970."

But she wasn't listening to him. "He was glad, too—that's what I wanted to say. It meant a lot to him, your coming home."

Alexander couldn't help asking: "He said that?"

"Well, not—"

"Not in so many words. I know."

When she didn't say anything then, he knew she was wishing she had lied to him—had just said, "Yes, he said that." But he wouldn't have believed her anyway. This wasn't the sort of thing his father said.

That was why she hadn't lied, of course. She knew he wouldn't have believed her. She tried now to think of what Bartha *had* said after Alexander had left yesterday. Had they talked at all? She remembered that he had been silent when they left the restaurant after the birthday lunch, directly from which Alexander had left for the airport, and that when they'd returned to the house they'd gone their separate ways, as usual—she into her study, he into his studio. When they met in the kitchen for a light evening meal (fruit, cheese, salad, bread), she was sure that he had mentioned how good lunch had been, and that she had agreed. Had anything else passed between them before they had parted again after dinner? She could not recall. And by the time she set down her drawing pad and markers and turned off the stereo and went upstairs to bed, he was fast asleep. And then she was, too, and once she was sleeping, nothing bothered her, nothing could wake her before morning. Before what *she* considered morning: ten o'clock, ten thirty. For Bartha, morning was the crack of dawn. Which was why, when she woke up this morning and he was still there beside her, she knew. She knew right away. Without touching him—without even really looking at him. He was there. And so she knew before she knew.

"It's funny you were so insistent," Alexander said. "As if you knew."

Startled, Esther said, "But I didn't tell you that, did I?"

"Tell me? You didn't have to tell me. It was obvious."

"What was obvious?"

"*Mom.* Come on. His birthday. And my being there. You know. And now it seems as if you...you know, *knew.*"

"No," she said. Sometimes she was almost sure that he could read her mind, but even at her surest she could never tell if this troubled or pleased her. "I didn't *know,*" she told him. "Not if what you mean by that is did I have a premonition."

"So why'd you beg me to come?"

"Did I beg you? I didn't mean to. I just meant to ask you."

"You *asked* six or seven times."

"Because you said no the first five or six times."

"Exactly," Alexander said.

But she hadn't realized she was begging. "It's just an idea," she remembered saying when she'd asked him—the first time she'd asked him (she didn't think she'd framed

108

the question in the same way when she had repeated it)—
to come home "just this once" for his father's birthday. If
he'd asked her why, would she have had an answer? But
he hadn't asked; he'd only told her no five or six different
ways (it wasn't a good time for him to take a break from his
work, he despised the Midwest at this time of year, he had
theater tickets for that weekend for a play a friend of his
was in—she knew better than to try to refute any of these
explanations, so she changed the subject and then didn't
ask again until midway through their next conversation,
four or five days later) before he had given in.

Why *had* she been so set on "doing something"—
so she had presented it, to him and Bartha both—for
Bartha's birthday this year, "whether or not," she had said
to Alexander, "he wants us to do it"?

"Do people have premonitions without knowing that
they're having them?" she asked her son now.

"I don't think so, Mom. I think the 'knowing' is pretty
much the point of premonitions."

"I suppose so," she said, but she wondered. What
could have inspired her to make a fuss ("a quiet fuss," as
she had promised Bartha) over this occasion when she had
not done so for so many years? He had told her long ago
that he disliked "commotion" on his birthday, and after
he'd tolerated her first few attempts at celebration in his
honor, he had said one year, while Alexander was still small,
"Please, let this be the end. No more. For me this is not
pleasure," and she'd given up. She'd let his birthdays pass,
from then on, as he wished them to—by doing, saying
nothing.

Until this one. When she had proposed a celebration
("no commotion, no balloons and flowers, just a nice lunch
for the three of us") he'd groaned and closed his eyes and

he had murmured, "Esther, Esther," but he had not said, "No, I forbid it. Absolutely not," and she had taken this to mean he would permit it. And he had. He had permitted her to ask (to beg?) Alexander to come home, and he had permitted them a birthday lunch. He had even allowed them the singing, in stage-whispers, of the "Happy Birthday" song over a piece of pastry (although he'd held up one hand when she'd made a move to insert into its top crust the candle she had carried with her, wrapped in tissue, in her purse). He had consented to receive, over dessert and coffee, the gifts they had brought: from her a salmon-colored cashmere scarf, and from Alexander a small crate of tiny jars of jellies and preserves ("made by monks," Bartha had reported as he held up one jar of blood-dark sour cherries, reading aloud from its label with a grin that she saw for herself pleased Alexander very much) and a new recording of *Tristan and Isolde* with Birgit Nilsson and Wolfgang Windgassen.

He had permitted all of this, in fact, with such grace and good spirits that she'd wondered, as they stood outside the restaurant waving goodbye to Alexander, if they might not have celebrated with him, celebrated *him*, all along—if she had only thought before this year to make an effort to contain her own impulses toward…well, toward *commotion*.

Her own impulses, and her son's. She'd watched Alexander's taxi turn the corner, disappear—and in her mind then, once he was out of her sight, he was already back in his loft in New York—before she'd said, softly, "I'm so sorry I did not think of this sooner." Bartha had smiled. He had taken her arm and drawn her quite near him as they started home, on foot, as usual. But had he understood? He hadn't asked her to explain herself, and she had not asked *him*, as people do, if he knew what she meant—nor had she gone on to tell him, for she was too busy thinking of the great fuss with which she and Alexander had for so long marked each other's birthdays (the notes that said *it's your day!* left in strategic spots throughout the house, the jars full of flowers from her garden not just on the kitchen table but on dressertops and bathroom counters, the elaborate homemade cards and store-bought decorated cakes, the gifts marked for opening on "birthday eve" or "birthday morning") and how, each year, Bartha had stood by and watched them celebrate. She knew—she *guessed*—that he did not approve. She guessed—she had to guess; he'd never said—that what he didn't want himself he didn't want for them. She guessed (there were so many things about which she could only guess) that he held her responsible for Alexander's inclinations toward excess and extravagance. High drama, Alexander called it. What *he*, Bartha, called commotion.

And she *was* responsible. She'd taught Alexander, early on, to make the sort of fuss she'd always wanted made over her own birthday—over herself—all through her childhood. In *his* childhood, she had filled the house with streamers and balloons after he went to sleep the night before his birthday, so that when he woke up the next morning his whole world would seem transformed. She'd set her alarm clock and she'd be down in the kitchen early: he would come downstairs to find pancakes (made from a mix—she'd never really learned to cook—but he'd never minded that the way his father had) stacked high on a plate and studded with lit candles; when he was still very small she'd also put a drop or two of blue food coloring in his milk ("A glass of the sky," she'd tell him solemnly, "which I've fetched for you in honor of your birthday"). Always there would be a little pile of presents on the table, and a card she'd made herself, with glued-on bits of sequins, shiny hearts, and tiny moons and stars.

He was not yet out of grade school when he began imitating her—reciprocating. She remembered clearly the first year she had awakened to a bedroomful of drooping, crisscrossed pink and yellow streamers, twin bouquets of white balloons tied to the bedposts, and, an instant later, Alexander peeking at her from the doorway, where he had been spying, waiting for her to wake up, bringing her a lukewarm cup of tea. Downstairs there were pancakes, no worse than her own, which he had perforated with pink and white candles—an entire box of each, it seemed—and she cried when she saw them. This was one of the last times, in fact, that she could recall having cried. Bartha disliked it so much when she cried. She tried hard, always, not to. The year Alexander thought of cutting flowers from her garden—whatever was still blooming in mid-fall—and setting juice jars and milk cartons full of them in every room she'd have to walk through to begin the day, she'd almost cried—she remembered that. But she hadn't. She had kissed and hugged her son, but she'd remained dry-eyed.

All the birthday fuss was well-established custom by now. Even after he'd left home he'd nearly always managed to be back for his own birthday and for hers. Indeed, for some time now, ever since he'd finished college, these had been his only visits home—just these two each year. She couldn't put her finger on how this had come about—other children came home for Thanksgiving and for Christmas. But she'd never made much of those holidays, and so it wasn't as if he missed anything, staying in New York and celebrating with his friends. Or so she reminded herself every year. What he had said, that first September after graduation, when he'd announced that he would come home in October for a full week for her birthday (and, "if Dad will consent to a small, quiet dinner in its honor," his parents' anniversary), was that "liberated from the rigors of a school-break schedule," he would very likely not return to Omaha before late spring that year—that he saw "no point in enduring Omaha in late fall or winter or what tries and fails so miserably each year to represent itself as early spring there."

As it happened, he did not come home again until July fourth, his own birthday, and he stayed just for the long weekend they'd joked about when he was growing up—the whole country taking time off to commemorate his birth. She'd asked him once or twice—perhaps three times— during the months before that if he'd think about a visit, just a short one, but he'd always had a reason why it was impracticable. And then the second year that he was out of school passed in the same way, and somehow the habit of the birthday visits and no others became fixed.

She tried hard not to envy women whose grown, far-flung children came home more often (Clara's daughters, for example, came home not just for Thanksgiving and for Christmas but for three-day February weekends and for Easter and sometimes for no reason at all). She would tell herself: *All right, so Clara's girls come home four, five times every year, but do they ever come home for her birthday? No, never! Who else's child but her own would even think of doing that?* But this did nothing to stop her from missing him from mid-fall until early summer, every year.

Guiltily, she wondered now if she had *used* Bartha's birthday this year to get Alexander to come home. And if she had, if her own need, or her desire (she could not decide which of the two, under the circumstances, was more selfish) to see Alexander had been at the root of her determination to "do something" after all these years for Bartha's birthday, did that undermine the good deed she had done in giving him, at last, a celebration he'd seemed to enjoy? She wanted to ask Alexander, but that was impossible. She'd never even told him how much she wished that he would come home more often, or how much it pained her that he didn't. If he knew that she had tried for years to come up with a reason good enough to bring him home between the visits he made willingly—if he knew that the only explanation for her never asking him to come home was that she'd never been sure, until this last *(last!)* birthday of his father's, that eventually he'd have to give in—he would be astonished. He had no idea that she was capable of scheming.

But *had* she been scheming? She could not be certain. And if she were to ask him, he would laugh and reassure her that scheming, like premonitions, *required* knowing. She was not so sure herself.

"It doesn't really matter, Mom," Alexander said, and she felt that strange thrill she often felt—a mix of fear and pleasure: he *could* tell what she was thinking.

"What doesn't?" she asked him carefully.

"Whether or not you 'knew' anything. Whatever motivated you. It doesn't matter. I'm just glad I came home. It was the right thing to do, and I'm sorry I was such a jerk about it, sorry you were forced to beg me to be there."

"I'm sorry, too," she said.

"There's nothing you need to be sorry for."

"Well, I am. I'm sorry for begging. And also for making you turn around and come right back here now."

"Oh, Mom, please. It's bad enough already. Let's not make it worse."

"I'm not trying to make it worse," she said. "I'm trying to apologize."

"Don't apologize for that. Jesus. Don't even think about that." He sighed. "It's a punishment, I guess."

Her heart gave a jolt. "What is?"

"My having to turn around and come right back. It's a small punishment, obviously. A very small one. Maybe just the first of many small ones. I certainly deserve it."

"You deserve to be punished?" Esther said. "For what?"

"For being such a crappy son."

To whom? she came *this* close to asking. But of course he'd meant to Bartha. The little flash of jealousy this sparked in her was a shock. So many little patches of guilt hidden everywhere! Did she really feel guilty over being jealous of the guilt that Alexander felt over his father? It was ridiculous. It wasn't as if she wanted him to feel guilty about her instead.

Oh, but she did.

"*Mom*," Alexander said. "I'm kidding. Not about being a crappy son. That's true enough." And then he said, "I've got to ask you something. Do you feel as bad as I do all of a sudden that we never did anything for his birthday before?"

"Oh, yes—yes, I was thinking about that myself. But I also know, and you know this, too, that he never wanted it."

"And I also know that even if he'd wanted it, he'd never have said so."

Esther didn't say anything. But it was true.

"Listen, Mom, I'll just call the airline and then I'll call you back and let you know what time I'm getting in, okay?"

All she had to say was "okay" but she didn't. "I'm hanging up now," Alexander said. "I'll see you later."

When he hung up, she did too. Then she made herself get busy. She called Vilmos, who cried and said he would "take care of everything"—which confused her (did he mean to have her move in with him and Clara?), but when she said, doubtfully, "Such as…?", he interrupted his own weeping with a hoarse burst of laughter like a dog's bark and said, "Esther, my dear! Have you not thought about what needs now to be done? Someone must call the undertaker and call back the hospital, someone must make arrangements for a funeral." "A funeral," she repeated— how could she not have thought of it? "Oh, yes," she said. "Thank you. Of course, a funeral." Next, at Vilmos's request, she searched for "a list or an address book or some other record" Bartha might have kept that would provide him with the names and phone numbers of former students, and then she had to call him back to say that she'd found what he wanted—a stack of index cards wrapped in a rubber band, in the top right-hand desk drawer in the studio—and then it was time to call Clara (who, Vilmos had told her when they talked for the second time, was waiting for her call). Clara offered to leave work and come sit with her if she didn't want to be alone. But she did want to be alone, "at least for the moment," she told Clara. "Is that all right?" she asked her. And Clara said, "Naturally it's all right. Whatever you want is all right." And Esther wanted to ask her, "Is there something wrong with me? Should I *not* want to be alone?" but she restrained herself. She didn't want to hear the answer.

After promising Clara that she would call if she changed her mind, she returned to the studio with a broom and a dustpan and a rag. When she'd gone in there to look for names of students, she had noticed how badly it needed to be cleaned. She could not even remember the last time

Bartha had allowed her to clean in his studio. He couldn't stand even the minutest rearrangement of his things (books in stacks replaced in not precisely the same order, piles of sheet music tidied so that their edges lined up) and it made no difference how hard she tried to remember exactly how and where everything had been before she swept, dusted, polished—she always failed. But now it didn't matter.

She worked in the studio for a long time, and once she had finished there, she kept on going. She went to the basement and put in a load of laundry, then she went upstairs and made up both beds with fresh sheets—first Bartha's and hers, and then Alexander's, whose bed she had stripped and left bare even before he had left (*just yesterday*, she reminded herself, because this did not seem possible), before they had gone out for Bartha's birthday lunch—and then she went back downstairs and began to clean the kitchen. Sweeping. Mopping. Scrubbing counters. Putting things away. Clara's offer to "come sit with" her had made her shiver and she'd thought it was because—only because—she didn't want to have to talk, she wanted to be alone with her own thoughts, but there was more to it even than that; it was also that she had to keep moving. No *sitting*, alone or in company. Sitting would be unbearable. And although she'd never been the sort of person for whom housework was a source of satisfaction, or even good busywork to keep her "mind off things," the way her mother used to say—*she* had cleaned only because she had to, and always with resentment, because it was the kind of work that didn't stay done, that became undone almost as soon you had finished it—she felt at this moment that making everything as clean and neat as she could was necessary. No, more than necessary. The only right thing to do.

While she scoured and wiped and swept and tidied, she sang—light-hearted songs, songs that were easy to sing— songs she had not sung in years. It was not the cleaning but the singing that helped keep her mind "off things." Mama should have tried that, she thought.

"The vittles we et were good, you bet," she sang as she sponged off the kitchen table. *"The company was the same."* She hadn't sung in a long time. Her voice sounded very loud to her, but she didn't mind that. She was just glad no one else was there to hear it. Or to see her cleaning.

She wiped the front of the refrigerator, scrubbed all the counters and the stove. Even Clara, who had been her closest friend for over twenty years, would think she had become unhinged, singing *All I want is a room somewhere* at the top of her lungs (but wouldn't she be taken by surprise to find out that Esther had a voice!) and cleaning the house. Even Alexander wouldn't like it, Esther thought. He would be worried that she wasn't doing what she should be doing, whatever that was (she was sure he did not know either) and in fact when he called back to tell her what time he would be arriving, he said, "Mom, you're out of breath," and he sounded suspicious when he asked her what she had been up to. "Nothing," she said. "Sitting. Waiting for you. I'm not out of breath."

But it did not occur to him that she was lying. His mind was elsewhere.

He was the one who'd been unable to stop thinking about how he had to make a trip to Omaha when he had just left there—but not because he resented it, the way his mother seemed to think he did, and not because he had been lying to her when he'd said that he was only kidding about it being his punishment (though he *had* been lying: it did seem a punishment, albeit a small one). What he could not stop thinking of was what had crossed his mind while making reservations for the trip, right after he had spoken to her for the first time, and that was how absolutely like his father it was to require this of him—how it was as if he had arranged it. The old man had always kept them on their toes. He was forever doing unexpected things and doing everything in unexpected ways, ways that complicated everybody else's life and required everyone around him to make sacrifices.

Even that the trip Alexander was about to make would cost three times what the first pre-planned roundtrip ticket had cost, even with the price break for "bereavement"—for which the clerk on the phone had told him he would have to produce a copy of his father's death certificate ("Are you serious?" he'd asked her. "Who would lie about this?" And she'd said, "Are *you* serious?")—even this seemed fitting. It was his father's kind of joke.

He had finished packing, called his mother back, called two friends to tell them what had happened (and reached answering machines and hung up, both times, without leaving messages), then hesitated for so long with the receiver in his hand that a recorded operator's voice told him that it was off the hook and urged him to hang up first if he'd like to make a call before he at last punched in the number of the woman he'd been seeing for the past few months (four months, almost exactly—four months and four days, he knew, but he had the idea that it was better not to let her know he knew, and better even to pretend to himself that he wasn't keeping track), half hoping he'd get *her* machine but reaching her instead—and telling her his news and finding her to be as sweetly sympathetic, without being sentimental or intrusive, as he could have wished (and on the mental list that he was tabulating about her, he recorded two more checkmarks on the plus side), going so far as to offer to come with him if he thought he might need her there—and had locked up and gone downstairs and walked over to Hudson Street and hailed a cab and was already *in* the cab, in transit, on his way to La Guardia, when it occurred to him that he was angry.

Still angry. Or again angry. He couldn't tell which. What difference did it make?

So it was the old man's style. So it was fitting. So *what?* That was just it.

As the cab swayed and jolted him, zigzagging through Tribeca and SoHo, he even found himself considering the possibility that the old man had *known* all weekend long what was about to happen and concealed it from him— from him and his mother. For effect. Because that was just like him, too. To hold off, to keep the knowledge secret, to wait until almost the very minute Alexander was no longer there, and then to slip away.

The taxi bumped, pothole to pothole, along Houston Street, and Alexander in the backseat brought his fists down on his knees. But what's this? he thought. This wasn't like him. A cliché—to be angry with your old man for "abandoning" you. An imperfect cliché in this case, too. For one could not abandon a place one had never been.

The cab shuddered, clanked and roared, and hurled itself onto the FDR. Alexander, flung sideways, shut his eyes and let himself fall toward the window, let his head thump against the glass. What's all this? he wondered. Angry with whom, then? His father, or himself?

It wasn't his fault that his father hadn't "been there" for him. *Been there*—now there was a turn of phrase for you. He'd once broken up with someone because after she had used it he couldn't see her in the same light he had

120

before—as smart and interesting and original—the sort of phrase that Mari, the woman he'd been seeing, would never think of uttering. It was the kind of thing she mocked. Just as the old man had. "A caring person," his father would repeat back to his mother if she made the mistake of saying this about someone. "A person who cares about what? Everything? Surely this is not possible." Or, as he sat reading the newspaper, he'd mutter, "Mothering? Fathering? Why is it that Americans enjoy making verbs out of every useful noun?" Or: "Oh, here is something! Caregiving! This is a verb? The noun itself is quite terrible enough, is it not?" He would shake his head. This strange people! This strange world!

After how many years in this country? In the backseat of the taxi, Alexander shook *his* head, conscious even as he did that it was his father's gesture. The gesture of the puzzled visitor, the observer who wasn't sure what to make of what he observed. One wanted to ask, "So, how do you like it here? What do you make of it so far?"

Even in his own home, his father was detached, amused—half there, half somewhere else. Alexander used to want to tug on him, to say, "Pay attention, please. You live here."

And to make him take *him* seriously. To get him to stop being so perplexed and amused by everything around him. To behave in a more serious manner.

But whose idea was that? Alexander wondered now. It was possible his mother had put it in his head. She was forever saying to his father, "But this isn't funny."

But very often it *was* funny. His father kept himself amused by making mischief—crazy mischief. Surprises, half baked schemes, strange doings. It was as if he had decided years ago to make sure he did not become too easily predictable to his wife and his son. His life was thoroughly routine in all its small particulars (he'd eaten the same breakfast every morning for as long as Alexander could remember: two cups of tea with lemon and a drop of honey, and two slices of whole wheat toast with four kinds of jam—the jam applied bit by bit just as he prepared to take each bite of toast, so that Alexander even as a two-year-old, according to his mother, could recite the order of his father's breakfast: a sip, a dab of strawberry, a bite; a sip, a dab of blueberry, a bite; and so on, until the second cup of tea and the second piece of toast were finished— and he'd drink two cups of coffee with hot milk and sugar every afternoon along with lunch; he kept the same hours in his studio, from eight AM to noon and from one to four forty-five, six days a week, even long after he had stopped giving lessons; he went to bed at the same time each night and woke at the same time each morning—and when he woke up he walked each day to the one place just barely within walking distance where it was possible to buy *The New York Times,* which he read over breakfast, saving the first part of it to read last), and yet he still managed to take Alexander and his mother by surprise so often that they had come to expect to be surprised, too.

He'd once bought a car without having mentioned it to them beforehand and without knowing how to drive (it sat in the garage for years, unregistered and uninsured). He used to disappear, first thing on a Sunday morning perhaps once a month, then call hours later from Des Moines or Kansas City or St. Louis, anywhere that he could get to by late afternoon or early evening on a bus, and say, "Tonight there is a concert I would like to hear"—or there was a performance of an opera by a company that he admired, passing through the town, or a lecture would be given that night by someone whose book he'd read and liked, or there was an exhibit he was interested in at the art museum—"so I will see you tomorrow. I will come on the first bus." Once he had announced that they were going on "a nice vacation in a wooden cabin" only hours before the vacation was to begin.

The taxi ribboned through three lanes of traffic, its imperfectly tuned radio spitting out static-laced "light and mellow" versions of the standards and show tunes his mother used to sing to him. He was calm now—he was himself again. *Sober* was the word that came to him.

At the airport, he picked up his ticket and made it to the gate with six minutes still to spare before the flight took off. "Hurry on, there's just time," he was told, and he smiled benevolently (in the old man's honor, he thought— *he* had never let himself be rushed) as he boarded.

He fished inside the pockets of his bag for the book he had been reading on his flight home yesterday and settled down with it, the bag stuffed into the bin overhead and he himself buckled in tightly. But when the plane had left the ground and the book, which he was sure he had found interesting yesterday (and there was evidence of this: two penciled checkmarks and an exclamation point in the left margin of the page that had its corner turned down), had been open on his lap for fifteen or twenty minutes during which he had read one long sentence again and again without making any sense of it, he had no choice but to admit to himself that he was still uneasy. Not angry— it would be absurd to be angry. It would be particularly absurd to be angry at his father. He had always felt that where his father was concerned, anger made no sense— where his father was concerned, what he felt was either charmed or irritated (one or the other, sometimes one immediately following the other)—and to be angry *now*? That made something less than sense.

So, not angry, he told himself. Only unsettled.

His mother was always saying of his father's antics—her word for them—that they made no sense. "What sense does it make?" she would murmur when his father vanished for a day—when he called from Iowa City to say he was going to attend a reading by a poet and would see them tomorrow. "A whole day's bus ride, by himself," she would say to Alexander, "just to hear an hour of poetry that he could sit and read at home."

Alexander had learned early which things made sense and which didn't. These were his mother's divisions, he saw later, but by then it was too late, for her ideas about his father were so well-entrenched in him there was no going back—no undoing of that, any of that, even if he'd wanted to. Still, there was something he'd begun to see as he grew older, that his mother could not, or would not, see—which was how often his father's nonsense had turned *into* sense, how often the crazy things he'd done had settled so completely into their lives that it was hard to remember afterwards how *un*settling they had once been.

The car that he had bought, for instance, which he had never learned to drive, telling them it wasn't "strictly necessary" for him, was the one in which both Alexander and his mother eventually learned to drive, and which Alexander drove all through high school (without it, he knew now—he had been dimly aware even then—he would have been even more of an outcast than he was then).

Ignoring his book, a treatise on ideas of beauty, and the pilot's disembodied voice as he spoke of the weather and their flight path, he thought now about the day, the summer he turned five, when his father went out for a walk after his last student and came home, just in time for dinner, in a stranger's car with seven mixed-breed, ten-week-old puppies—a whole litter—in a basket. "Now, this is too foolish," Alexander's mother said. "No one takes in seven pets at once. It makes no sense. Let's choose the nicest one and give the rest back." But his father insisted that they keep them all. "Not everything must make sense," he told her, and he nodded at Alexander, who'd been perched on the end of his chair, waiting for a sign that it was all right for him to approach the basket on the floor (he remembered how he'd run to it then and sat down crosslegged next to it, scooping out one after another of the puppies—two copper-brown with black paws and one streaked and spotted, copper over black; one glossy black all over and one mostly brown, with a scattering of freckles; one improbably, starkly white; and one penny-colored with black loopy rings around her chest and legs that looked like necklaces and bracelets—and setting them all in his lap, letting them chew on his fingers and his wrists and lick his knees and tug on his shorts and tee shirt: he remembered his helpless pleasure at the warmth and softness of them, at the way they climbed and slid and toppled over one another, at the scratchy hot feel of their tongues on his skin).

Those puppies! They had become almost immediately so essential to his happiness that he had been unable to imagine what his life would have been like without them. And the truth was that after the first two or three weeks it had not just not seemed odd to have so many of them, but it had seemed odd to him that other people had just one (who must, he'd thought, be very lonely). And later, during seventh and eighth grades especially, when he didn't have a single friend, the little pack of dogs that tagged along with

125

him wherever he went made him feel distinctive and helped him to bear his isolation—indeed, kept him from feeling the full weight of it. The dogs had seemed to understand this too, and when the last one, Mister Snow, died toward the end of Alexander's senior year of high school, it was as if he knew that his job was done, that Alexander was about to leave home, change his life for good.

Even his father's Sunday disappearances had become, somewhere along the line, the impetus and the occasion for his mother's own adventures. By the time Alexander was in eighth or ninth grade, on the Sundays that his father went out for his morning walk and did not come back when he was expected—his customary walk took no more than an hour, enough time to buy the newspaper and make a full circle around the neighborhood—his mother would set out herself, on foot (even after she had learned to drive, she didn't like it). She'd let Alexander take his father's call. "Tell him I'm out. Tell him you don't know where"— which was the truth. He never knew till later, when she came home to eat Campbell's soup or scrambled eggs or sandwiches with him—the sort of dinner that they never had when his father was at home—and reported on her day. She'd walked down to the Old Market and had lunch at the new Chinese-French restaurant or window-shopped in the boutiques. Or she had gone over to Dundee and poked through the antique shops there. Or she'd gone to the Josyln—*she* didn't have to travel all day on a Greyhound bus to go to an art museum, she'd say. She didn't have to stay out overnight; she didn't have to vanish without warning. She never strayed farther than she could walk.

Before she left the house, she'd always ask Alexander if he wanted to come with her, but he knew she didn't really mean for him to come, and he never wanted to go, anyway. Those Sundays were the only times that he could count on having the house to himself. Not that either of his parents bothered him, exactly, when they were both home. Most often when all three of them were in the house at the same time, they were in separate rooms: his mother in her study, his father in his studio, and he in his bedroom upstairs, the door closed, while he worked (or "fooled around," as he had called it then) and listened to music. He'd just liked knowing that there was nobody else around. He'd liked leaving his door open for a change, and being able to turn up his stereo—since for once his music wouldn't be in competition with the music emanating from two other rooms downstairs—and most of all he'd liked not having to stiffen and stop what he was doing (not that he had to; not that he was ever doing anything wrong—but he couldn't help it) whenever he heard footsteps in the hall or on the stairs.

It was funny, he thought as he declined a tray of food, but those Sunday outings of his father's—he'd never thought of it this way before—*because* they had inspired his mother to take off as well, had permanently left their mark on him. He still thought of Sunday as a time for him to be alone, to work all day in the studio without having to answer to anybody. This was one reason—of the multiple reasons—he had been reluctant to return to Omaha to celebrate his father's birthday, though he hadn't told his mother this because it made him feel too guilty (*selfish*, as more than one of his former girlfriends had said of his refusal to "give up a Sunday"). He thought now that he might have admitted it if it had ever crossed his mind before that in a roundabout way his "private little goddamned holy Sundays"—a coinage of his most recent ex-, Diana the printmaker/day care teacher—was his

127

mother's own fault. Hers and his father's.

Certainly, if he had never given any thought to why Sundays had emerged, early on, as his best workdays—to why, on a good Sunday, he could accomplish more than he had in the six days that preceded it—he had been *made* aware that keeping Sundays for himself was more than (read: worse than) eccentric. It seemed to be common knowledge in New York that Sundays were supposed to be reserved for all-day dates (there was a rigid protocol for these dates, too, he'd learned—for on each occasion, in each new relationship, when he'd felt he had to make the gesture and spent a whole Sunday with the woman with whom he believed himself to be in love, the day took precisely the same form: the Sunday *Times* in bed, with bagels or croissants and coffee; brunch, either alone or with another couple, in the afternoon; a foreign movie matinee or else a visit to an art museum—the latter something for which he preferred always to be alone; then dinner at a restaurant. On each of these long Sunday dates, it had struck him at some point in the proceedings that his father would have been pleased by the role meals played in them, but he had kept this observation to himself).

"Are you sure you won't have anything to eat?" a flight attendant asked him, and he laughed before he thanked her and said he was quite sure. "A cup of coffee would be nice, though," he said, not because he wanted it but because he didn't want her to think he had been laughing at her. "A cup of coffee would be wonderful." Now she laughed. "I can pretty much guarantee that it won't be wonderful."

When she brought him the cup of lukewarm coffee, he accepted everything she offered with it—two packets of nondairy creamer and two packets of sugar—and put *In and Out of Art* on the empty seat beside him. He unlatched his tray, and as he set his cup down and stirred both white powders into it, he considered that one of the less dramatic pleasures of his relationship with Mari—less dramatic than her beauty, which was startling enough, in its great-eyed, Victorian way (the pale skin, the tower of pinned-up hair), less dramatic than her delicate sexiness or her gift for making ordinary moments artful (the way she would sit naked in the center of his bed and unpin and unwind that extravagant hair, dropping into his outstretched hand bobby pins affixed with tiny pearls or rhinestones, tortoise shell barrettes, and what seemed like a hundred V-shaped plain black metal hairpins, then shaking her head until waves of dark hair draped all around her, covering her to her knees), less dramatic than her talent as an actress, her intelligence, her grace, and how interesting and how pleasant it was to have conversations with her—was that finally he had a girlfriend who was perfectly content to spend Sundays without him. They saw each other every night *but* Sunday, at his place or hers, most nights meeting at ten thirty or eleven, since at least one of them was generally working until then. They would eat Chinese takeout or frozen pot pies or canned soup and crackers (yet another source of pleasure for him: that she was as indifferent as he was to what, when, where, and how they ate), they would talk, and then they'd go to bed. On the rare evening that she was not performing and he felt he'd had a good enough day to quit early, they'd go out, to a concert or a movie, for pizza or cheap Indian or falafel.

Mari said it seemed to her that they saw plenty of each other and that it was nice to have "a day off." The phrase itself delighted him. It was the one his mother had used for the Sundays she had spent without his father—and even now, though she had not had a "day off" in years, she still referred to them that way. *I can't tell you how I miss those Sundays off,* she had written to him only recently. *I keep thinking I'll get used to it, but somehow I just don't. Is this terrible of me?*

When he'd written back he had been tempted to tell her about Mari, but he had quelled that impulse. All he'd said was that he understood, that it wasn't "terrible" at all, and he asked her if she'd ever told his father how she felt. It was not until after he'd mailed the letter that he realized what a stupid question that had been, that she could not have told his father since he had never admitted that he'd given up *his* Sunday outings—and how could he have, when he had never spoken of them in the first place? The illusion, always, had been that he'd gone wherever he went, whenever he went, on a whim that had come over him while he was circling the neighborhood, as he did every morning—that he himself was not sure why or how he'd ended up in the place he was calling from when he called home hours later. The illusion was that he had taken off without having decided to.

The illusion.

But this had never crossed his mind before.

Of course it had been an illusion. Would his father have boarded a bus on a whim, at random, hoping that wherever he got off would happen to be hosting an important orchestra or opera company that night? Alexander took a sip of coffee from the paper cup and set it down at once—it was undrinkable, even for him. This explanation wasn't plausible. It was inconceivable. His father's Sunday jaunts around the Midwest would have required him to find out what was scheduled to happen where *before* he walked downtown to the bus station. They would have required him to get in touch with at least some of Monday's students in advance, or else to bring a list of their phone numbers with him when he set out on what he pretended (to himself too?) was his morning walk—for he would not have left them to turn up on Monday morning, puzzled by his absence; he would not have (he had never, after all) left his wife or his son to answer the door and explain that Bartha wasn't in—which meant, Alexander understood for the first time, that although his father's family knew nothing of his plans when he walked out the door on Sunday mornings, there were housewives, college students, a few serious musicians, and a high school girl or two scheduled for lessons after school who must have known where he was going and when he'd be back.

So much for his father's *impulses*, thought Alexander. Impulses that had required research. Impulses about which strangers scattered around Omaha were well-informed, while he and his mother remained in the dark.

But this wasn't news, he told himself as absently he took another sip of coffee (his father would have called the flight attendant—"stewardess"—to his seat and complained; he was tempted to press the call bell himself, simply to ask her politely to take it away before he accidentally drank any more of it). How could this be news to him? He had known for years how carefully his father had planned some of his apparent vagaries. When he was fourteen and his father told them he'd rented a house for a month on Lake Okoboji ("It's time to pack," was what he said. "We are leaving today for a nice vacation in a wooden cabin"), he was old enough already to know that this must have been in the works for some time, that plans had been made— papers signed, a sum of money given over—and then kept a secret only for the sake of keeping them a secret (why else would he have sprung it on them that way?).

131

This was how his father did things. It had never troubled him before. When more than ten years after he'd brought home those puppies (which had certainly seemed an act of pure impulse, the result of a moment of weakness—which, family legend had long had it, only his pride had not allowed him to recant) his father had at last admitted—in what must have been a true moment of weakness—that he'd picked out the puppies in advance and even bought the wicker basket days before, secreting it in the garage and making off with it when he went out that evening "for a walk," Alexander had been more amused than shocked. The idea that his father had spent weeks circling ads headed FREE TO GOOD HOME in the *World Herald* and making calls in search of (as he confessed, a decade later) "the best situation" had pleased him—indeed, had charmed him. His mother had been less sanguine. "'Situation'?" she had said. "What 'situation'? What could you have been thinking of? Seven dogs at the same time! In what way was this 'best'?" But his father hadn't answered her. His interest in the subject exhausted, he'd excused himself, went into his studio, and never spoke of it again.

That he'd brought it up at all after so many years was what had surprised Alexander, as had his mother's reaction to what he told them. What did explanations matter anymore? he had thought. Over half the dogs were gone by then—two lost, one run over, one put to sleep when she became so sick she had trouble breathing. The day they had adopted them was history. But he had imagined that what troubled his mother was being reminded of her opposition to adopting the dogs, of the debate she'd lost (and he'd wanted to say, *It all worked out, so what's the problem?* and had kept silent only because he feared that if he spoke he'd make her angry with him, too). That wasn't it at all,

132

he thought now. She'd been angry that he'd made his plans and kept them secret. *Once again*, he thought. *As usual.*

It stood to reason that this would have angered her. On the day his father had told them to pack up for a month at the lake, and he saw that his mother was displeased (just as he was), he had not considered that she might not be feeling *what* he was—dismayed by the thought of spending a whole month in a cabin in the woods, reluctant to leave town (he hadn't paused to wonder either why this seemed so awful to him, when it was not as if he had been having any fun at home so far that summer). Why would his mother not have welcomed a vacation?

And she *did* welcome it—he remembered this very well. Her mood had lightened at her first sight of Lake Okoboji. He, however, had squandered the whole of his first week there, hanging around the cabin, grumbling. It was she who'd forced him out of doors ("Enough," she said, and took his book out of his hands; she had even latched the door behind him), where he had at once bumped into the girl in the cabin next to theirs—wisecracking, tomboy-pretty sixteen-year-old Pamela, from Council Bluffs—and promptly fallen in love, so that the three weeks following that first wasted, gloomy one were among the happiest he could remember of his life. Indeed—he thought, and shook his head—you had to hand it to the old man: this had turned out to be another time his father had, in his odd, crafty way, done something for him that made special sense—for those three weeks had made more sense to Alexander than anything that had happened to him up to then.

Pamela! He had not thought of her in years. She had not only been his first girlfriend—and his first, of a long line, of "older woman" (two years older; at the age they'd been, those two years might have been a decade)—she was also the first person he had ever met who talked about fleeing the Midwest, at least as great a revelation to him as was love (or what passed for sex between them during those three weeks). He had no idea if she had ever managed her escape—no idea, in fact, what had become of her. They'd lost touch almost immediately after their vacation, once they both returned to their "real lives" at home, even though Council Bluffs was just across the river, not a half hour's drive away. But he'd started plotting his escape, too, then—once he'd seen that it was possible, that it might be planned. Might be done.

By the time he was sixteen, he had already written to every art school on the East Coast for catalogues and applications, without telling anyone—not his parents or his friends or the girlfriend he had by then, who was a year ahead of him in school and like everyone he knew by then was talking about getting out but hadn't come up with an escape route beyond a blurry idea of someday becoming famous, though for what she wasn't sure (*she* had never left; he'd heard that she'd married young, while she was still at UNO, driving her parents' white Dodge Dart to classes, sophomore or maybe junior year; his mother had run into her mother a year or two ago and she'd reported that Danielle already had two kids and a big ranch house in West Fairacres).

He started working part time, after school and all day Saturdays and Sundays, and saving every cent he made. His mother asked him if he was sure he could get his schoolwork done while working at a job so many hours. "Not that I don't think it's admirable," she said. "You know, I used to work on Saturdays and after school myself" (Daring him to ask her more? She said so little about her life in New York, and always before this he'd risen to the bait whenever it was offered—but now he was preoccupied with his own plans, with his future, not her past.) She asked if there was "something special" that he needed money for, because if so she would be glad to simply give it to him. He shrugged. "I'm fine," he said. "Don't worry about it."

Even when it came time to make choices, to spread out the catalogues and brochures on his bedroom floor and make stacks—yes and no—and whittle down the yes stack to the four schools he most wanted to get into, plus one "safe" school he was sure would take him, and to fill out applications and financial aid forms using the old tax returns he found in the file cabinet in his father's studio one Sunday afternoon when both parents were on their "outings," and working on his portfolio, making new pieces and photographing them, and then finally to send everything off, it was still easier for him to keep his plans a secret than to talk about them beyond the few words he was obliged to exchange with his school's all-purpose "art teacher" (she also taught music, coached the glee and drama clubs, and was faculty advisor for the student newspaper) and the "college advisor" (who taught English, too, badly, and offered no actual advice), whom he had no choice but to ask for letters of recommendation.

Who would he have talked to, even if he'd felt like talking? Not to any of his friends, who by that time didn't want to talk about the future anymore—to admit that they'd sent applications no farther away than Lincoln (or, like Danielle, who by then was midway through her freshman year, practically around the corner)—and not in any meaningful way to any of his teachers, not a single one of whom he trusted or respected (especially objectionable was the so-called art teacher, who began each class sitting chummily on the edge of a table at the front of the art and music room, telling them to "draw anything" they felt like drawing, then spent the rest of the hour sitting on the piano bench and reading paperback romances, occasionally looking up to remind them to "focus on your *feelings*") or the college advisor who scheduled ten minutes with each senior who requested it (most didn't); least of all not to his parents, who hadn't asked him any questions about what he would be doing after graduation, who seemed to have no idea that the time had come (come, and gone) for him to make decisions about the rest of his life. He still wondered sometimes what his parents had imagined he'd be doing after high school, or if they had ever thought of it at all.

He had sprung the news on them at the last minute— just the way his father always had, he'd recognized even then, but he did not think *imitation*, much less *homage*. He did not see it as ironic, either. What he had told himself was that what he'd done was completely different from his father's antics, that this was his *life* and not a trick or game. *He* had not been trying to catch anyone off guard. Unlike his father, who had always seemed to take more pleasure in surprising them than in the doing of whatever he'd surprised them with, he didn't *want* to surprise them. He hadn't talked things over with his parents (not until it was too late—until it didn't matter what they said because everything had been decided) because he'd known that they would be no help. He'd known that even if he had reminded them that it was time for him to think about, to make choices about, what would become of him, they would not have had the slightest idea what his choices should be based on, for they seemed to have no idea where his talents or his interests lay. He had been nearly that old, after all—fifteen, perhaps—when his father had brought

136

home a flute, a violin, and (most surprising, in the midst of this particular surprise) an electric guitar and a miniature amplifier, and told him to choose his instrument. Surely the old man should have known by then that he had no interest in taking up any instrument, that he had no gift for music. But surely, too, he saw now, it should have occurred to *him* that he could—that he should—have said, "No thanks," that he could have spelled it out himself for his old man. But no. His father had said "choose" and choose he did—predictably, the glossy red-and-black guitar and the square pig-nose amp. He told himself it was what any boy his age would have picked—that it was impossible to resist. But the truth was that he hadn't wanted to have to tell his father that he had no interest in making music—he wanted his father to *know*. To know without being told. And he had wanted—as he always wanted, as his mother always wanted—to please him. Not enough perhaps to choose the violin. Perhaps to please him in a way that had a little bit of sting in it—to have it both ways, then. But the old man betrayed nothing. He said only, "Yes, good. Now I will arrange for lessons," and left with the two rejected instruments, presumably to take them back to the store where he had bought them. It was a matter of months before even the semblance of an effort Alexander had been making to play the guitar was finished and the instrument was relegated to a corner of his closet, where it remained to this day, exactly where he'd left it twelve or thirteen years ago, after his final hopeless lesson.

If only his father had consulted him before he'd gone out shopping, he could have told him not to bother—he could have told him that there was no point. He might have resented having to tell him, but if he'd had the chance to—if the old man had spoken, just this once, of what he had in mind to do instead of being so determined to pull off another of his big surprises—he would have had the chance also to tell him what he *was* good at, what mattered to him. Then his father would not have been so stunned by Alexander's own big news, by his announcement that he would be leaving in September for New York, where he would study sculpture. Where he had a tuition scholarship—where someone else, more than one person, perhaps many people, had noticed what he was good at.

But his father never consulted anyone. He never spoke of what he had in mind to do and never asked for anyone's opinion, not even when what he was planning would affect somebody else more than it would affect him. He was always certain he knew what was best for everybody—certain he knew what to do and the best way to do it. That was another difference between them, thought Alexander as he absently drank his cold, terrible coffee. He was never certain he knew what to do—all he was certain of was that nobody else knew any better than he did.

No one in his family, he reflected as he drained his cup, had ever believed in "talking things over." For one reason or another—for different reasons, he thought—they all kept whatever they were up to to themselves.

And yet—as if she didn't understand this, as if she'd never been surprised before—how furious his mother had been when he announced that he was leaving. "But you *can't,*" she told him. "A boy your age can't just decide to go, and go." "I think I can," he told her. "There was no place on the application for a parent's permission."

"I don't like your sarcasm," his mother had said. "And I don't like your attitude. Or your secrecy. Or your arrogance. Not a word to us!" She'd actually thumped the kitchen table with her fist. "Not a single word!" She looked at his father—they were sitting at the table, all three of them, over dinner that no one was eating—but his father was no help to her. Even as she thumped and shouted, he was silent and showed no sign of intending to break his silence. Dumbfounded, Alexander thought. Without meaning to, he'd beaten his father at his own game. "Not a word to us," his mother had repeated. "That's what I can't understand. That's what makes me angry."

But if not having been consulted was something that made her angry, why had she not been angrier with her own husband? She had never argued with *him*, never worked so hard to make *him* feel ashamed and guilty, even though what he had sprung on her over the years had nearly always had a more direct effect on her than Alexander's having sent an application to and gotten into (and then written back, still secretly, to say he would attend) the college of *his* choice. He pointed this out to his mother sometime in the course of their long argument (it went on—on and off, all day, each day—until the day he left) and she shouted, "One thing has nothing to do with the other."

It made him proud to recall that he had not been boorish enough to say what he had thought of saying: "You just don't want me to leave you. *That's* why this 'one thing' has nothing to do with 'the other.'" Instead he continued protesting that he'd done nothing wrong, as if the argument they were having was about what it seemed to be about.

His father stayed out of it. Throughout the weeks of shouting between Alexander and his mother, and the ceasefire they agreed to silently the day he left (after which neither of them ever spoke again of what had passed between them that summer—the only serious, prolonged discord there had ever been between them), his father managed to behave toward him exactly as he always had—pleasantly, if distantly, with the same indeterminate, mild brand of fondness and regard he had expressed toward him for as long as Alexander could remember. He would pat his arm when they passed in the kitchen, and when Alexander came home from his summer job each evening—the earnings from which, along with what he'd saved all year, turned out to be just about enough to pay for his first month of housing and food in New York City (so much for his plan to take no money at all from the old man)—his father would say, "So was everything all right at work?" In the morning, he would ask him, kindly, how he'd slept. Sometimes he would read aloud from the newspaper, and then say, "Well? What do you think?" He never said a word about his leaving.

Alexander crushed his empty paper cup. The pilot's voice was floating overhead again, talking once again about the weather—*Snow flurries predicted west and north of St. Louis*—and as he shook his head (a habit kicking in: *oh, yes*, he thought reflexively—derisively—*the great Midwest*) he all at once remembered how, after he and his parents had driven to the airport on the day that he had left for school (Alexander did the driving, going to the airport; his mother would have to drive home—a sacrificial gesture, he had understood, of reconciliation, for there were few things that his mother hated more than driving), his father had climbed out of the car as soon as he'd pulled up to the curb, and stood on the sidewalk waiting as if he had something urgent to say. Alexander jumped out of the driver's seat—he should have known better but he had the idea that the old man might be about to tell him something important—but then when Alexander reached him, he just smiled and put one hand on his arm and held it there, an inch or two below his elbow, for what seemed like a long time, and then he said, "Good luck to you."

And what had *he* said, in response? Alexander closed his eyes. He had said—of course he had said—"Thank you." What else was there to say? He and his father had always been unfailingly polite to each other. He would not have dreamed of telling him that he was disappointed. Angry? Hurt? It wasn't possible to say such a thing to his father. The reserve between them kept him from such declarations, it kept him—kept both of them, he supposed—from even the kind of companionable, trivial grumbling about how they felt that went on all the time between him and his mother. In fact, he thought, what was between him and his father was *so* genteel, so polite—so nebulous—he could never even be sure he *was* angry with him, much less display it. He had never in his life shouted at his father. Shouted? He'd never even slightly raised his voice. He'd never argued with him over anything—he'd never even questioned him, or criticized him. He'd never objected to a single thing that the old man had ever done or said.

And now? Now he thought that if the old man were here—*here*, right now, in the empty seat beside him—he would object all right. He would object to everything. He'd tell the old man off for all the things he'd never told him off for, all his life. Not just for never bothering to notice that he hadn't the makings of a musician, or for thinking that he could still turn him into one at fifteen—or for being so impossible to read that Alexander *still* didn't know which was true, whether his father had been dense and inattentive or the world's most arrogant procrastinator— and not just for all the secret-keeping and surprises and the show of spontaneity that went along with them, which he

141

and his mother were supposed to pretend they believed; not just for *Good luck to you,* and not just for never calling, never writing—never even asking to speak to him when his mother had him on the phone and he passed through the room where she was talking—not just for all that, but for this weekend, too. For sitting in that corny restaurant at lunch yesterday afternoon and acting as if everything were fine, for making a big fuss over what they would order, as if it made any difference—for eating two portions of dumplings and two pieces of strudel, saying that he couldn't let them go to waste if Alexander and his mother didn't want them. For the pretense that nothing extraordinary was about to happen. For the *years* of pretense, Alexander thought, that nothing extraordinary was about to happen. Or had ever happened. Or was happening right then.

For the way that he would take his hands and smile when Alexander visited, and ask him how his work was going. For the way he listened calmly and politely to the answer and yet never seemed to have heard anything his son had said. And how could he? He never looked directly at him and his mind seemed always to be somewhere else. Certainly he never listened hard enough to understand, or to remember even a few minutes later what he had been told. Hell, how could he remember what his son had said when he hardly managed to remember that he *had* a son?

It was true, he thought—it was true. Suddenly he was breathing hard. He felt as if he'd been blindsided, and for a moment, as if he really had just been in a collision (the one he dreaded, the one for which he was prepared, every time he had to drive—because he hated to drive as much as his mother did; the only difference between them was that he'd always kept how *he* felt secret), he wasn't sure he had survived intact, and he took stock: was he all there? still breathing, heart still beating? Yes, all there. He was all there, all right, and altogether certain—as certain as if he'd known all his life and simply hadn't *known* that he had known—that his father's genial, abstracted, charming act, which he had for so long imagined was directed pointedly toward him (just as he had imagined that the pretense yesterday—the pretense all weekend long—of light-hearted ordinariness was meant to throw him off, to make this last surprise as much of a surprise as possible), was not an act at all. That when his father acted as if it were nice enough to see his son but nothing so out of the ordinary that it was worth getting stirred up over, it was not a pretense—not an effort not to be unseemly. It was how he felt.

Of course it was. And why then would any effort of pretense have been directed toward him? How could it have been, when the old man hardly ever gave him any thought at all—except when he was forced, by his presence itself, to think of him? Each time he visited, it seemed to him that when his father first set eyes on him he started, taken by surprise. There was a pause, a heartbeat long, before he said—too quickly, but quite pleasantly—"Why, Alexander, how are you?"

Even when he was a child, a small child (he remembered this so clearly that it shocked him, for he couldn't have been much more than a baby), he had so often felt that he'd surprised his father when he crossed his path that he had asked his mother once if there were somewhere else he was supposed to be (and he remembered what she'd said, too—so precisely it was as if he had heard her say it two and a half hours instead of two and a half decades ago: "No, sweetpea, you're just where you should be"). It was as if his father had to see him to recall the fact of his existence—as if in his absence he was able to entirely forget about him. As if in his absence, for his father, he did not exist.

This was what was on his mind as the plane began its descent into St. Louis. It was still on his mind as he made his way through the airport there, and he supposed it was what made him think of something he'd forgotten, or supposed he had forgotten: that when he was very young—no more than three or four, perhaps even the same age he had been when he had asked that question of his mother and she'd answered him so swiftly and so cheerfully, without having to ask him why he'd asked the question—he had had the idea that his *father* ceased to be when he was not with him, that there was magic involved somehow, so that his own presence called his father into being and that at all other times he simply was *not:* there was no such person.

He stopped, so abruptly that someone behind him, moving too quickly to stop himself, bumped into him. He was too stunned to say, "Excuse me." Everywhere around him people rushed to catch their planes or get out of the airport or meet someone who had just arrived from somewhere else, but he set his bag down where he stood and let himself be jostled and spun.

People muttered apologies as they pushed past him, setting him off balance so that he had to keep righting himself. But no one yelled at him or cursed him, and this seemed strange. He had forgotten where he was, forgotten that he was no longer in New York, that he had landed in the great Midwest. That he had less than half an hour before his connecting flight and he should be rushing, too.

He shivered. He was sweating. It was as if he had just now understood what his mother had told him—as if just now, this very instant, he'd realized that the old man was dead. But something else too. As if what he'd believed in when he was a little boy had turned out to be true.

That magic. *He* had not been present—and his father had ceased to exist.

three

The funeral, arranged by Vilmos, was set for first thing the next morning. That made perfect sense, Esther and Alexander told each other over poached eggs on toast quarters, which for a quarter of a century had been her standard meal for him when he was sick or disappointed (he almost asked her, when she set the plate before him, which category this event fell into, but he stopped himself in time and said, instead, as he'd said all his life, "Thanks, Mom, that's just what I need"). In fact they both had their doubts, which neither mentioned.

In the hour and three-quarters that Alexander had been there, Esther had twice said that since nobody else was coming in from out of town, there was no reason to wait. Both times, Alexander had agreed with her. He didn't ask why Vilmos's twin daughters weren't coming, since he was certain that they would have made the trip if they'd been asked—or, rather, if they hadn't been asked *not* to make it. His father had liked them—indeed, they'd been special pets of his. "I should have had daughters," he used to say sometimes after they had visited. This had always irritated his mother, Alexander knew, and he could easily imagine her having told Vilmos that he was not to "inconvenience" the girls, just as he could picture Vilmos protesting, but too weakly to do any good (telling himself, and then having to tell Clara, that this was no time for an argument). Alexander's mother had never thought much of those girls.

Of course, he had never liked them either, not even when they all were children and were forced by circumstances into one another's company. He was just as glad that they would not be coming to the funeral. He listened to himself agree (three times? four?) that there was no point putting off "something like this"—and asked himself, to pass the time while murmuring, "Yes, certainly," "Indeed," and "Absolutely," what there was in all the world that might be the least bit "like this"—and really, he knew, there *was* no point. No reasonable argument could be made in favor of waiting. And yet he had the feeling that arranging for his father's funeral should have been more difficult, more complicated and time-consuming than it seemed to have been. He was afraid that what Vilmos had planned would seem rushed and paltry.

As was Esther. Despite what she said, and kept saying, she was thinking that it might have been better not to have a funeral at all than to have one that Bartha would have hated. Or (worse, possibly) one he would have been amused by, one he would have gently mocked throughout. As Alexander nodded (she'd just said, for the second time, that she didn't know what she would have done without Vilmos, that she never would have managed the arrangements on her own), the absurd thought came to her that they should have gone back to New York for the funeral.

Imagine if she said this to her son, who had been trying to persuade them to come for a visit since his first year there! Persuade *her*, for Bartha had never made a secret of his own desire to see New York again. That he hadn't made the trip without her was something she had never understood. He'd made all those little trips of his alone, apparently without a qualm—not to mention without warning—and for years he'd said that if she didn't change her mind ("so stubborn!" he'd say, and she would

147

answer, "on this one subject, yes") he *would* go to New York alone. He'd been saying this since Alexander's second birthday, which he had suggested might be celebrated with a trip. Perhaps, he'd said then, they might go to see her family. "Enough time has passed," he'd said, and she had disagreed—although she hadn't said what she'd known even then: *enough time will never have passed.*

When Alexander at eighteen began to call home urging them to "come back" to New York to see him—"for a weekend, why not? It would be fun for you"—she had been sure Bartha would go alone at last. Was it in deference to her that he had not? Or had he decided that a visit would cause him to miss the city more, perhaps too much to bear (or that after all there was no point in *visiting*)? Or had he, after so many years, lost interest in the very notion of returning, speaking of it out of habit only? How could she know? She couldn't. Now she never would.

"Never will what?" Alexander said.

"I didn't say that out loud, did I?" she asked him.

"Somebody did."

For some reason this struck both of them as funny. They were both a little drunk, which might (though this occurred to neither of them) have been the reason. They'd added half an inch of Scotch to the first cup of tea they'd each had with the eggs and toast—*instead* of the eggs and toast, since neither one of them had taken a single bite—and a bit more than that to each succeeding cup. By now they each had had three cups of the doctored tea—and Alexander had been slightly drunk already on arrival, having had a drink on the second leg of his trip. By then he'd figured out that he had to shut his mind off, and he'd done it too. The drink had helped—that, and the magazines the flight attendant handed him, "men's magazines" that might

148

have been published on some other planet, their obsessions were so alien to him: *Dressing for Casual Friday. Which Sports Car is You? The Fit Traveler: Where to Run in Sixteen European Cities.* By the time he landed he was woozy, his head stuffed with useless information—a pleasant sensation.

His mother, on the other hand, when he got there, was manic. She was out the front door of the house before he'd even opened up the back door of the cab. She thought she was all right, thought she was calm. She told him that when he asked her, alarmed not only by the way she'd shot out of the house and by the way she looked, in high heels and jewelry and makeup, everything slightly askew, as if she'd dressed in a hurry for a party, but because she'd used the *front* door, for the first time in his memory. She'd been telling herself, too, for the last few hours, how calm she was. She'd finished cleaning, singing much of "The King and I" and "Oklahoma," "State Fair" and "Camelot" and "Brigadoon" as she did—skipping all the ballads, singing only the liveliest songs from each—pausing only to accept the phone calls that had started coming after Vilmos made his calls. She thanked everybody and said yes, she'd see them tomorrow, thanks again, all right now, and went back to her singing and her cleaning. Afterwards she took a shower—which was as unusual for her as singing out loud: she took baths, not showers, and she took them late at night, right before she went to bed—and then she dressed again, in a bright, flowered blouse and a silk skirt, hose, good shoes, and she brushed her hair and put on lipstick and eye shadow and mascara and even a pair of earrings and a string of glossy black beads and two bracelets she'd bought long ago in the Old Market, and thought *All dressed up, no place to go.* She began to wander through the house then, touching things as she walked past them. She wasn't

149

singing but she wasn't thinking either. She was waiting, taking stock. She thought she was very calm. But when she heard the cab pull up outside, she ran downstairs—she had just started touching things in Alexander's room—and flew through Bartha's studio, the quickest way out, and flung open the door, and as soon as she saw Alexander, she began to talk, she could not stop talking, and she spoke so quickly he could hardly understand her. By the time she slowed down, she was almost finished with the blow-by-blow account of everything that had transpired since she'd woken up that morning, right up to her calling him, telling him the things she hadn't told him on the phone as well as the things she had (or must have, he thought, when he wasn't listening).

Now, as if her laughter had shamed her, she backed up and said, again, "A heart attack. That's what the doctor said. Although without an autopsy he couldn't know for sure. Thank goodness he said that wouldn't be necessary. Unless we requested it. Which I didn't, of course. Why would I? The doctor said, 'To go the way he did, at his age, in his sleep, is not so unexpected.'"

"No," Alexander said, as he'd said while he watched her poach the eggs. "Not to the doctor, anyway."

"Do you know what the doctor said? He said, 'It's what we all should hope for—to live to see our ninety-eighth birthday, healthy to the end, and then die in our sleep peacefully.'"

"Peacefully," Alexander murmured. He could not imagine that his father had died *peacefully*. His death hadn't woken his mother, yes. But nothing woke her, as far as he knew, until she was ready to wake up. And nothing happened peacefully to his father. Silently, perhaps, but never peacefully. Peacefully suggested uneventfulness.

And everything his father ever did—sipped a glass a wine, buttoned a shirt, shopped for groceries—he did with a certain flair, a certain quiet drama. Everything was an event. An *artful* event.

Once more he thought that what was required tomorrow was something grand and elegant. Something hard to plan and harder to pull off. Hundreds of guests. Good music. Excellent food. But as he thought this, he could hear his father saying, one white eyebrow raised dramatically, *Oh, yes? And where do you propose to find* that?

Alexander shook his head and drank what remained in his teacup. The tea was standard issue with the poached eggs. The addition of the Scotch had been his idea. The old man always added Scotch to his tea when he felt chilled— at least that was how he explained it. He kept a bottle in the cupboard for this purpose. "To ward off illness," he would say as he stirred lemon, honey, and a shotglassful of Scotch into his cup. "Preventive medicine."

"He was never sick," said Alexander. "Was he?"

"No, never," his mother said. "I can't think of a single time. The doctor didn't believe me, I could tell, when I said that."

Alexander raised his empty teacup and his mother smiled. He was grateful for the smile.

"It *is* amazing," she said, "when you think about it. I suppose I never did."

He had never thought about it either—it was just part of the way his father was. But it was true that the old man never got sick the way other people did. Never had a cold, a headache, a sore throat. Nothing. Even past ninety he had not developed high blood pressure, despite decades of sitting down every night to a dishful of salt into which he dipped things—a hard boiled egg, a stalk of celery, a sliced turnip, a whole tomato from the garden. He was not arthritic or a diabetic. He had not grown hard of hearing. He had never had a kidney stone, a gallstone.

In all these years, Alexander thought, his mother had never had to hold his father's hand as he lay in the bed, feverish or aching. She'd never had to fix *him* poached eggs on toast. "I am a little bit chilled," he might say, and make himself a tea and whiskey. That was the only indication that he ever felt anything less than perfectly fit and comfortable.

They were both silent for a while then. Alexander considered pouring a little more Scotch into his cup, and never mind the tea. Esther considered clearing the table of the food they hadn't eaten.

"Are you tired?" he asked her finally. She looked as if she were.

"Yes, very," she said. "For once, I might even go to bed early."

"That's a good idea," he told her. He felt guilty for feeling so relieved. "I'm pretty tired, too."

They both looked at the table, the untouched plates of food.

They rose together and cleaned up together, without talking. When there was nothing left to do, he kissed her and told her to get some sleep. "Tomorrow will be hard," he said, although really he had no idea what to expect, no idea what a funeral would be like. He was lucky, he knew. Mari's parents were both dead. And her grandparents, all of whom she'd known—which itself was unimaginable to him—had died, one by one, starting when she was in high school. And she had lost friends, too. Two of them to AIDS and one to cancer. One in a car wreck. He should have asked her about funerals.

"Get some sleep," he said again. "I'll see you in the

morning." And then, because he was still doubtful, he said, "It was good of Vilmos to take care of everything."

"Yes, wasn't it?" she said. Alexander thought that what she meant was, *You were the one who should have done it.* But what she was thinking was that there was no chance that she'd cancel what Vilmos had planned and instead take Bartha to New York. Take him home, twenty-five years after he had first suggested it.

Alexander went upstairs. He thought he'd try to read in bed, but as he flipped through the pages of his book, the scattering of checks and asterisks and exclamation points, the scribbled "no!"s and question marks along the margins all disheartened him. He set the book aside. For a while he surveyed the walls—the posters, the clippings and the postcards still affixed to them; he paused to contemplate a series of postcards, photographs of Mycenaean terra cotta animals, he had taped in a straight row above the headboard of the bed, his last year of high school—and then he turned off the light. He was too tired to do anything else. So he hadn't been lying—that was his last thought before he fell asleep.

His mother was also tired—she'd been telling the truth, too—but she wasn't ready to go to upstairs, to bed. She hadn't even let herself think yet about what that would feel like. She was used to waking up alone—she always woke up alone—but when had she last climbed into an empty bed?

In her study, where she knelt looking through her record albums, trying to find something—the right thing—to put on the turntable, Esther tried to remember. It would have been the last time Bartha had gone on one of his trips and stayed overnight. When had that been? Years ago now. She sat back on her heels, realizing—she'd never thought of it before—that she had never taken note of it, the last time, because she hadn't known that that was what it was. Had he? she wondered. Had he known—decided in advance? Or was it only afterwards, when he began to contemplate another trip (*did* he contemplate them? She'd always wondered but had never asked) that he made his decision not to go? Never to go again? Had something happened on that last trip?

How could there be so many things she didn't know? After twenty-seven and a half years of marriage you'd think you'd know everything. Small things and big.

She put on a record and sat down to listen to it but she couldn't—she could not sit still. After a minute she got up to change it.

She had never slept well when he was gone overnight. She'd liked the freedom of those days off—she had *learned* to like the freedom they provided her—but she'd never learned to like going to sleep in the empty bed.

Now she'd have to, wouldn't she. Not to like it, maybe. But to do it.

She kept changing records. She felt sure that there was something, some specific thing, she wanted to hear. What, though? Perhaps it was something they didn't have? She'd put a record on the turntable and listen, restless and dissatisfied, for less than a minute before she got up and moved the needle to another place on the same record, and then thirty, forty seconds later she'd get up and move the needle somewhere else. Then she'd give up, take the record off and put another on.

She changed records at least a dozen times before she settled on something, an aria—*In des Lebens Frühlingstagen*, from *Fidelio*—that Bartha used to sing to her and Alexander long ago, before he gave up singing altogether, before he decided that he could no longer stand the sound of his own voice. She could hear his singing voice in her mind, still, though the last time he had sung for her had been so long ago that Alexander had no memory of ever having heard it.

Listening to someone else—whom, she didn't know; she didn't bother checking—singing what she could remember even now, quite clearly, sung by Bartha to her and the baby was peculiarly comforting. Of course, it was a pity they had no recordings of *his* voice. His voice in his prime—how she would have loved to hear that. But he hadn't cared—he had said he didn't care. Lost forever, long ago. In another world.

She'd stopped feeling restless, though she did not return to her chair but instead sat on the floor, beside the turntable, shoes off, her legs tucked beneath her. Each time the aria came to an end, she replaced the needle at its start and listened to it again, sung by someone younger and in stronger voice—decades' stronger than Bartha's had been when he'd sung for her. She had no idea how many times she listened to it. Again and again and again.

By the time she checked on Alexander, she was tired enough to sleep, she thought. For once, she'd skip her bath; she'd taken that shower, after all. She stood for a moment watching Alexander sleep, and thinking of how, when he was a baby—when they were still in the little house they'd rented after leaving Vilmos and Clara's, before they had bought this one—after she'd put him to bed and knew that he would sleep for at least two, and maybe three, hours before he'd wake up for the first time, she would tidy up and drink a glass of warm milk and then get into the bath and lay there for so long that Bartha, who had gone to bed himself long before, would stand outside the bathroom door, half asleep, and whisper, "Esther? *Still* you're in the bath?" and she would call back, softly, "Shh. It's all right, I'm fine. You go back to bed. I'll be there soon."

When Alexander was a baby, this hour and a half had been the only truly quiet, private time she'd had. And she had grown used to it—to depend on it—and as the years had passed it had turned into a ritual. She would lie there thinking things over, adding hot water as necessary. For years, she'd felt that she did her best, her calmest, thinking in the tub. No matter how late it was, she never thought of skipping her bath.

But tonight? She hesitated in the doorway of what Bartha had always referred to as "the child's" room, even after Alexander had grown up and gone away. It was not so easy to break a habit of so many years. And if she did, if she started altering her routine now (already! she thought guiltily—as if she'd just been waiting for a chance to make a change!), would she soon find herself with no routine at all? Roaming through the house at midday in a nightgown, wandering into the kitchen to eat standing up before the stove, spooning something out right from a pot? Her routines—her morning tea, her bedtime bath—gave shape to her days. How many alterations could she make before she lost her sense of how a day was meant to go? Before she lost her sense of what a day *was*?

She would take her bath, she thought. And as she drew away from Alexander's doorway and went down the hall, past her own bedroom—*her own* (she paused to consider this: not only a bed to herself now but her own bedroom for the first time in her life—for even before the birth of her sister, there had been her grandmother, and for a time she'd shared the small bedroom with both of them, her baby sister Sylvia and Grandma Lili)—she told herself that she would not stay in the bath for long. A compromise.

The compromise bath—shallower and cooler, too, than usual—felt like a burden. And all the while, she kept her eyes on the little clock that Bartha kept on the glass shelf over the sink. He'd put a clock in every room—he never wore a watch, but he liked to keep track of time. The lovely wristwatch she had bought him years ago—a birthday present—he kept on the piano in the studio. The pocket watch—another birthday, later on—had never left his nightstand. Alexander was the same way. One could buy him watches, but he wouldn't wear them. She wondered if he too surrounded himself with clocks.

When the second hand made its ninth full revolution she rose from the bath, dried off, put on her robe. One-tenth of her customary time. But this was not a night for thinking—the last thing she had any interest in tonight was thinking—and she could not lie any longer in lukewarm water staring at the small round silver-framed face of a clock .

In her bathrobe, she went once more to Alexander's room. Again she paused in the doorway, but this time, though she hadn't planned to, she tiptoed in, stopping after every few steps on the wood floor to make sure she hadn't woken him. She went to the armchair in the corner by the window—his reading chair, square-backed and thickly cushioned (which, along with "a good lamp to read by," he had asked for, leaving her and Bartha briefly speechless, for his tenth birthday)—and sat down. If he'd awakened at that instant and asked her what she was doing there, she could not have said. But for the first time all day, it seemed to her that she was in the right place, doing the right thing.

She turned on the lamp. Undisturbed, Alexander slept on, and now she could see him—she could see his face, turned toward her, as if he could see her with his eyes closed. As if he could see her in his sleep.

He found her in the chair when he woke up, hours earlier than was his habit—the sun had not yet finished rising—and because he saw her first, saw her even before he had taken in where he was, and why, he felt for that first groggy moment as if he were a small child. In childhood he had often woken in her presence. He would call out for her in the night, and she would come to comfort him and fall asleep. The memory of waking to find her in the bed beside him or curled up on the carpet by the bed—or later, in the chair he had insisted that he needed—was so powerful, so thick, he felt he had to push through it as if it were mud or snow.

She must have been unable to sleep in her own room, he thought once he'd pushed all the way through and was fully awake. He turned off the lamp behind her and covered her with the blanket from his bed before he went into the bathroom. There was still plenty of time before he'd have to get her up if she didn't wake up on her own.

He made coffee for himself and put the kettle on, over a low flame, for his mother, so that when she came downstairs he could hand her a cup of tea immediately. Even under the best of circumstances she was hard to talk to in the morning before she'd had her first cup of tea.

At seven, drinking his third cup of coffee, he called Vilmos. He'd be up by now, Alexander knew. And worried, probably. Guiltily, he thought he should have called last night.

"Oh, my boy," Vilmos said when he heard Alexander's voice. He dismissed his apology for not having called him sooner. "No, no, your mother needs all your attention. Watch her carefully. She doesn't know herself how shaken up she is. She is sleeping now, I hope?"

Alexander assured him that she was. He didn't mention the armchair in his room.

"Good, good," Vilmos said, and his voice broke. "Oh, already I miss him so very much!"

"I know, Vilmos. You've been a good friend to him. To all of us."

"A whole era is gone now with him. A whole world is lost. Somehow I was unprepared. And now…"

"I know," Alexander said again. "None of us were really prepared."

"And now only you and my own girls and Elise's little girl, my beautiful granddaughter Annette—oh, Alexander, you must see her! She is a marvel, a wonder—this is all that remains of my blood relations. There is no one else." And now he was crying. Alexander waited. He wanted to ask him what time they should meet, and where exactly—and what would happen when they got there, if he could find a way to ask this without sounding like a child—but he thought he'd better wait. As it was, he felt callous, listening to Vilmos's sobbing. Shouldn't he be the one weeping? But his father had always said that Vilmos had "feelings enough for all of us." His cousin, he would say dryly, had been "given the job of expressing all necessary emotion, to relieve the rest of us from this terrible burden." Given the job by whom? Alexander wondered now. Surely his father hadn't meant God. He never talked about God. Evidently that also had been Vilmos's department.

When the weeping began to taper off, Alexander said gently, "Excuse me, Vilmos, but I'm wondering what time you have in mind for us to meet. Also, I'm afraid my mother doesn't seem to know where—"

"To meet?" Vilmos interrupted him. He was agitated. "To meet? No meeting! I'll come to you. Nine thirty I will be there. The limousine too."

"What limousine?"

"For you and your mother. I'll follow behind."

"That hardly seems necessary."

"Oh, yes. I asked. It's only right."

"At least you and Clara could ride with us in it. Surely it's big enough."

"No. This is not the way it's done." Stubbornly. "I *asked*," he said again. "Now. Listen to me. You wait there. We'll come. The limousine will come. Nine thirty. Funeral at ten. Let Mother sleep until eight thirty if she can."

Alexander gave up. He said goodbye—he could hear, as he hung up, that Vilmos had begun to cry again—but even after he'd put the receiver down (a receiver with a dial, not buttons; it was probably a rental from the phone company—that was how long they'd had it; but his mother, he bet, still thought of it as the latest thing: a phone with a dial right in the handle!), he stood looking at the phone. It was too easy to imagine Vilmos, at his end, standing by his phone, head bent, still sobbing.

It wasn't as if Vilmos intended to make him feel deficient —Alexander knew, in fact, that if Vilmos had discerned that he'd had this effect on him, he'd make an effort to contain himself from this point on. All this heartbreak was genuine. It would not occur to Vilmos to put on a show, to make an effort to make his grief noisier, more visible. Alexander knew it wasn't reasonable to be

160

irritated. Yet he stood in his mother's kitchen shaking his head at her Trimline phone and thinking: All this *keening*. This chest-beating. And for what? For a nearly hundred-year-old man whose own emotions, if he'd ever had them, hadn't ever risen even close enough to that impenetrable surface for anyone, *anyone*, to guess what they might be.

What was it in him that his cousin would miss—that he already missed—so fiercely? That required such lament? It was unfathomable. Not that Vilmos had loved his father— that was not unfathomable. Alexander had, too. He *had*. So had his mother. She'd loved him enough to change her life—to abandon her life. To change the course of her life forever. Alexander loved that story. He *told* that story. He'd used that story for seduction. Not cynically—not cynically where his mother was concerned (it was perhaps a bit cynical of him to dust the story off and bring it out again each time he did)—no, he admired the young woman, the girl, his mother must have been, and he could imagine how appealing, how charming and elegant and interesting a man such as his father would have been to her.

The way her mother told the story, he had swept her off her feet. The age difference didn't matter to her— "Honestly, I hardly noticed it." There was no question that she'd loved him. But *she* wasn't heartbroken. She was sad, a little shaken—he, unlike Vilmos, believed she knew *exactly* how shaken she was (she had known enough to come to his room when she couldn't sleep in hers, hadn't she? She hadn't simply lain awake on her side of the bed in which her husband had died silently the night before)—but she was not done in. She wasn't *broken*. She would be all right, just as she'd said she'd be. She might even be thinking that now she'd have all the days off she could ever want.

It was only when he saw her, when she came into the

kitchen fifteen minutes later, confused and sleepy-looking in her bathrobe, her eyes not altogether open, her hair tangled, that he understood how harsh, how ungenerous, that thought had been. He hugged her and offered her a cup of tea, which she took without speaking.

"I assumed I'd have to wake you up. This is early for you, isn't it?"

But it was too soon for her to talk. She'd always woken very slowly. When he was a child this had amused him, especially because it was so different from the way his father woke: his father opened his eyes and he was alert at once, ready to see what the day had in store for him.

He, child of the extremes, had landed in the middle. It took him a few minutes, during which he had to fight his way awake, and then he was up to speed. Mari said that watching him rise out of sleep was like watching someone being born. She half expected him to let out a cry when he took in where and what he was. So she said, sweetly. Grinning.

A sudden, sharp pang of regret ran through him now: he should have taken her up on her offer to come with him. He hadn't even let himself consider it. It would have been the first time he had ever brought a woman home, and wouldn't this have been the worst possible occasion for it? His mother would need all of his attention and support. He hadn't even had to think about it. But now he was sorry. For himself. He yearned to talk to her. She would know exactly what to do and say.

Even with the time difference, it was much too early to call her. She was like his mother—she slept late. But he might sneak in a quick call just before they left for the funeral. He could ask her what to expect. And she would either tell him, seriously and in great detail, or she'd refuse

162

to tell him anything. It would depend on whether she believed he should or shouldn't know. He trusted her to figure this out. She was always a step or two ahead of him, which should perhaps have made him uncomfortable but instead it pleased him. He felt soothed by it; he had the idea that she knew exactly what needed to be known. He had been anxious for most of his life, and with Mari he felt calm.

Just thinking about her had soothed him, he realized. He was no longer angry. Who was there to be angry with, after all? Poor Vilmos, for his broken heart? His mother— he watched her drink her tea—because hers remained *un*broken? If Mari were here, he thought, she would say, sagely, *Think again. You're leaving someone out.*

Himself? His father? (*Again*, he thought, his father?) It occurred to him, with some amusement, that he'd learned to ask the questions Mari asked. He just didn't know their proper answers. Of course, she always insisted that there weren't any. And yet even so she seemed to have them. She'd coax him along until he found his way to them, too. There were always proper answers to the questions she taught him to ask.

He looked at his mother. Even dazed with sleep, she looked happy to see him, happy to have him sitting across the table from her. And she *was* happy. She was so happy and grateful, she felt guilty—a tangled, sleepy sort of guilt. And she'd had a tangled, sleepy, guilty thought just before she'd come downstairs. She *had* in fact thought (fleetingly, but still she'd thought it, hadn't she?) what Alexander had imagined or supposed (and then quickly unimagined, unsupposed) her to be thinking. She'd been in the bathroom, splashing water on her face and singing to herself—sleepily, half humming, half singing something from "Paint Your Wagon" to which she didn't even know all the words, murmuring the song, really, as she scooped up handfuls of cool water to make herself wake up—and it struck her forcefully that she didn't have to murmur, she could sing all she wanted to now, quietly or loudly, as she chose, She could sing anything she wanted to. Then the other thought had edged into her mind, dislodged by this one. An unseemly thought. She blushed now, over her teacup, and brushed the thought away. *Days off* indeed.

Alexander took a sip of coffee, his fourth or fifth cup—he'd lost count. Usually it took him half a day to drink this much coffee. His mother was working steadily on her first cup of tea, still trying to wake up. Her hair fell over her eyes as she took small sips, one after another without pause, like a child making her way through an obligatory cup of milk.

And she looked like a child, too. She raised her eyes now, smiling at him shyly. "More?" he said. She nodded, handed him the empty cup. He stood up and fixed another cup of tea.

Friends spoke of going home and turning into children in their parents' presence, but his mother became a child whenever he came home. It was not a role reversal, either—he'd tried to explain this to Mari—for it wasn't as if he were the adult and she the child. They were both children—they were children together. His father was the grown-up.

And why do you assume that she becomes *a child?*

But Mari hadn't asked him that. He asked himself now. He'd never thought of it before—had never wondered. What *was* his mother like when he was not around, when it was just the two of them? When she was all alone here with his father?

Which she would never be again.

Which she would never be again.

And did that mean that there was some way she had been that she would never *be* again? That she would never be herself again? Or that she would never be *other* than herself again?

Which was it?

The question—all these questions—made his head ache. He would never know. And why should he know? It was none of his business to know.

He had said this so often when Mari asked him questions! Questions about her, about them.

Not that he minded her asking. He liked that she was interested. Even if he didn't want to answer, or even to think about an answer, he liked that she had asked, that she took nothing at face value. She was the first girlfriend he had ever had who wasn't simply charmed by the fairy tale he told about his parents, about how they got together and then ran away. She wondered over it. She made *him* wonder over it. She made him think about things in a way that both confused him, undermining the ideas he'd had for practically his whole life, and at the same time gave him hope. Things didn't have to be what they seemed to be. Things didn't have to be what you'd always thought they were. It was news to him.

It was possible, he thought now—*let* himself think now—that he loved her. She was beautiful, she was brilliant, she had work she loved and was very good at. And she cared about him. She wouldn't ask so many questions if she didn't. It was corny, but he had the sense that he mattered to her in a way he hadn't mattered to anybody else he'd dated. In a way he hadn't mattered to anybody since—except—his mother.

That was a sobering thought. He was not an idiot

(he told himself this as he watched his mother drain her teacup and once more hand it to him): the significance of the age difference between them had not escaped him. He had never been interested in girls or women his own age or younger, the way his friends were, but Mari wasn't two years or four years or six years older, like other women he had dated. Thirteen years was no small difference. Thirteen years meant she was closer in age to his mother than she was to him.

This didn't *bother* him. On the contrary—he gave his mother back her cup, refilled—it was one more item on the plus side. And it didn't bother Mari either—or at least he didn't think it did. She made cheerful jokes about it that suggested she was genuinely amused. She acted as if what she called his devotion to his mother (the "birthday thing," as she referred to it, for instance, or the frequency of his mother's letters and phone calls), even if it had "spoiled him for girls"—she'd said this to him once while sitting on his lap, her arms around his neck—had been "*ideal* preparation for a fabulous romance with a middle-aged babe like myself." She loved to call herself middle-aged. She loved to call herself a babe. He could not imagine how she had become so confident and sane. "Years of psychoanalysis," she said, and he couldn't tell if she were serious or not. He asked and she just laughed.

She laughed a lot. At him? He wasn't sure about that either. "No," she would say. "Not at you. Near you." She laughed, she recited poetry—whole poems from memory—and quoted to him from contemporary novels, novels by Saul Bellow or Milan Kundera or J.M. Coetzee. ("'There's no more reason to trust the heart than to trust reason'—that's Coetzee," she had said out of the blue one day, and when all he managed in response was a neutral,

166

"Is it?" and "I keep meaning to read him," she said, "But what do you *think*? Do you agree?" He told her it wasn't something he'd given a lot of thought to. "Maybe you should," she said. And then she kissed him.)

Or she'd quote Karen Horney. Or Van Gogh, from his letters. Or something from a play she'd been in—Chekhov, Pinter, Tennessee Williams. It was hard to keep up with everything she had memorized. She'd recite the lyrics of Ira Gershwin or Johnny Mercer or Oscar Hammerstein. Or she'd sing them. That was another thing—she could sing. The first time he'd overheard her in the shower in his loft one morning singing "Something Wonderful"—*He may not always say what you would have him say*—his heart had clenched in a way that both alarmed and thrilled him. He'd never dated anyone before who could sing. Not anyone who could *really* sing, the way his mother could. Mari had even been in a couple of revivals of the musicals his mother loved so much—and she had been amazed when, after she had told him which shows, he began reciting lyrics, rapid-fire. It had amazed him, too—he'd had no idea how much he had retained of his mother's favorite songs.

She was the only woman he had ever dated who had laughed—the only one who'd even understood—when he had told her that the names of his beloved childhood dogs had been Tony, Maria, Laurey, Professor Hill, Mister Snow, Julie Jordan, and Nellie Forbush. "For years, I didn't know myself that we had named them after characters in musicals. I thought my mother had made up those stories. She used to tell me them at bedtime, songs and all."

"'West Side Story' and 'Carousel' are kind of heavy bedtime fare, no?"

"No worse than most fairy tales."

"Your mom must have been a real character herself."

"Oh, she still is. Trust me."

He was smiling, he realized, thinking of Mari. And his mother was smiling back at him.

"Let's have breakfast," he told her. "I take it you're awake now?"

"Awake enough."

"I'll cook," he said. "It's my turn." His mother looked skeptical. "I can cook as well as you can."

She laughed. "I suppose that's true. You know, your father tried, years and years ago, to teach me."

"To cook?" Alexander had already opened the refrigerator and was peering into it. He turned back to his mother. "But he couldn't really, either, could he?"

"No. That's what was so funny. But when we were first married, when you were still a little baby, maybe four or five months old at most—we were living still in Vilmos and Clara's basement—he took it into his head that I should learn to cook. We had to wait till they'd finished their dinner and cleaned up before we could begin." A small sigh escaped from her: she was remembering sitting in the basement, Alexander in her arms, and listening to the noises that came from the kitchen, just above their heads, and waiting. It was amazing how clearly she remembered, considering that she hadn't thought of this in years—in decades. Vilmos and Clara would have their dinner at five thirty, "Middle Western-style"—a habit Bartha had disdained the first few years they'd lived here and then, slowly, grew accustomed to himself, so that by the time they'd bought this house at last, she, like Clara, would be at the stove by five o'clock. "I used to sit on a chair and watch him cook a chicken, while Vilmos and Clara watched television in their bedroom, and I would try to memorize what I saw him do."

Alexander took out eggs, a loaf of bread, a quart of milk. "And?"

"It was hopeless. The meals he made were so bad even *I* could tell that they were bad. He was accustomed to eating in restaurants. What did he know about cooking? Still, we would sit together in Clara's dinette, and sometimes it would be eight o'clock before everything was ready, and we were both so tired we could hardly sit up straight, but he would set the table very carefully with our own dishes and cutlery and glasses and real napkins—it bothered him so that Clara and Vilmos used paper!—and we would have our terrible meal and he would ask me questions to make sure I'd paid attention. And he'd say—he knew, of course, that he'd done something wrong, only he didn't know what—'But not *exactly* that way, you understand. You should do this, and this too, but do it a little'"—Esther waved both her hands in the air expressively, in Bartha's manner—"'a little *better*.'" She laughed and shook her head. Those "cooking lessons" had gone on for weeks, perhaps months, but between his lack of knowledge and her lack of interest or aptitude, naturally they had failed. Finally he gave up, she swallowed her pride as she'd already done a dozen times by then and asked Clara for advice, and armed with a Betty Crocker cookbook, she had learned to cook without his help. Simple things only, and it had been dull work for her. She'd never taken pleasure in it. But no one had starved.

"I make pretty good French toast," Alexander said. "How does that sound to you?"

"It sounds fine. But you don't have to cook for me."

"I want to," he said. "And you don't even have to take notes. You can set the table."

He got to work on the French toast, which Mari had taught him to make—it was one of the few things *she* ever cooked—and as his mother stood and began taking plates out of the cabinet, he was startled to hear her singing, very softly. He stopped beating eggs and listened. When had he last heard her sing? He hadn't even noticed that she'd stopped—not until now, hearing her again.

His mother put forks and napkins on the table. He added cinnamon, vanilla, and a pinch of salt to the eggs and milk; he whisked, still listening. He listened hard. He had to, she was singing that softly. "*Common sense may tell you,*" she sang, "*that the ending will be sad.*"

His mother added water from the still-boiling kettle to her cup, dipped another teabag in, stirred, sang.

Mari sang this one, too.

When his mother had sung the song's last line, he said, "That's pretty, Mom. It's nice to hear you singing."

She blushed and turned away—another surprise. "How long till breakfast's ready? Suddenly I'm starving."

They made small talk as they ate. When they were almost finished, he remembered to tell her that he had talked to Vilmos. "That's good," she said. "He's taking this hard. He was very attached to your father, from the moment we arrived in Omaha. Even before, when they didn't really know each other. It was as if he made a decision to love him."

"He stuck by it."

"Yes. Now he's having trouble taking this in. He seems to have thought—"

"That Dad would live forever," Alexander said. "I know. Who didn't?"

His mother looked at him curiously. He waited for her to say what she was thinking but she didn't say anything.

"You know, you might have let him ask Elise and Jill to come home for the funeral." He stopped then, surprised.

He hadn't known that he would say this. He didn't know why he had.

His mother was surprised too. "Elise and Jill?" She said it as if she'd never heard their names before.

"They might have been a comfort to him," Alexander said. "Certainly more than Clara will be."

"Oh, Clara has her ways. She's—"

"Not what she seems. So you've told me all my life."

His mother looked down at her empty plate—apparently it had been true that she'd been starving—and said, "He offered yesterday to ask the girls to make the trip. But they were just here for Easter, and it isn't easy for either of them to get away. Jill has her classes, and Elise is busy with the baby now. To make another trip here now, on such short notice, seemed a lot to ask." She looked up at him. "I didn't think it would be fair to them. And it wasn't as if they were close to your father. He didn't care very much for them, you know. Although naturally I didn't say that to Vilmos."

"Dad didn't care much for them?" Alexander was shocked into laughter. "*Dad* liked them fine. Dad was crazy about them. I never understood it. It seemed so out of character for him to be so fond of girls who used smiley faces to dot the 'i's in their names."

"Fond of them? Your father?"

"You'd know better than I would," he said, "but, yes, I always had the idea that he was. That he was the only one around here who was."

"Oh, don't be silly, Alex. They're lovely girls. I've always said so."

He heard the "Alex," but he let it go. For now. "So you have," he said.

Esther couldn't decide if that was sarcasm she heard

171

in his voice. The truth was that as close as she and Clara had become over the years—a closeness born, she knew, of Clara's having *had* her girls, for that was when it had begun—she'd never felt at ease with them. She'd never understood them, and for her that meant that she could not begin to like them. Even as babies, they had been too sunny, too unworried, too *simple*. They had slept through the night contentedly. They seemed to have no moods. Neither of them suffered in the dark, or cried at being parted from their mother (though until their middle teens they'd hated to be taken from each other); neither of them ever threw a tantrum, the way Alexander had, nearly continuously, between ages two and three. Neither of them ever had rebelled the way he had. (Alexander, she knew, would insist he hadn't either. Any time she'd spoken of this he had laughed at her. "Oh, yes, some rebel I was," he would say. "I was docile and devoted all my life. The only independent thing I ever did was go to art school. You should have tried being someone else's mother, then you'd know what rebellion is.")

Neither of them had ever really *left* Clara. Even though they lived in distant cities now, both girls were reliably in reach in a way that Alexander never was. They called Clara daily and they came home often. Jill would almost certainly return to Omaha when she was through with college in Ohio. Elise had been there too, at the same school, until last year. Now she lived in New Orleans, where on a spring break visit she had met the man who had become her husband; she'd dropped out of school before the year was over, married him, and moved to New Orleans for good.

Clara had been stoic at the time, and Vilmos spoke to Esther privately about how "brave" she was, how well she was hiding her poor broken heart. But it seemed to Esther there had been no breaking of hearts. Elise's husband was a nice young man, the baby they had had was reliably sweet, and even with her whole new life so many miles away Elise managed to call her mother every night. She had brought her baby here already five or six times since her birth. And Jill? Jill came home for summers and for every holiday, even if it were just a long weekend. They *were* good girls, both of them. She should make more of an effort with them, Esther told herself. It was not too late.

"They both called me yesterday, you know," she told Alexander. "While I was waiting for you to get here. They were very kind."

"I'm sure they were, Mom. I never said they weren't kind. In fact, I've never known anyone as concerned as those two are about other people having a nice day. To tell you the truth, I've never understood how Clara, grumpy as she is, could have produced such daughters."

"You don't understand Clara at all," Esther told him. And then, without thinking about how this would sound, she added, "I should have had a daughter."

Alexander was not offended. He laughed. "Yes, ma'am, you certainly should have. So why didn't you?"

"One isn't given a choice," she said. "Or did I leave that part out when I explained to you how—"

"I meant later." He had turned serious, she saw. He leaned forward, over his plate. It looked as if he hadn't eaten more than two or three bites of his French toast. She resisted the impulse to tell him to eat a little more, or to offer to make something else for him. "I mean it, Mom," he said. "Why didn't you?"

"Are you asking for a sister?" she said lightly. "This is some time to put in a request. You might have done that twenty, twenty-five years ago. It's a little late to change your

173

mind." And because he looked puzzled, she added, "Do you mean to tell me you don't remember what you used to say? From the time you were, oh, two or three years old?"

"What did I say?"

"You'd say, 'Oh, I hope there won't be any more babies in this family. One child is quite enough.' You said this all the time. And then, as you got older—six or so, somewhere around the time Vilmos and Clara's girls were born—you were a little bit more subtle. You'd say things like, 'I don't know why anyone thinks an only child is lonely. An only child *likes* being alone.'"

"Are you telling me you let *me* decide?"

"It wasn't a hard decision," she said. "You were plenty for me. I never felt I needed another child. For a while your father would ask me, he wanted to make sure." She didn't tell Alexander *how* he'd asked—so hopeful that she would say no: "You don't feel that you should have another baby, Esther?" he would say, when Alexander was still very young. Then he stopped asking, and she never brought it up herself. What she'd just told Alexander was the truth. He *had* been plenty. She had adored him; she hadn't needed anybody else. "You were more than enough, to be honest," she said. "You were a handful, Alex, always." She stood and began to collect their dishes, to put them in the sink. "And I have never seriously regretted not having another child. Not even not having had a daughter. I wasn't much of a daughter myself, so why should I imagine my own daughter would have been more dutiful? I would not have had a Jill or an Elise. I would have had a little Esther or a female Alex."

"Mom," he said. "You just did it again. Twice."

"Did what?"

"*Alex*," he said. "You called me Alex."

She began to wash the dishes. Without turning around, she said, "Did I? That's funny, no? I haven't in a long time, have I?"

"Except for the last couple of days, no."

She glanced over her shoulder. "It bothers you?" But she didn't wait for him to answer. "Your father hated it. That's why I stopped. But then"—she paused; she made a sound halfway between a laugh and a sigh—"it's also why I began."

"What does that mean?"

"Well, while you were still very small he started calling you Sandor, and I had—"

"That I don't remember at all."

"Oh, he did, trust me. Sandor! How I hated that! But I didn't have the nerve to tell him. So this was the way I let him know. I called you by a name I knew he'd dislike just as much. And I was right. From the beginning, from the first time he heard me call you Alex, he objected. He said that *Alex* sounded to his ear 'American in the most foolish way.' He said it reminded him of something from the television. But I kept on. Every time he called you Sandor, I called you Alex. And finally—oh, months went by, or a year—one day when he objected to Alex I said what I'd been thinking all along. 'Sandor is better? He does not live in Budapest in the year 1905 with those vanished cousins of yours.' In the end, I agreed to give up Alex if he gave up Sandor. I said, 'We'll both call him by his right name, the name we agreed upon.'"

"The two of you made a deal."

"Yes, a deal."

"I had the idea that he'd forbidden you to call me Alex." But until he heard himself say this he hadn't known that he remembered it that way. And of course it made no

175

sense. When had his father ever "forbidden" anything? But he was disappointed. It was as if he'd secretly been holding on to the idea that just this once the old man had been so stirred up about something concerning him he *had* taken a stand. *A deal*, Alexander thought—well, at least he hadn't simply given way; at least he hadn't shrugged and smiled and said, "As you like, Esther," with that little bow of his head.

"He made a deal with you," Alexander said.

"That's what I just said." But she sounded cautious now. Once, when as a boy of twelve or thirteen he'd protested her swift, cool, definitive rejection of a "yes" he'd slyly (or so he'd imagined then) extracted from his father, she had said, "We each have our spheres of influence." He could not remember now what the issue at hand had been. A rock concert or some other outing? An overnight stay at a friend's house? It didn't matter. She made all the rules; she set the tone. His father never once put up a fight.

"Well, a deal's a deal," he said. "Besides, I don't like it either."

"Don't like what, sweetheart?"

"*Alex.*" His eyes filled, which took him by surprise. "Don't do it anymore, Mom, please? Don't call me that."

She turned off the water and reached for the dish towel to dry her hands. She faced him. "All right. I'll be more careful from now on."

"Thank you."

She came back to the table and sat down, the towel still in her hands. She looked troubled. She had that searching look she used on him when something had transpired between them that she didn't understand, a look she'd used on him his whole life. But she didn't speak, and he was grateful. He had a feeling that if he were forced to speak himself, to answer her, he'd cry. He hated the thought of it.

He fixed his gaze out the window. His mother's eyes followed his and they sat silently, both looking out. The day was gray. The grayest city on earth, his father used to say. "I once thought this was true of Warsaw. How little I knew then." He'd said this again and again.

Today the sky was like a dome covering the city. He had heard somewhere that it was supposed to snow. But how could he have heard this? A radio forecast? Perhaps his mother had mentioned it last night. No. He remembered now. He heard the pilot's voice. *Snow in Missouri, Kansas, and Nebraska.*

He waited, staring out into the grayness until his eyes cleared and he was certain his voice wouldn't break. Then he said, "Wasn't it supposed to snow?"

"Snow!" His mother sounded shocked. But then she repeated it, softly this time, and reached for his hand. "Oh, yes," she said. "Yes, indeed. Snow." She squeezed his hand and smiled. "I haven't lost my mind, don't worry. It's just that you made me remember something. Your father told me it was going to snow."

"Oh, yes?"

She laughed, as if she could tell that he was bracing himself for the news that his father had come to her in a dream last night to give her the weather report. "The night before…before he was gone. As he was going up to bed. I'd been thinking that we didn't talk at all that night, but we did. I'm just glad I remembered."

"What else did you talk about?"

"We didn't talk about anything. He just told me it was going to snow."

Alexander didn't understand—she could see that he didn't understand. But it didn't matter. For once, it didn't

177

matter. She was only grateful that she remembered. And now that she remembered, she could not imagine how she had forgotten these few words they had exchanged. He always put his head into her study right before he went upstairs to bed, to say goodnight and tell her, "Don't stay up too late," but on this night he'd had something to tell her first. He had been listening to the radio, he said. He thought she'd want to know that snow had been predicted for tomorrow. "A light dusting," he said. And then, in response to what must have been her look of dismay, "Not a blizzard, Esther. Only one last quite small gasp of winter."

She remembered the wave of irritation that had passed through her when he said this—not because she blamed him for the weather, but because of his defense of it, because of the implication that he and winter were now in cahoots (since when? she had wanted to say). She was glad now that she had suppressed what she had felt. She'd sighed, that was all, and murmured, "Snow, so late in the season."

"So you say every year. You used to enjoy the last snowfall of the year."

"That was a long time ago," she told him. "I used to like surprises better than I like them now."

"One would think by now you wouldn't be so much surprised." He smiled at her. "Still, it's nice that you are. Nature loves surprises."

"My poor narcissus," she said.

He blew her a kiss. He said goodnight. He said, "Don't stay up too late."

I shouldn't have, she thought—or thought she thought. She must have said it out loud, because Alexander said, "Shouldn't have what, Mom?"

"Shouldn't have stayed up. I should have gone to bed when he did." Before he could say anything else, she went on, quickly, "I should have said something out loud to *him* about the days long ago when I would be so happy to hear that it was going to snow, I'd jump up and down like a little girl. I *was* practically a little girl then. I'd bundle you up and scoot you outside, running right behind you, just as soon as the snow started. Do you remember?"

"Sure," her son said.

"This was back during our first years here, when we were living in that little rented house—do you remember that house?" But she didn't give him time to answer. "Before you started school, before I started gardening. Before I started waiting out the winter like my tulips."

She had begun to cry. Alexander's eyes widened, and that made her angry. Why shouldn't she cry? She was supposed to cry. Her husband was dead. Her son should be crying too.

Alexander didn't cry. He was a silent for a little while, and then he said, "I remember making snow angels in the yard. That was at the old house, right? We had that tiny yard, and when it snowed it would just be a square patch of white, just big enough for the two of us to lie down in and spread our arms."

"That's right," she said. Tears were slipping down her cheeks but she wasn't making any noise. The tears were as steady as rain, though. There was nothing to do but wait for them to stop falling, wait for the storm to pass.

"We should get ready to go," he said.

"You're right, we should." But she didn't move.

Gently, he said, "You go on up. Get dressed. I'm going to go up and get ready in a minute, too."

She nodded, and this time she rose, slowly, and started

out of the kitchen. She was still crying silently. From behind, just now, she looked like an old woman.

He called Mari from the kitchen phone. He got her machine. "I just wanted to say hello," he said. "We're leaving for the funeral shortly. I'll call you later." He hesitated. "Thinking of you. Wishing I'd said yes when you offered to come."

If she'd meant it when she'd made the offer, he thought as he hung up. Had she meant it? When he'd said *No, that's okay, it isn't necessary*, it had crossed his mind that she'd known in advance that he'd refuse, that she'd felt safe asking if he needed her because she'd known that he'd say no.

Don't be so cynical. Don't be a jerk.

She'd meant it. Why wouldn't she have meant it? He went upstairs to dress. He'd call her later, as soon as he had another minute alone.

Half an hour later Vilmos tapped on the back door—Esther's door, his father had always called it—and Alexander and his mother both went to open it. Clara, in gray instead of black, and stone-faced to match, was at her husband's side in the doorway. Alexander kept an eye on his mother, who had emerged from her bedroom in a long black silky-looking dress he had a feeling she'd had since he was a child, and black high heels, her hair in a tight bun at the nape of her neck. She was dry-eyed and pale. She hadn't said a word to him.

She and Clara hugged but didn't speak. Vilmos hugged Alexander. "The girls would have come, you know," he said. "Your mother insisted it wasn't necessary for them to make the trip."

"It wasn't," Alexander said. "But I know they would have. They're lovely girls. Mom was saying so just this morning."

The limousine arrived then—they heard it pull up and Alexander and Vilmos exchanged glances. There was a bit of fussing over checking to make sure that nothing in the house had been left on—stove, coffee maker—and locking the door and stashing his mother's key in Alexander's pocket. Then they went round to the front, walking two by two—the women behind the men—and Vilmos leaned his head close to Alexander's and whispered to him. He wanted to know if there was anything they'd need at the house besides what had already been arranged for.

"At the house?"

"For afterwards. You know. Cold cuts. Rolls, cake, soda pop. Everything's arranged. But I'm worrying that I might have forgotten something."

"I didn't know we were going to have a party," Alexander said. They had reached the front curb. The limo driver was holding the back door open for him and his mother.

"That's all right," Vilmos said, as if Alexander had apologized. "I understand. But it's what people do. I asked."

Asked whom? Alexander thought, but he said, "Well, if that's what people do. Of course."

His mother and Clara stood holding hands.

"Do you think we should have wine?" Vilmos whispered to him. "That's what I'm wondering. I wasn't sure."

"Oh, wine, yes." Alexander refused to whisper. "Dad would expect it, wouldn't he?"

Vilmos's laugh sounded dangerously like a sob.

"And a bottle of brandy," Alexander said, louder still. "While you're at it. And plain club soda."

Brandy and soda was Mari's drink. Before he'd met her,

he'd never known what to order. One couldn't very well ask for a tea and Scotch, and he always felt foolish ordering a glass of wine. As if he were trying to be his father. An impostor.

Now he was thinking: If we're going to have a party, I might as well get drunk.

"All right. Good," said Vilmos. He gestured at the limo. "I'll be right behind you."

"Are you sure you don't want to get in with us?"

"No, it—"

"I know, I know. You asked and it isn't done. All right."

Vilmos and Clara got into their own car and Alexander and his mother climbed into the backseat of the limo. It seemed tacky to him, despite Vilmos's assurance on the phone that he had "asked." His father, Alexander thought, would have been amused. By the limo, by the party at the house that Vilmos had planned—by Vilmos's sober assertions that he'd checked out every detail and was certain that it all was just right, as it should be.

Still, as they slid forward, he was glad not to have to drive. He supposed it was a family trait, hating to drive. He'd pretended to enjoy it when he was in high school— like his attempt to play the guitar, it had seemed to be a necessary part of teenage boyhood—but once he'd left home he had been grateful to give up driving except for the occasional weekend rental with a girlfriend—and even then, he always urged the woman to drive if she "wanted to." Women considered this gallant in a feminist manner and were impressed, they told him, since most men insisted on driving. Rarely did the woman he was with decline to drive.

His mother not only hated to drive, she was terrible at it and she knew it, and since Alexander had left for college, the car had mostly sat in the garage, just as it had the first few years after his father had bought it. (To this day Alexander didn't know where it had come from, or how his father had pulled off buying it without a driver's license— from a dealer, or from someone on the street who had been driving around with a sign taped to one of its windows?) For years, ever since it had been made clear that Alexander wasn't coming "home," his mother had been after his father to sell it, telling him that it was silly to keep it, silly to keep spending money to insure and register it, just to keep it sitting in the garage, where she hardly had room for her garden tools, her sacks of mulch and peat moss and fertilizer. But he would say, "No, no. One needs a car." If she pointed out—as she reported to Alexander—that *they* didn't, that she walked everywhere, that he didn't drive himself and disliked being a passenger, that Alexander came home rarely and even when he did he hardly ever took the car from the garage ("I also hate to drive, you know," he'd intercede and she would say, impatiently, "Yes, yes, I know, exactly"), his father would just smile, she said, and shrug, and then repeat, maddeningly, "One needs a car." And then he'd say what he almost always said to end a discussion when they disagreed. "Sometime, Esther, you might change your mind."

But about the car, as about most things, she did not. She continued to ignore its presence among her gardening things—as much as it was possible to ignore so huge and intrusive a machine in what she considered her gardening shed—and to walk, or take a bus when walking wasn't feasible (and when it was impossible to get where she was going on foot or by bus, she'd call a taxi before she would take the Impala out herself). Everywhere she went she took a collapsible shopping cart of the kind her own mother had used in Brooklyn. She bragged to Alexander that she was the only one in Omaha who *did* walk, that the baggers at the Hinky Dinky never failed to be surprised when she asked them to load her groceries directly into her own ancient cart and declined their offer of "help out to your car, ma'am?"

His mother still had not spoken, and as he watched the parade of gas stations and fast food restaurants along Dodge Street, he wondered what she thought about the limo. Did *she* think he should have driven them in the Impala? Or was she afraid that if she spoke she'd start to cry again?

He was still somewhat unnerved by the tears she had shed this morning. Of course, he'd been half wishing all along that she would cry, wishing that Vilmos wasn't the only one shedding tears for his father. But he hadn't seen her cry in such a long time. Not since his own childhood. Not since *he*'d stopped crying. As if they had grown out of it together.

In his childhood, his mother had cried easily and often. She'd cried whenever *he* was crying, which had never failed to make him cry that much harder. And if his father happened to be about, he'd throw up his hands and say, "Now what? Now what?" This made them both cry harder.

Alexander stared out the window of the limousine. Along this part of Dodge, there were patches of small shops clustered together—old-fashioned drug stores, hardware stores, beauty "salons." All with dusty windows and hand-painted signs. And here among them, suddenly, was the funeral parlor. They pulled up and his mother spoke for the first time since she'd left the kitchen. "Pretty dismal, no?"

"That's what Dad always said."

"Especially on a gray day like this. He'd say, 'Omaha at its grandest.'"

"He always said it was like Warsaw. 'A gray city, a city without charm.'"

"He hadn't seen Warsaw in fifty years and still he kept saying it."

"Warsaw probably hasn't changed that much since the war. Omaha probably hasn't, either." The driver had gone around to open his mother's door for her, and Alexander got out on his side and went around to meet her. He offered her his arm. "It's funny. In New York, even when I'm gone just for a weekend, I sometimes come back feeling as if the whole city's changed. I mean, whole blocks change over in just a few days. Chinese restaurants turn Mexican, dry cleaners turn into...I don't know, sock boutiques. Or sushi take-out places."

"Well." His mother paused at the threshold of the funeral parlor. "Do you remember when that sushi place opened here? What a big event that was? Dad took us but he was the only one who ate the sushi. You and I ate fried shrimp, fried vegetables, fried ice cream. It was in the place that used to be that pancake restaurant. Where that girl got shot, do you remember? So in fact things do change a little here, just bit by bit."

He spotted Vilmos's car coming up the street and he lingered in the doorway. "I remember that restaurant. Is it still here?"

"I don't know. We never went back."

Alexander laughed. It was a nice surprise, to laugh. "For all Dad's talk about restaurants, he stuck to the same few, didn't he?"

"He said there were only a few worth going to. He got tired of trying new ones and being disappointed."

"And fighting with Clara over it."

"Yes. She was always dragging him downtown. And he so hated downtown."

They smiled conspiratorially at each other. Clara and Vilmos were pulling into a parking space.

"'A mockery of a city,' he would say," said Alexander, with his father's accent. "'And now they are building a big parking lot! For what? For whom?'" His mother laughed. When he was young, he could always count on this imitation of his father to make her laugh, as long as the old man was out of earshot.

"He was right," his mother said. "No one goes downtown. All those little pagodas they put up—"

"With the corn motifs!" Alexander could not resist imitating the old man again. "'For whom are these pagodas? For ghosts waiting on empty streets in front of empty stores as empty buses rattle by?'"

But he stopped then. This was not the time for this. Though it was possible that his father would have been amused, even pleased, that he was saying what he would have said if he were here, saying it in his own voice. Standing in for him.

Vilmos and Clara approached.

Alexander took a deep breath. He saw his mother take one too.

"Come, let's go in," said Vilmos.

As soon as they stepped in, people started coming over to them, telling them how sorry they were, how much they'd miss his father. How they'd cried when they heard. How much he had meant to them. His father's students, mostly, Alexander guessed. Their parents, too. And other people who looked familiar but whose names he didn't know— whose names he was sure he'd never known. Neighbors.

186

Storekeepers. There was one man he thought might have been their mailman when he was growing up.

They just kept coming as Alexander tried to walk his mother through the front room, into the chapel. More people by far than he would have guessed had known his father well enough to care. More people than he'd had any idea his father had been on speaking terms with. People he could not imagine his father speaking to.

His mother didn't seem surprised. But she didn't speak to any of the people who approached them, either; she left that to him. And he just kept saying, "It was kind of you to come. It would have pleased my father." This sounded to him like something he'd heard spoken in a movie, or read in a novel. Everyone nodded solemnly when he said this, and looked as gratified as it was possible to look without smiling. Then they backed away and let him and his mother through. Vilmos and Clara followed. Another step or two, and someone else approached.

In this way, it took some time before they made it to the chapel and down the center aisle to the first row. Once they were sitting, people left them alone. He took his mother's hand. Clara was on her other side.

There was a minister—Alexander guessed he was a minister—at a podium.

He'd never met his father, that much was clear from the start. He mispronounced his first name, and then he got everything else wrong, too. Alexander squeezed his mother's hand. She nodded without turning toward him. (Did that mean that she objected to this, too? Or that she didn't?). *A fine man. Devoted to his family. Beloved by his students*—well, that he was, apparently. *A good Christian. A member of our community for nearly thirty years: "He made this his home, though he was born on a distant shore."* Alexander snorted.

187

He couldn't help it. His mother didn't look at him, but he saw her mouth twitch.

It would have to be endured. It would be over soon enough. It didn't matter if it was meaningless, if it had nothing to do with his father. Really, he thought, it wouldn't have mattered what sort of funeral it had been. Whatever they did would have been beside the point. He wasn't even certain what the point was. But surely something more than—or other than—the funeral itself. Coping with the death? He grimaced. That was the kind of talk he detested. The kind of talk his father had taught him to detest. *Coping. Caring. Being open. Sharing.*

The minister talked this way. *Sharing our grief. Coping with it. Coming to terms.* There was nothing to come to terms with—that was what Alexander wished the minister would say if he had to say anything. His father had been close to a hundred years old. Men didn't live forever.

That was what this joker at the podium should be saying. *He lived a long time. Now he's gone. And that, my friends, is that.*

He was proud of himself, suddenly, thinking this way about it. His father would have been proud of him. He felt calm, cool, collected. Mature. Out of reach of all this—all this nonsense, all this talk, all these gerunds. He felt like his father. Distant and amused. Except that he was tempted to point this out to his mother, which the old man wouldn't have done, wouldn't have approved of. Still it was hard to resist the urge to draw her attention to how well he'd risen to the occasion. He'd dressed properly; he'd stumbled on the right tone, the right words. He'd been doing all the talking, on her behalf as well as his. He wanted her to acknowledge this.

He didn't say any of this, of course. He didn't say

anything. He just kept sitting there, only half listening now. He'd never asked for praise from her, not even as a small boy. Not even at those times when everyone else, in the course of things, looked to their parents for approval. He'd never been the sort of child who demanded admiration. Perhaps because he'd so steadily been granted it by his mother, whether or not he had earned it, and never (even when he knew he *had* earned it) from his father—so that, in his mother's case he didn't have to ask, and in his father's he knew that it wasn't worth the trouble?

It made no sense that he was always wondering if his mother had noticed how well he was doing. The trouble was that she seemed so impressed by everything he did, she didn't seem to know the difference between insignificant and significant achievements. As far as he could see, she didn't differentiate between his having won first place in the children's art category at the county fair and his having his first solo show in SoHo. He never had to wonder if she'd be impressed when he sent her a postcard announcing a show, or a clipping from the *Times* or elsewhere that reviewed his work—but he always asked himself if she knew how impressed she was supposed to be. He had no clue if she knew how well he was handling things today, especially as measured against how prepared he'd been—*not at all*, he wanted to tell her—and how competent he'd felt. Still felt. Not competent. Not *equipped*. And yet he'd managed, hadn't he?

His mother gave him no sign that she had noticed. She'd assumed that he would manage, and that he would manage well. Mari would say that he should be glad, grateful that he had her confidence. He *was* glad, he told himself. He meant to be glad. It embarrassed him to wish that it be harder to win her regard. How she had spoiled him!

Oddly enough, his mother was thinking, just then, that she hadn't spoiled him—that despite both Bartha's and Clara's constant admonitions that she was, she must have done right by him, for he'd turned out so well. And in fact she was thinking about how nicely he was handling this business of the funeral, and fighting an unseemly urge to whisper into Clara's ear, *Look how nicely he's managing all this. Remember how you used to tell me he'd grow up without manners, without a thought to anyone's well-being but his own? That I gave him too much attention? You and his father both!* Of course, Clara had changed her tune—or at least she'd gone silent on the subject—once she had children of her own. Bartha, on the other hand, had simply given up. *Do as you wish, Esther. But a little less fuss over the boy would not be so terrible, it seems to me. Nor would a little discipline.*

Why was it that he had failed to understand—to notice!—that their son had not required her discipline? He disciplined himself. She could not recall ever having had to punish him. From the youngest age, he'd taken it upon himself to issue his own punishments: when he did something he considered "wrong," he was much sterner with himself than she could have been even if she'd chosen to be stern with him. If he lost his temper, if he broke something, he took himself into a corner. He withheld his own pleasures. She used to laugh to herself when she read in "parenting" magazines, in the doctor's or the dentist's office, about sending children to their room to think over their crimes. Nobody had to tell Alexander to think things over, to apologize.

How sober he had been, how self-possessed. She used to think he would grow up to be a scientist, a scholar. Or a judge—even that had crossed her mind. He was so intelligent and earnest. She had never for an instant imagined that he would turn out to be an artist, and she had never gotten over it—how wrong she'd been, how she had failed to see what was ahead. Failed to see what had been there already, or so Alexander had said bluntly when he'd made his announcement of his plan to study sculpture. "You want to become a *sculptor*?" she had asked, amazed. "Since when?"

"I don't want to *become* a sculptor. I am one."

"You are? Since when?"

He hadn't even answered. He had looked at her with what she thought was pity as much as contempt. She had never forgotten what it felt like, having him look at her that way.

Bartha had also been caught off-guard. Often in the years since then, he had said to her, "We should have known. He had always the temperament of an artist, even when he was small. So sensitive, so anxious! So self-serious! We should have seen it."

But they had seen nothing. That he had no gift for music, Bartha said, must have distracted them. Esther didn't bother to point out that he, not she, had been insisting for years that the boy "must have" inherited musical talent, that this was inevitable, "as certain as gravity," Bartha had assured her. Gravity indeed. *She* had acknowledged years ago that the child could not sing a note. But even after the disastrous business when he was a teenager—that guitar!—Bartha had remained stubbornly certain that music would prevail. What had finally caused him to give up, a year or so after the foolishness about the guitar, in which Alexander had not even pretended to be interested for more than a few months, Esther didn't know. But it seemed to her that when he did give up at last on music, he gave up also on the boy himself. He had never paid him very much attention, but during that last year that Alexander lived at home with them, he paid him none at all.

But *she* had always paid attention. She had no excuse. Nothing had distracted her. She simply hadn't ever taken seriously the child's habit of sitting in his room all day and "making stuff"—that was what he always told her, with a shrug, when she asked what he'd been doing up there for so long, so quietly. She'd misunderstood. She had assumed that this was something children did. Now she couldn't think why she'd made this assumption. *She* hadn't sat alone hour after hour at the age of eight or ten or twelve—certainly not at fourteen, at sixteen—gluing feathers onto lumps of clay and twisted wire, building up strange, leaning towers made of chunks of wood. Those long Sundays, when she used to take off on her own, while Bartha walked the streets of some other Midwestern city, Alexander would spend by himself up in his room, with strips of metal and wood scraps and shavings, clay and wax and balls of wire. She didn't worry about the mess—she'd never been the sort of mother to worry about messes. But she'd never thought about it, either.

It had surprised her that in high school, with a girlfriend and a group of other boys and girls with whom he went to parties and rock concerts, he still "played in his room" alone. She was ashamed that this was how she'd thought of it. Thank goodness she had never told him that. How stunned she had been by his announcement! And she was still surprised, more than a decade later, every time she found herself standing at the mailbox with a postcard that displayed a photograph of something he had made, or a catalogue with pictures in it from a group show at a gallery, or an exhibit in a small museum in Maine or Vermont or Massachusetts.

She would study Alexander's work—figures made, according to the line of type beneath the photos, of lead and wire and concrete, carved wood, iron, fabric, "dried, stretched skins"—and try to reconcile this with the boy she knew better than any other human being on the earth. She tried to fathom that it was Alexander who had made them. But she could not make heads or tails of them. She had told him once, tentatively, that they were "a little hard" for her to understand, and he had laughed and said, "Don't take it personally, Mom. There was a review of that last show—the one I called Fairy Tales?—where a guy said my work was beautiful 'in its way,' but 'finally incomprehensible to the human mind.'" He laughed again then, and she couldn't tell if he was joking—if he'd just made this up— or if someone had really written this in a newspaper (and if someone had, was *that* meant to be a joke?). She asked if he would send her the review, but he said, "Not a chance. It'd just confuse you more." She hung up the phone without daring to confess that she didn't think that was possible.

There was silence in the chapel; then a rustling, which gave way at once to a hushed commotion of coughs, whispers, creaks and thumps. The tribute, such as it had been, thought Esther, must be over. She looked at Alexander. He was already looking at her, waiting.

"Ready?" he asked, and hooked his arm through hers. She rose with him, guiltily. How could she have allowed herself to miss most of her husband's funeral? What sort of wife—no: what sort of *widow*, she had to force herself to think the word—would let herself become distracted at a time like this?

Alexander hadn't noticed, couldn't know, that she had not been listening. The way he looked at her suggested nothing but concern—love, tenderness, anxiety. She let him lead her up the aisle as if she couldn't manage on her own. It was possible, it occurred to her, that she could not. In fact she could not imagine having to proceed through the chapel, up the path that had respectfully been made for them, all by herself. Alexander led her forward, past murmurs and bowed heads that he acknowledged silently, with nods, and once more she found herself admiring him. Who would have guessed that he would turn out as a young man to be so like his father—that he would be decisive, graceful, elegant?

All the way out to the cemetery, out near Boys Town, she held on to Alexander. She sat very close to him in the backseat of the limousine and closed her eyes. She was determined not to think—not to be distracted now. To concentrate on what was before her, nothing else.

At the cemetery, she and Alexander joined a circle—not too large, mercifully—around the coffin Vilmos had chosen. She could see that Vilmos wanted to ask her if he had done all right but was keeping himself from speaking. She nodded at him—she tried her best to imitate the nod, the dignified and grateful look, that Alexander had employed all morning. Sweet Vilmos looked relieved.

The graveside ceremony was short and scriptural. It wasn't hard to pay attention, as long as Bartha wasn't being talked about in ways that made no sense. Someone must have informed the minister of the correct pronunciation of his name, so that when it was spoken this time, it came out properly. That helped, too. She kept her head bowed and simply listened. Alexander held her hand.

On the ride back to the house neither she nor Alexander spoke. The house would soon be full of people, she knew, and she dreaded this. Vilmos had explained it, patiently, not once but three or even four times, but still she didn't understand why it was necessary. Why, she had asked Vilmos, would this comfort her? "A houseful of people? I can't think of anything I'd dislike more at such a time."

"Everybody does this," he had said. Perhaps so. She could not imagine why.

Alexander too was dreading the onslaught of strangers in the house. Vilmos had sworn that he'd handle everything, but even so it wasn't as if *he* could vanish—as if, leaving Vilmos in charge, he could go up to his room and close the door, the way he might have when he was fifteen. Though it was tempting. Would there at least be time, he wondered, before people started coming, to leave his mother with Vilmos and Clara and take a short break, take ten or fifteen minutes to be by himself?

Esther was now asking herself the same question. She was calculating the time it would take to get to the house (though this was hard to do, since she could not be sure where they were now, as nothing out the window of the limo looked familiar) and the extent to which she could push Vilmos's famous patience if she were to disappear at the beginning of his party (for how else was she to think of this event?) for just a little while. Might she not steal fifteen or twenty minutes before things got underway? She saw herself stretched out on her bed—lying on her back, the covers undisturbed beneath her, wrists and ankles crossed. Lights off, shades and curtains drawn. Silence, darkness.

She sighed. Then she heard Alexander sigh beside her and despite her gloom and her anxiety she smiled a little. Him too, she thought. Poor thing.

And once they'd both concluded, at the same time, that it would not be possible to steal a bit of privacy, each of them thought fleetingly of running away, of telling the driver to keep going, to take them somewhere else—

anywhere else, anywhere at all but to the house that would be full of people.

They didn't, naturally. And somehow Vilmos and Clara, who had stopped on their way to the house to pick up wine, brandy, and plain soda, had contrived to get there just as they did (and as he climbed out of the limo it occurred to Alexander that Vilmos must have handled this too—must have told the driver not to take him and his mother straight home, but to take a roundabout route, killing enough time so that Vilmos could be sure they wouldn't get there before he and Clara did).

The four of them had only stepped inside and started to unpack the bottles in the kitchen when the doorbell rang—a man bringing the platters of food and the soda pop Vilmos had ordered—and after that it kept on ringing, so that within minutes of their own arrival the house was full. Where had all these people come from? There seemed to be a bigger crowd than there'd been at the funeral. Had Vilmos announced an open house in the *World-Herald*? Alexander took him aside and asked him, but Vilmos took the question as a joke, laughing as he patted Alexander's arm, and Alexander had no way to tell which joke it was, exactly: that he would have done such a thing, or that he would have failed to?

They were all milling around in the only room in the house suitable for a crowd, the room that would have been the living room in anyone else's house—not just the largest of the rooms on the ground floor, but the one into which the front door opened. Unfortunately, this was his father's studio. What would have been difficult to bear in any case, thought Alexander, was made that much harder by the presence of guests—of strangers—in this of all rooms. *He* was a guest in this room. His mother, too. How much time had they ever spent in it before today? Five minutes here, five minutes there. One had to walk through this room to get to the stairs that led up to the second floor. A minute in the morning, and at night. A minute after school each day.

His mother didn't even clean this room—his father kept it clean himself. He kept his own broom and dustpan, his own feather duster, his own soft rag for wiping off the piano keys, in here. Alexander had never been able to imagine his father with a broom in his hand, had thought his insistence on taking care of it himself was only his way of keeping his mother away. But the room was quite clean, he noticed now. He looked around curiously. As he stood beside the piano, shaking hands with strangers, saying thank you for their sympathy, he was acutely aware that he'd already spent more time in this room, just today, than he'd ever had before. He tried to keep an eye out for his mother, on the ancient couch against the wall where she sat holding hands with Clara, but people kept getting in his way. How could *she* bear it? He searched the crowd for Vilmos: he wanted to ask him how long this would go on.

When the crowd thinned, the platters of food Vilmos had set up on every surface—including card tables he had brought in from somewhere—disarranged so thoroughly that even though there seemed still to be plenty of sliced meats and cheese and cake and bread left on them, everything looked unappealing, Alexander managed to excuse himself and slip upstairs to call Mari again. He went into his parents' room—the only room upstairs where there was a telephone—and sat on the bed, his father's side, without thinking. Then when he thought about it he stood up. The cord was long enough to pull the phone around to the other side, long enough to take the phone into the hall (or even into his own room, as he'd done as a

197

teenager) if he wanted to, but instead he kept standing, by his father's nightstand, while he dialed. (*Dialed*—they still had a dial phone up here too, the old squat heavy black one. For his mother's birthday last year he had bought her a new phone with pushbuttons and a built-in answering machine, a pale rose-colored one to match the curtains and the bedspread and the carpet, which he'd been so sure she'd like and which had been hard to find in just that color. It was probably still in the box, on a shelf in the closet.) He reached Mari's machine again, and this time he hung up.

Reluctantly, he started down the stairs. There were only a few people left, thank God. He counted—six people now. His mother was still on the couch with Clara beside her. They weren't talking but they were still holding hands. His mother had had someone, him or Clara, holding her hand all day. What would happen when he left, when he went back to New York? Clara could not hold his mother's hand full time. He paused on the third step down. What was wrong with him? Why had he not thought about this— what it would be like for his mother after he left?

But even now that he had begun to think about it, he didn't know what he was supposed to do. Was there something he could do for her, to help her—help her to do what? "Settle herself" was what he thought, but without a clear idea of what he meant. And what about afterwards, when he was back in New York? He could call her every day, of course—he could. He would, he promised himself. But a daily phone call from him would not be enough to fill the hours of her days.

As he forced himself down the stairs, back into his father's studio, as he watched his mother sitting on his father's beautiful old velvet-covered couch ("the only piece of furniture remaining from my studio in Brooklyn," his father had once told him, although Alexander hadn't asked; it was one of the few times his father had ever spoken of what Alexander thought of as *back then*, his mother's phrase for life in Brooklyn, for "before"—and when he volunteered this information, Alexander asked, not curiously but politely, "What happened to the rest of it?" "Who knows?" his father said, but said that was where he left it, that was the end of the conversation), he thought of what her life would be like in the days to come, once he was gone. She would see Clara, she'd thumb through her catalogues, and when the ground thawed she'd work in her garden. She'd read, listen to records. How could this be enough? And what of waking up each day in an empty house, and each night going to sleep alone—the simple day-to-day business of living alone?

Unless it turned out that she liked it.

He had reached the couch, reached her. Clara stood and discreetly slipped away. His mother patted the cushion beside her and he had no choice but to sit down. But the unexpected thought had ambushed him. It was as if it were already true—she was enjoying being all alone. When she touched his arm, he flinched. He had to hold himself still when she drew her arm through his and rested her head on his shoulder. "Almost over," she said quietly. "Five people to go. Not counting Clara and Vilmos."

He nodded. But why should she not end up enjoying living by herself? She had never had the chance to—perhaps she would enjoy it as much as he did. He had not expected to enjoy living alone. He had been full of trepidation when he'd moved out of the dorm and into an apartment (a room, really—a tiny, furnished room) in his junior year. He had thought it would be good for him, the logical next step after the move away from home, but he'd assumed it would be difficult. He had been certain that he would be lonely, that a period of misery would precede whatever peace he might make finally with solitude. Instead, from the beginning, he had thrived on it. He remembered very well how stunned he'd been, that first night in his own place, to find himself not only not unhappy but elated. He had so decisively preferred living alone that it was hard now to imagine himself ever living with another person. Even Mari.

But this too was a thought that came as an assault to him. *Even Mari?* Was he considering this—living with her? This was the first time the possibility of it had crossed his mind. Had *she* been thinking of it? She'd lived alone far longer than he had. Since a very early marriage and divorce, both while she was still in college, she had lived alone— surely she was in no hurry to change that.

But he saw the illogic in this protestation, for even if she had been thinking that they might move in together someday, this could not by any means be characterized as "hurrying"—not after almost twenty years of living by herself. And why shouldn't she be thinking of it—and why shouldn't he? He had searched for reasons to think less of her, to find fault with her, and he had been unable to. And she teased him about how he must be hiding from her all of his "unlovable traits." ("It's never taken me so long to find the bad things out about a man I'm seeing," she said. "And then I have to make excuses for them, and so on. It's time to get that process underway. But where are you keeping them," she asked, mock-sternly.)

But he wasn't hiding anything from her. This also was remarkable.

He felt at home with Mari. He took pleasure in the sound of her voice, in watching her work. He even liked sitting with her in her studio apartment, the same small apartment in the Village she'd been living in for fifteen years, reading in a chair while she read a script. He'd look up sometimes to watch her for a moment, highlighter in hand, concentrating fiercely—he loved to watch her concentrating. And when they were going out, he liked calling for her early enough to watch her get ready, to sit beside her as she piled and wound and pinned up her amazing hair with hairpins from a fancy cut glass jar she kept on her dresser.

He liked very much that she had not bought him a mug with something written on it, that she had said she found his mug collection irritating—"all those slogans, first thing in the morning, how can you bear it?"—and had declared that if the two of them were still together on his birthday (she grinned; she was always prefacing things with the phrase *If we're still together*, but she she always grinned when she said it, as if to say, *but isn't it silly to think that we won't be?*), she'd buy him a set of plain white mugs. They would be waiting for him, she said, when he came back from his usual celebration in Nebraska. He thought of saying, then, "If we're still together, maybe we'll both go," but he didn't. He couldn't picture it—Mari in Omaha with him and his parents.

Which would now never happen.

Mari in Omaha with him and his mother.

This was hard to picture, too. Harder, perhaps. His father would have turned on his old-world charm, would have told stories, poured wine. What would his mother do with Mari? What would *he* do, sitting between the two of them? He tried to think of a single thing he might say in the company of them both.

He sighed. Beside him, his mother shifted, lifted her

head to look at him—he could feel her looking at him, even without turning his face toward her—and then with a little sigh of her own she set her head back down.

It would have to happen someday, he thought.

And just like that, he saw it: if he were to live with anybody, ever, it would be with her, Mari. And if it were strange that he hadn't thought of this before, it was stranger still to be thinking of it for the first time *now*. Wouldn't it be something if he stopped living alone just as his mother started? If they traded places?

Strange did not begin, however, to describe how he felt as this thought passed through him. Everything that worked inside him seemed to have sped up. His heartbeat, his breathing—even his blood seemed to be flowing faster. There was so much movement in him, all of it arrhythmic (his heart thumping one way, his lungs squeezing out their own unnatural pulse), he thought he might be about to faint. Or worse.

He kept himself as still as possible. It's an anxiety attack, he told himself. That's all it is. It's panic, it's not physical. He'd never had one this bad, but he knew what it was—he wasn't stupid. He'd just have to wait for it to pass. He wasn't going to die. He said this to himself as calmly as he could, but he was sweating and so close to hyperventilating it was hard to be convincing.

How was it that his mother hadn't noticed? Her head felt very heavy on his shoulder. Perhaps she was falling asleep. He sat rigidly, his gaze on the few people who remained in the room. Just at this moment all of them were still—a man, his paper cup poised near his lips, stood inches away from a woman whose arms were folded protectively, nervously, across her chest; another woman stood alone beside the piano, only her eyes moving as she took in what was left around her; an old couple stood stock still so close to Vilmos the man's shoulder might actually have been pressing Vilmos's, the old woman holding tightly to her husband's elbow—and Alexander felt himself begin to ease, to slow down and return to normal, calmed by the tableau before him and the vision that came filtering through it, rising from it now like steam: a group of figures arranged just this way, ghostly white (bandaged? he thought; or—no—plaster over mesh), with fragile looking towers (but he'd make them sturdy; they would only seem precarious and delicate) scattered here and there among them—thin, uneven spires of something silvery, perhaps of stacked-up tiny squares of lead?

His breathing had settled down; likewise, his heart. He tucked away the image in his mind—he'd think about it later. But what had happened to him? The only time he could remember ever feeling like this had been a night five years ago, when he'd been mugged while walking home after a movie he'd gone to alone. He'd been punched once, ferociously, on his right cheek—a hard enough blow to knock him down. It had happened too fast for him even to be properly scared, until afterwards, when he sat alone on the sidewalk for the minute or two it had taken before someone walked by and helped him up, asked him what had happened. He remembered wishing aloud—like a child! (and he'd begun to cry then, too)—that he'd stayed home that night, as he had originally planned, or that he'd chosen to walk home by another route, or even that he'd just obeyed his own first instinct when he'd had the sense that he might be in danger, and ducked into the bar that was just a few yards away, or even crossed the street. A hopeless wish to undo, to go backwards.

What he wished now, with a force more than equal to

the humiliating, tearful longing he'd voiced to that stranger as he'd staggered to his feet five years ago on Astor Place, was that things stay as they were, as they'd been. Between him and Mari, he knew, everything would change if they were to live together. *He* would change; he would change toward her. He remembered how, when he had still lived here, in this house with his parents, he'd returned from school each day filled with a sort of desperate hope that no one would be at home, that he'd have the place all to himself. It never happened. Both of them were always there—his father in this very room, hiding behind the flimsy sliding doors they had installed to block the room off from the rest of the ground floor; his mother in the kitchen or in her own ground floor room, her "study"—waiting for him. No matter how quietly he entered, she would fly out of her room, she would greet him as if she hadn't seen him in days, weeks. Years. She had questions for him, she had things to tell him, and here he was at last!

It was not as if he wasn't glad enough to sit and talk with his mother when he came home from school—it was not as if he didn't love her. It was not even as if he minded telling her about his day, hearing about hers. But to be alone! To *not* be under that constant watchful, searching love of hers—that tenderness, that solicitude, that endless devotion.

He imagined hearing a key scrape in his own lock—Mari coming "home." Stopping his work. Sitting down with her and talking.

He imagined his mother, thirteen hundred miles away, alone in the house he had so often, so fervently, longed to be alone in. Remembered his pleasure on those Sundays when both parents had gone wandering. Thought of his mother, here, in this silent house, remembering those

Sundays too. Ashamed now of how she'd thought of them as her "days off." Ashamed that she had missed them.

His mother lifted her head then and looked at him, and this time he turned to her. Her face was so near his he couldn't see it clearly. But even blurred by nearness he could recognize the love that shone on him—that familiar, steady, unswerving love. He felt it tugging on him, as surely as a hand.

"You should come back with me," he said.

She sat up straight. He could see her very clearly now. "Come back?"

"To New York. You know. When I go."

She looked so confused, he added, "Where I live."

"I know that's where you live, sweetheart," she said. "I'm just trying to figure out what you mean."

He wasn't sure himself. He'd had no idea he was going to say it until he had. Now he blushed. "I mean, you could come for a visit. Stay as long as you want, as long as you need to."

His mother looked grave. "I couldn't."

"That's ridiculous, Mom. You could if you wanted to. What's stopping you?"

His mother was shaking her head.

"What is it?" Vilmos said as he walked toward them. "What is happening here that you are both so red in your faces?" He looked from one to the other. "Are you having a quarrel?"

"No, of course not," Alexander said. His mother touched her own cheek. He suspected it was hot, for Vilmos was right—it was flushed.

"If you're not quarreling, what then?"

Alexander shrugged. He knew he looked sullen but he didn't care. His mother said, "Alexander wants me to visit

New York. I was telling him I couldn't possibly."

Vilmos nodded as if this made sense to him. But Vilmos always treated his mother this way, as if everything she said or did made sense. It was his version of respect. He had treated Alexander's father the same way.

"I wasn't asking her to visit New York," Alexander said. "I was asking her to visit me."

Vilmos looked from him to his mother as if considering whether to allow himself to be drawn into this business between them. Then he smiled at both of them and said that he had not intended to interrupt their conversation, he'd just wanted to point out that everyone was gone.

Alexander blinked. It was true—the room was empty now except for Clara, carrying a stack of paper cups in one hand and, in the other, a platter strewn with crumpled paper napkins and used plastic forks atop the ruins of what had been rows of ham and turkey, cheese, salami, bread. He saw that Vilmos held in one of his hands an enormous black trashbag; in his other hand was a dish towel. His sleeves were rolled up.

"You're cleaning?" Alexander said. Vilmos began to answer but Alexander said, "I wish you wouldn't. I'm sure Mom feels this, too. You've done more than enough for us."

"You want us out of your way?"

"No, of course not," he said again. Perhaps he could put that sentence on repeat. He glanced at his mother, whose thoughts were obviously elsewhere. "I just mean we can handle it—*I* can handle it myself. There isn't really all that much to do. We used paper plates and cups, no? So there can't be more than—"

Before he could finish, Vilmos bent to pat his knee. "Good. Okay. So we'll go." He kissed the top of Esther's head. "Don't worry, I understand." He called to Clara, "Come. These two need to be alone. Leave those things in the kitchen, they'll be fine." And then, to Alexander, who had begun to rise from the couch: "No, no, don't get up. We'll get our own coats and we'll let ourselves out. Call later if you need us."

And then they were gone—through the kitchen, out the back door. His mother's way.

The silence in the house was shocking.

Alexander looked at his mother. She was looking down at her hands, which were clasped in her lap, resting in the folds of black silk.

She knew he was watching her. She almost gave in and told him—almost confessed that just before, as she had watched him standing on the stairs looking so worried, and then coming toward her with that grave and anxious air about him that reminded her so much of when he was a child, she had been wishing that he wouldn't go back to New York, that he would stay here with her indefinitely. It hadn't seemed to matter at that moment that this was a wholly unreasonable wish—she'd remembered that it was, but it hadn't troubled her, it had seemed to her an obstacle that might easily be overcome. And when he had sat down beside her and allowed her to lean on him even though he was distraught himself, she'd gone even further. She had let herself wish that he'd never leave her side, that he would stay for good. It had seemed quite possible that he would do this for her.

She'd felt his pulse leaping under her as her head rested on his shoulder and she'd heard, not only felt, his rapid breathing—she had even heard, or she'd imagined she could hear, the wild cadence of his heart—and she had closed her eyes and made her wish, the way a child would have. The way she used to, when she was a child. With all her heart. With perfect faith.

But reason had returned almost as soon as she had finished wishing—reason that drained faith as suddenly as if a plug had been pulled (pulled *because* she'd been too full of hope, she thought: the foolish kind, the kind that Bartha used to tell her, teasingly, "makes your heart swell so, my dearest Esther, that it interferes with your mind's proper working")—and now, upright again beside her son, the house so still around them (what she'd wanted, she had to remind herself), what she was wishing was not so specific, though it was more desperate, she thought: a wish without hope, a wish *born* of hopelessness.

To have nothing else change—that was what she longed for now. Just as she had wished for change, for movement—for excitement, feeling, drama—as a girl, she wished now for *nothing*. Enough change, she thought. Whatever might come next, she didn't want. She didn't want to have to make her way through *next*.

No hope in it and no hope for it either. What Alexander had come home for was all done. He'd leave tomorrow, she guessed, or at best the day after. That curious discussion—debate, dispute—about New York would lie between them like a half built wall that one of them would have to have been brave enough to climb and then jump down from.

Nothing stayed the same. If only she had known that long ago, her life might have unfolded in another way entirely. She hadn't had to leap, to rush after change. Change followed you. Change raced at your heels.

She remembered how, when Alexander was a baby, helplessly all hers, it had been as if there were no one else in all the world but them, and no place in the world but that small basement room they'd lived in. There'd been nothing he had needed that she couldn't give him as they lay curled up together in the fold-out bed, taking their catnaps nose to nose, forehead to forehead, his baby heat against her, his fingers closed around whatever he had grabbed for blindly or she had put in them for him. Her hair. Her ear. Her outstretched finger.

She could not get up to get a glass of water or her clothes, could not move from his side for half a minute without his eyes following her anxiously, without his waiting impatiently, tensely, for nothing more than for her to return. Hour after hour, day after day, week after week. Weeks that passed as slowly as years. *This is my life.* It had made her proud—joyful and certain of herself—even as it made her restless too. She had not been able to conceive then of a time, a version of herself, when this joy and certainty and restlessness would not define her. She *had* no self that was apart from what he needed of her. In his world, she was everything—she *was* the world.

And then bit by bit that world had vanished. It had vanished, and everything had changed. Everything, she thought, except for one pure fact that she acknowledged now, turning away from her son so that he would not see her grief.

If not for him, she would have had a different life entirely. A life now unimaginable.

"Mom? Mom, what is it?" Because she had begun to cry. "Oh, Mom. Don't cry."

"Why not?" she said. She turned to face him. "Why shouldn't I? A widow is supposed to cry. Don't tell me 'don't.'"

He flinched. "You're right. I'm sorry."

"No," she said. She had already stopped crying. "*I'm* sorry. I didn't mean to speak so sharply."

"We're both worn out," he said. "It's hard to know what to say, isn't it? Even to each other."

"I suppose it is." She took his hand. "We could talk about when you might come back for a visit."

He frowned—involuntarily, and so briefly that if she had not been watching him so carefully she would not have seen it. "Well, Mom," he said, with a brightness so forced her eyes began to fill again, "you know, I haven't left this time yet."

"I know," she said. And then she couldn't help herself. "That brings up a good question. When will that be, exactly? You haven't mentioned."

"That's because I'm not sure." With his free hand he patted their linked hands, which rested on her right knee. "I have a flight booked for the day after tomorrow. But I don't *have* to take that flight. I can stay as long as you need me to."

"Oh, you need to get back, I know. You have things to do. I just wondered what your plans were." She said this briskly, pleasantly. She was proud of herself. She smiled and squeezed his hand. "I just didn't want to be suddenly abandoned." She had meant this to come out as a light, rather clever remark—a little joke—and she was every bit as surprised as he when she burst into tears again.

"Oh, no," she managed to say as she wept.

"It's all right, Mom. You said it yourself. You're supposed to cry."

"It's *not* all right. For twenty years I haven't cried. Now look at me—so many times in one day. Your father would have been horrified."

"I don't think so. I think even Dad would have said it was all right for you to cry on the day we buried him."

"Once, maybe," she said. "Not three times." And then

she added, "I'm serious," because that *had* sounded like a joke and it wasn't.

But now Alexander was laughing. "Christ, I just remembered. Not twenty years. Ten. You cried when I told you I was going off to school in New York. You said I was abandoning you then, too."

"Did I?"

"Did you what? Cry or accuse me of abandoning you?"

"Both."

"Both."

Now she began to laugh, too—although she was also still crying. Alexander watched her closely, trying to figure out whether he was supposed to be relieved or alarmed by the laughter. The tears just kept rolling down her face. "I'm sorry," she said. "For then and now both."

All right, he thought, he'd be relieved.

She kept laughing while the tears slowed down, then stopped. When both the crying and the laughter seemed to be finished, he said, "What would you say to a cup of tea? I'm thinking we ought to get the hell out of this room."

"Oh, yes," she said. "What a good idea." She stood up before he did.

In the kitchen, she waved him into his chair. "Let me," she said. "I need to be doing something."

They didn't talk while she made tea. And when she sat down with him, putting two cups between them on the table, they still didn't talk. They looked out the window together. The sky was pearl-gray, sober. The predicted snow had not materialized. Around the bottom edges of the grayness, Alexander noticed now, this year's beginnings of his mother's garden were in evidence. Her antidote for the drabness all around her.

He admired his mother's garden. He always had, from

the beginning. He liked the way it mixed wildness and calm, zaniness and sobriety—the springing up of beautiful surprises everywhere in the orderly curved rows along the path she'd put in years ago. He had described his mother's garden to Mari as "a sort of stately self-conscious drama that periodically convulses into screwball comedy—think Merchant-Ivory meets Preston Sturges." And she'd liked that. She had laughed and said she'd have to see it for herself then one of these days, which pleased him (she had not added *if we're still together*, either). But it struck him now that he had reduced his mother's garden to a witticism, which diminished it, and he was ashamed of himself.

The garden was a miracle, really. Even now, so early in the season, when it was nothing more than a preliminary sketch of what it would be later on, it was something worth seeing. If you knew how to look, if you knew what to look for.

And he knew enough, too, to guess how little this rough sketch of this year's garden resembled what she'd cooked up for it since last fall, over the heartless, relentlessly gray Nebraska winter. The actual sketches she had made—drawing and labeling groups of flowers (ten, twelve, fifteen different kinds in every group) and then redrawing, reorganizing the groupings, fifty or more times—never bore much resemblance to the garden itself once spring came. Her impulses, he knew, were always infringing on her plans—and he loved that about the garden, too, loved the way she *let* her impulses derail her plans. When he was a child it had exhilarated him. She would show him her drawings, drawing after drawing, talking him through them, pointing out the changes she was making from last year, and come spring there was the pleasure of walking with her through the garden itself as she pointed out (cheerfully, laughing at herself) how little had survived the careful plans she'd made. And all through spring and summer, into early fall, they would notice together the difference between what she had intended and what she had done.

He sometimes thought he had learned more about how to be an artist from these walks through his mother's garden than from anything he had learned in art school. But he could never think of how to tell her this.

He loved, too, in his mother's garden, the mix of delicacy and longevity, sturdiness, *history*. All those strange and glamorous new tulips (black and purple and every shade of pink, feathery and plump, fringed and flame-shaped—mysterious, fragile-looking, exotic) amid the stolid, waxy-looking red and yellow ones that for all he knew sprang from the very bulbs he had helped her put in when he was a child. The primroses that returned year after year, the outcroppings of semi-contained wildflowers, the buttercups and bee balm, flowers that nothing could prevent from blooming, and the delphiniums that needed to be fussed over and nearly always died off for good at season's end, that had to be chosen and coaxed into life again the following spring. The hybrid tea roses that required almost daily tending—like spoiled, oversensitive children, his mother used to say (adding, with a little smile, "Not that I would know anything about that") or vain, needful women (the way, his mother said, she used to think of Clara, before she came to understand her—to understand that the need was real, the "vanity" a cover for a failure of tolerance and affection for herself, and Alexander had wanted to say, "Isn't it always? All needfulness real? All vanity a cover?" but he didn't, because his mother's story of her journey from dislike to love of Clara was precious to her, and was one of the few stories she ever told—that one and the one about how his father had swept her off her feet—and he believed it would be hurtful to undermine it in any way).

Alexander hadn't seen his mother's garden in full spring bloom, when she was proudest of it, in years. But even in early summer, when he was at home to see it, the garden was lovely. Early summer was, in fact, when he liked it best, he told her. This made his mother laugh. She said he'd always loved what was available to him, what was nearest at hand, that in this way—*this one way*, she meant—he had always been easy to please. But he didn't think this was true at all. Or perhaps it had once been true—long ago, when he was a child—and had ceased to be so while he was still too young to remember it. Perhaps his mother had never noticed that as he grew up, he'd changed. Or perhaps she'd just decided not to believe even what she could see for herself.

In early summer, his mother's beloved tulips, both the showy new ones and the sturdy ancient ones, were gone; the hedge she had constructed out of *hibiscus syriacus*, which so delighted her and which he had disliked since childhood, was weeks away from flowering. He had learned when he was young enough for it to have made a deep impression upon him how unreliable the pretty, red-eyed, trumpet-shaped pink flowers were. On the first day of school one year—he must have been in second or third grade—while she was still asleep, he had gone out and cut dozens of branches with her pruning shears as a surprise for her. He put them in a tall vase he filled carefully with lukewarm water into which he dropped an aspirin and a penny, just as she had taught him when she brought in armfuls of tulips or daffodils or zinnias. The bouquet, which he set in the center of the kitchen table, was meant to cheer her up. For days she had been saying (in a false-bright voice that was supposed to let him know it was a joke), "Oh, dear, what will I do without my little sidekick?" He knew that it was not a joke, that she was sad (she said this at the start of every new school year and after Christmas and spring break, too, but she had never once fooled him into thinking that she wasn't sad). He was proud of himself for being old enough—clever enough finally—to do something about it. But although she said, "What a sweet thing to do!" and, "How nice to have our breakfast among such beautiful flowers," he could see that she was not cheered up at all. She seemed distracted as they ate their breakfast and talked about the day ahead: what his new teacher would be like, who was and was not in his class this year, the errands she planned to run while he was gone, the work she would do in the garden. When they stood up to go—oddly, he remembered this perfectly, two decades on—she touched one of the petals and murmured, "People call this 'Rose of Sharon,' but that's not its name. It's not the name of any real flower. Things should be called by their own names." She sounded so unhappy that he found himself thinking about it—how he'd failed her—on and off all day. When he got home he saw that every single bloom he'd cut had died.

His mother never said a word about it, not even as she watched him take the vase out back and dump it out into the trashcan, then return to the kitchen with it and wash and dry it himself and put it away in the cabinet where it belonged, slamming the cabinet door shut behind it, embarrassed by his stupidity, angry with *her* for not telling him that these were flowers that should not be cut and brought inside, and furious with the hedge itself.

In a day or two he had forgiven his mother, who had only been trying to protect his feelings, after all. But he was still embarrassed when he thought of his mistake, and he had never forgiven the hedge for its too-pretty deceitfulness.

What *he* loved in his mother's garden was the tangle of old roses like something out of an illustration from a book of fairy tales, and the winding rows of multicolored zinnias, the blue and white bellflowers, the tall red and orange poppies that were like celebrities, towering over everything else, movie-star gorgeous against the background of the velvety dark green of the vegetables his mother grew just for his father.

The garden was as close as anything had ever been to his mother's life's work. He had said this once to Mari and her response had disappointed him, though even now he wasn't sure what had he hoped for—that she would be impressed (or charmed or moved) by his mother's devotion to her garden? Or by his appreciation of her devotion? "She could have made it her real work," Mari had said. And when he asked her what on earth that meant, she said, "Oh, I don't know. Horticulture? Landscape design?"

"Don't be so literal-minded," he told her, and she said, "I'm taking you seriously. That's not the same as taking you literally." And when he did not respond to that, and she said, "I'm disappointed in you, Alexander," he had to resist the urge to say, "Same here." Mari sighed and took his hand. "You don't get it. I'm not suggesting that tending her own garden, just to make something beautiful of her own, doesn't matter because nobody paid her for doing it. *I've* worked plenty without pay. *You've* worked plenty without pay. But that's different." "Why is that different?" he said coldly. It was the closest they had ever come to arguing. "Come on. It's different because this was the work we chose to do. So we do it whether anyone pays us for

216

doing it or not." "And you think my mother didn't choose to have a garden? You think we forced her?" He laughed, but he knew it wasn't a friendly sounding laugh. "You think we cared if she had a garden or not?" Mari raised one eyebrow. "Cared? No. Forced? Also no."

Her phrasing and her intonation were so like his father's then that Alexander shuddered. Mari let go of his hand. "What, then?" he said. She shrugged. "I think she just ended up turning to it. Because what else was there?"

He looked at his mother, whose eyes were still on her garden. "What now, Mom?" he asked without meaning to.

His mother turned slowly toward him. She looked puzzled but not startled, as if she had been waiting for him to speak, but when he had spoken finally it hadn't been to say what she'd been waiting to hear. "What do you mean?"

"I guess I mean, what will it be *like* now?"

She still looked puzzled.

He wasn't sure himself what he meant to be asking her. "Well, I guess…this is a pretty big house. You know, to have all to yourself," he added lamely.

"Don't be silly," his mother said. "I've had this house all to myself since the day you left for college."

Of course she had. He could have said, *But that's ridiculous, Mom. Dad was here.* But he knew better, knew that day after day, year after year, his father had shut himself away in his studio. Had left her to her own devices. Such as they were.

He would be better off not speaking at all, Alexander thought.

But his mother was in fact wishing he would say more. She wanted to tell him this, wanted to beg him to say everything that was on his mind. She wished *she* felt free to say more. She hated the carefulness between them.

Esther remembered, with pleasure so deep, so sharp, it was like pain—an ecstasy of pain—when there had been no secrets, no caution, nothing careful, nothing *shaped*, between the two of them. When there had been no barriers between them, when everything flowed freely, back and forth and back again—so freely it was hard sometimes to tell which one of them was thinking, feeling what.

Alexander remembered something else. He *willed* himself to remember something else. When he thought of the time (so long ago he would have sworn it hardly counted: a lifetime ago, almost *his* whole lifetime ago—when he was too young to know anything, too young to *will* anything, too young for choices) that his mother recalled so longingly, he felt vaguely ashamed, vaguely horrified. What he remembered was what had come after that. How separate they had been. All three of them. How the house had never seemed to him quite big enough as he hid from both his mother and his father. Shut away in his own room, his anger muted but always just beneath the surface, he listened to the muted sounds of both parents going about their lives in their separate parts of the house. Each of them going about their own separate parts of their family's life.

He remembered his father tucked away in his studio, or off on one of his jaunts, far away. His mother in her own room with her own door closed, her loneliness seeping out around the edges of the door. Sometimes she would emerge to haunt the halls and empty rooms, the rooms no one was hiding in, as she went about her housekeeping, raising dust, poking into corners, making things tidy.

He had never let her clean his room. His father had never let her clean his studio.

He wondered for the first time if this had insulted her,

218

if she had felt excluded.

But the three of them had lived together in mutual exclusion. If his mother had been insulted, if she hadn't liked it, it meant that she would have been insulted all her life.

All his life, he corrected himself.

For she had had a life before him, before she had met his father. She would have a life now, with both of them gone. Each in his own way, gone.

But what sort of life?

"What will you *do*, Mom?" he heard himself asking her.

His mother laughed, and again he was sorry he had spoken.

Esther saw that she had insulted him—insulted or embarrassed him, she wasn't sure which (but either way she regretted it, as she had always regretted causing him pain or discomfort of any kind)—and so she spoke to him gently. "I suppose I'll have to get used to eating dinner alone. That will be hard." And mischievously, hoping to make him laugh—always one of her pleasures—she added, "Perhaps I'll start using the front door."

He did smile, wanly. But what he was thinking was how shocking it was how little his mother's life *would* be changed by his father's death.

And Esther was thinking: *Everything has changed. Everything has come to an end.*

Why had she married him? Alexander wondered, and wondered how it was that he had never thought to ask himself this question before. The old story—he had swept her off her feet! How could she have resisted? Why *would* she have resisted?—for the first time seemed unconvincing. He had taken it on faith all his life that she had loved his father. He had taken it on faith that it was a source of satisfaction to her to look after him, to make a home for him. It had to be, for that was what her whole life had been—caring for his father and for him.

But how did one care for someone who allowed no care to be taken of him, who kept himself so much apart?

Unless that was why she had loved him.

"Mom?"

She took a sip of tea. "It's not really hot anymore," she said. "I should make us fresh cups." But she didn't move and he didn't, either. How serious he looked! "Are you worrying about me again?" She reached for his hand but he was already shaking his head. "What is it, then, darling?"

"Have you ever wondered what it would have been like—what your life would have been like—if you'd married someone else, or—I don't know—if you hadn't gotten married at all? Or if you'd gone to—"

"Hadn't married!"

"It's not as if it's never been done. I'm just trying—"

"And done what? Stayed at home with my family?"

It was hard to tell which one of them was more incredulous.

"Those were the only options?"

"You don't know anything about it," she said bitterly.

"If I don't know anything, it's because you've never told me anything."

"There's nothing to tell."

"Mom," he said, "I just want—" But he stopped, because he didn't know what it was he wanted.

"You want, you want. You want *what?*"

"I think I just…I think I just want to…know." But even as he said it he realized that he didn't know *what* he wanted to know. The meaning of his mother's life? The meaning of his?

"It was a long time ago," his mother said.

"Not that long."

"Not that long! Longer than your whole life!"

"And that makes it ancient history." He smiled in a teasing way, a way meant to encourage her to talk, to tell him things. But what she was thinking now was of the stories Bartha used to tell her, the stories that took place so long before she was born. *Ancient history*. All his adventures and his triumphs, the mysteries and drama of his former life. Turning his life into a story for her—a mystery, a romance. One that seemed to have no end.

And then he had run out of stories. Or he had lost interest in telling them. And instead of stories, then, there was only life.

"It was a long time ago," Esther told her son again.

"Not really," Alexander said. "Not in the greater scheme of things."

"The greater scheme," she repeated after him. Wonderingly. Then she laughed, which surprised them both. She shook her head. "Oh, my," she said. "Is there one, then?"

"You got me, Mom."

They considered each other.

After a moment, he said, "Seriously, Mom. What *will* you do now?"

She didn't answer right away. She picked up her cup of tea as if to drink it—she held it for a while with both hands near her mouth—but then she set it down without taking a sip. She turned the cup this way and that; she tapped its handle. She looked at Alexander and she looked away. When finally she spoke, it was only to say, "Do you know that I can't even remember a time when your father and I didn't keep different hours? Isn't that something?" She paused, and there was nothing for Alexander to do but nod—yes, that was something. "Even when you were still young enough for me to have to get up early and get you ready for school," she said, "so that I would set the alarm clock and jump out of bed in the morning, even then your father was awake and in the studio already. It didn't matter how early I got up, he was always up first. Do you remember that?"

"I do," he said cautiously.

"And I always went to bed late. And *he* always went to bed early, earlier even than you. Do you remember that?"

"Yes, of course." But he felt as if she were trying to distract him, to tug him toward nostalgia.

His mother was smiling. "What a funny little boy you were. Your father would go to bed at eight o'clock, nine o'clock, and you were still up at eleven and fighting with me to stay up later still! And yet you always woke up early. In that way you were like him. The two of us battled it out in you—the one who stayed awake and the one who couldn't wait to become awake—and so, between the two, you never needed much sleep."

"That wasn't it at all," he said, surprised she didn't know this. "I needed sleep, all right. I just hated *to* sleep. I still do. I wish I could do without sleep altogether. Given the choice, I prefer to be awake. So I never get enough sleep, and I'm always tired."

But his mother wasn't listening. She was thinking of herself, last night, in the chair in Alexander's room, watching him sleep. And of how, w hen she had woken up, she had glanced at his bed, empty and already made, without thinking of what this meant. But it meant that he had woken first and seen her there. She wondered what he'd made of it. She hoped that he'd thought only that she had been resourceful, that she had tried and failed to sleep alone in the bed she had shared with Bartha and had fixed on this solution to get through the night. She hoped it hadn't crossed his mind that she might not even have tried, hoped he hadn't understood what she did, suddenly: that she had not felt she could entrust him to the custody of sleep.

And now it came to her that Bartha's death beside her in *his* sleep—beside her as she slept—had been what his life with her had been, that he had left her as he'd lived with her. Alongside and yet apart from her. Silently, in secret.

In secret. He had altered the course of her life, altered *her*, and she had never understood why. She had known why she'd allowed it—why she had *invited* it—but what could he have had in his mind? Certainly not what had come to pass. Well, and this was not what she had had in her mind either. She had yearned for beauty, for something bigger than her life, something extraordinary.

"Dad liked to sleep *and* to wake up," Alexander said.

"It's true," Esther said. She made an effort to smile. "He took great pleasure in falling asleep. He looked forward to it, as if it were a reward for him at the end of the day. Even after he gave up his students, you know, he put in a full day in the studio."

"What did he do in there?"

"Oh, it isn't hard to guess. He'd read and listen to records. Think. Daydream. He'd come out of there with things on his mind, I know. During dinner he was usually distracted—still daydreaming. Once, just once, I asked him what he was thinking about and he looked at me as if that were a strange question. 'Everything,' he said. And when I said, 'But what does that mean?' he said—"

"Don't tell me," Alexander said. "He said"—he used

his father's accent—"'Everything means everything.'"

"Naturally," said Esther. She used the accent too, and laughed. But then she said, "Still, toward the end—these last few weeks—he spent more and more of his time taking naps on that old couch. I could hear him snore. I never said anything about it. He never talked to me about how he spent his days and I never asked him. I think he would have been offended if I'd mentioned that he'd been asleep. And at the end of the day, every day, he was tired, he was ready for bed. He'd put in a good day, that was how he felt, I think. Whatever he had done, he'd put in a good day. And then the next day he'd be up at dawn, as always, wide awake and anxious to start the day. Like a farmer. Like the owner of a candy store that opened at six to sell the morning paper."

Like my father, she thought. And for an instant she was afraid she'd said it out loud. But Alexander's expression hadn't changed. So she allowed herself to think it again, in the safety of her own mind. *Like my father.*

How surprised she had been when she had first discovered this habit of her husband's. And how disappointed. She had imagined…oh, she had imagined that he'd sleep late, have breakfast in bed on a tray. But who had she supposed would have brought this tray to him? Servants? Herself?

Alexander said, "What's funny?"

"Nothing," she said. Had she laughed? She hadn't felt like laughing.

If she had been disappointed in Bartha, she thought, it was because she'd been so ill-prepared. She had imagined—she had expected—the impossible.

No, that was wrong. She had not *expected* anything. She had let things happen to her, and she had been surprised by everything as it unfolded. She had watched as it unfolded, bit by bit, an inch ahead of her. *Ah, so it's this,* she'd thought and run a little to catch up with it. And then another bit unfolded. *And now it's this. And this.*

Now it was all unfolded, all behind her.

"Everything turned out to be more ordinary than I thought it would," she said.

"That doesn't seem funny at all."

"No. I suppose it's not. And maybe…." She looked down at the table. She did not want him to see that her eyes were filling again. "Maybe I *made* him ordinary. Maybe that was my doing. But it wasn't what I had in mind to do."

Now she was crying—it could not be helped.

"Oh, Mom." He reached across their cold cups of tea and took her hand, as he had been taking her hand all day, it seemed to him. "You might want to think about getting out of Omaha. For good, I mean."

"Why would I do that?" Already the tears were stopping. She sat up very straight. "It was you who couldn't wait to leave. You and your father, you both hated it here so much! It always seemed ridiculous to me, your father's hatred, his constant complaints. It was his idea to live here, not mine. He brought me here when I was practically a child still! If he hated it so much he could have taken me somewhere else. What did I know? I would have done whatever he said. Once we got here and he saw he didn't like it, saw that he would never like it, why did we stay? We didn't have to stay."

"You don't have to stay now."

"Now? But I want to stay now. This is where I live.

There's nowhere else for me to go."

"That's not true, Mom. You could come back to New York with me."

"To live?" She was looking at him as if he'd lost his mind.

Had he? But he pressed on. "To live, why not? Not with me—I mean, for a while with me, sure"—he was improvising now—"while we find a place for you to live, while we figure things out...." But here he faltered because she was shaking her head, she was laughing at him. "What? Why is this funny?"

"It's not funny. It's ludicrous. There's a difference."

"Why is it ludicrous?" In for a penny, in for a pound, he thought. "It was once your home. It could be again. You have family there, don't you?"

His daring amazed him. He'd never said a word about her family before. Never asked a question, never speculated, never fished for information. He had never mentioned them because she never had, except to tell him they existed—or "probably did," she had said, on the one occasion she had spoken of them, when he was twelve or thirteen. "Probably?" he'd asked her, and even at that age he'd had the sense that this was some kind of fairy tale: they might be real, these people, or they might not be—this was what she meant by "probably." And then she changed the subject, and he understood that this was all she meant to say.

She didn't say anything now, either. "Well, don't you?" he said. And, more daringly, added, "Probably?" But this word meant nothing to her. She didn't remember. "You could go back to New York. There's nothing to stop you now."

"Alexander," she said, "there is no 'back' to New York.

New York is not my home, this is."

"But you do have family there." And when she did not respond, he said, "Somewhere in Brooklyn, right?"

Mari was from Brooklyn, too. He'd never told her that his mother's childhood had been spent there. She would have had questions for him, and he would not have had the answers to any of them. But that was not the only reason he had never told her. It was too hard to put the two together in his mind. Mari and his mother, both from the same place.

"I did once, yes," she said. She started to say something else, then stopped. *Wait*, he told himself. *She'll tell you.*

He waited.

"I write to them," she said. "But they don't answer. So who knows?"

She closed her eyes. She bowed her head.

She had never told anyone. She could not believe that she just had.

And Alexander could not believe what she had told him. "You write to them? When do you write to them?"

When? Surely that wasn't the right question. But he couldn't think of the right question, couldn't think of any questions—couldn't pluck one from the chaos of questions that seemed to boil down to just one, one that wasn't even a question. *Your family?* was all he could think. *Your family?*

"When?" She shrugged. "From time to time. Not so often anymore."

He stared at her. Not so often anymore? But often, once? Perhaps *when* was the right question after all. Long ago? How long ago?

He had assumed she never thought about her family. He had to assume that. She never spoke of them, which meant she never thought of them. He had always thought—she

227

had always said—that she talked to him about everything. "I can tell you anything," she used to say.

"Only once a year, the last few years," his mother was saying now. "Out of habit, mostly. But I used to write them all the time. Goodness, for years I think I wrote them at least once a month. And when you were a baby, once a week. On a bad week, twice or even three times. But later…"

Alexander must have groaned because she stopped, and finally she looked at him. He must have looked stricken, which his mother seemed to interpret as pity for her, or sorrow or revulsion at the way she'd been treated. "It doesn't bother me that they don't answer," she told him. "I don't know myself why I kept writing. It was just…once I started, I couldn't stop."

"And Dad? What did he know about this?"

"Dad! He didn't know anything about it. It wouldn't have made sense to him. It didn't make sense to *me*. I never told anyone." She emphasized the *anyone*. She understood how much it mattered to him that if she had not told him, she'd kept it to herself.

And this shamed him—that it mattered to him. He thought of something Mari had once said, about how everyone she'd ever known suffered from a yearning to be the most important person in the world. He hadn't understood what she meant. "But that's crazy," he said. "Why would anyone think he could be?" And Mari laughed. "*To* someone, I mean," she said gently. "But the thing is, you're the exception. That's why you don't get it. You're the first man I've ever gone out with who doesn't need to be at the center of the universe." She cocked her head and tapped her lip twice with her index finger, then raised it and shook it at him, like a college professor about to make

228

a point. "You already *are*," she told him. "You have been your whole life."

"What?" his mother said.

"What?"

"The look on your face."

He hesitated. But why should this be a secret? "I was thinking about someone. A girl—a woman. A woman I've been seeing."

"Oh, yes? And this woman is called what?"

"My girlfriend." His mother looked amused. "Oh. You mean her name. Her name is Mari. Mari Blum."

"Mari." His mother pronounced the name carefully, correctly, with the *a* sound like the *a* in *father* and the stress on the first syllable. Mari didn't care when he introduced her to someone and he said, "Marie, is it?" or "Mary" or "Merry," but he did. "Pretty name," his mother said. "Unusual."

"Actually"—he blushed—"I kind of made it up. I mean, she uses it too now, but I'm the one who started calling her that. It's short for Mariana."

He considered saying more—telling her how much it had disconcerted him, near the start of their relationship, when Mari told him that the name she went by was invented. She had been Anna. The Mariana was an innovation of her middle twenties. And Blum was not her name, either—not her family's name—but a shortening of Blumenthal, her married name. The only leftover, she told him, from that early and disastrous marriage. He had never told her that it bothered him that in her youth she'd had another name entirely from the one she used now. But the blurriness between what she had been given and what she had taken, what she'd kept and what she had discarded, made him uncomfortable. And he hated that she'd kept her married name, even only part of it. And then there was this: the implication that she had created herself, both by circumstances and by choice. Which suggested that she might again—might reinvent herself, leave the version she'd become (and leave *him*, too) behind. He wasn't thinking about staking a claim when he asked, impulsively, if anyone had ever called her Mari, but he supposed that was what he was doing, and when she introduced herself to someone now as Mari Blum and he was there to hear it, it made him happy. Partly it was because she'd let him call her something no one ever had before, and partly it was because *she* liked it enough to take it on in public. But something else occurred to him now, and he was surprised he hadn't thought of it before. She had once been Anna Kessler and then she had been Anna Blumenthal, then Anna Blum, then Mariana Blum—the *Mari* was the only part of her name that was all her own invention. It was as if he had decided to single out the part of her that she *wanted* to be.

But he didn't tell his mother any of this. Instead he said, "She's an actress. Also a singer."

"A singer!" his mother said. "What does she sing?"

"Oh, you'd like what she sings. She sings those songs you used to sing to me. She'll be pouring orange juice or buttering a piece of bread or tying her shoe and all of a sudden it's 'No Other Love' or—what's that one from 'The Music Man' you always liked? Not 'Till There Was You.' The other one."

"'Being in Love'?" His mother sang a line, softly: "*Being in love used to be my favorite dream, oh, yes.*"

"That's the one. She'll sing half the score of, say, *Brigadoon*, while she's doing her hair and putting on makeup. She sings songs I didn't even know I remembered, songs I didn't know I *knew*, until I hear her singing them."

"Ah," his mother said. "So. It sounds like you're seeing quite a lot of her. That is, if she's pouring juice and buttering toast and putting on her—"

"Yeah."

"I've embarrassed you?" She smiled. "So tell me about her."

"Wasn't that what I was just doing?"

"*Alexander.*"

"Okay." He took a deep breath. "She's smart, beautiful, funny. Confident. And she should be, too. She's a terrific actress—I've watched her. And she dresses like, I don't know, like someone out of an illustration in a nineteenth century storybook. Long things, lace, silk fringes, things that trail. And she has this kind of amazing hair." He was blushing again.

"She sounds lovely," his mother said.

"She is. But not *just* lovely. She's also, I don't know, very down to earth. I mean, she looks ethereal but she isn't— not a bit, really. Well"—he laughed—"she's a New Yorker. So, you know." His mother didn't look like she knew. "Actually"—Alexander paused, considering; but what did he have to lose?—"she's from Brooklyn. Like you."

"Is she?"

He watched her, but he couldn't read her face. "Yeah. Kings Highway, wherever the hell that is. She won't take me there. I keep asking her."

"Do you?" She said this noncommittally.

"So, how far is that from where you're from?"

"Not too."

"Which means what?"

"It means 'not too far from where I'm from.'"

Alexander shook his head. "It's funny. Neither one

231

of you will talk about where you're from. It's like some great Brooklyn conspiracy of silence." He laughed again, but his mother didn't even smile. "She won't take me there and she won't tell me anything about it. I've told her I'd like to see the place where she grew up, the schools she went to, all of that, but she refuses. 'It's not interesting,' she says. 'There's nothing there.' What she means, I think, is that there's no *one* there. She lost both her parents before she was out of her twenties." But that was a mistake, he thought. He didn't want his mother to register what he had said, to ask how long ago that was. He went on quickly: "For her, everything's about people. She doesn't see that what I'm interested in is the place itself, the look of things. I want to see the house she lived in, the streets she walked on on her way to school, the schoolyard—you know?" His mother didn't answer. "But maybe it would make her too sad. Maybe she hates the place. I don't know. She's never told me anything about it except that her subway stop was Kings Highway."

"Mine was Brighton Beach."

Alexander froze. "Was it?" He was careful not to sound excited. Not to sound particularly interested, even.

"Same line," she said. "The D train."

He held his breath. He told himself to proceed cautiously. He thought about the way you'd talk to a lost dog on the street, careful not to scare it off before you could get close enough to read the tags hanging from its collar—he'd had to do that plenty of times as a kid; he knew how to do that.

But his mother wasn't a stray, and he was too excited by this information—any information, any fact, anything at all—about her old life to be careful. He couldn't keep himself from saying, "You know, Mom, if you came to

New York, I could go with you to see your family. We could do that together."

He still couldn't read her expression—couldn't read her mind, though she had always said he could. And sometimes, when he was growing up, it had even seemed to *him* that he could.

Then she spoke, and it didn't help him. "Sweetheart," she said, "I think I need to go rest for a little while."

"Oh, God, of course," he told her. "You go on upstairs. Why don't you try to take a nap? I'll get things cleaned up in here."

"A nap?" She stood up quickly. "No, no, no nap. Just a little time alone, I think. I think maybe I'm just not used to so much...so much conversation." She patted his hand as she turned away from him. Then without turning back, she said, "And you should call your girl. The singer. Mari."

She fled to her study. And he hurried too, as soon as he heard the door of her study close behind her. Because—of course—he was going to call Mari.

His mother listened to him racing up the stairs and although she was still shaken by what he had proposed, she laughed a little when she heard her bedroom door close. Ah—he was calling his girlfriend from the phone upstairs, in her bedroom, so that there was no chance that she would hear him talking to her. As if she would eavesdrop on him! As if she could not guess for herself the kind of conversation two people in love might have.

She bent to choose a record to put on. She was shaking her head, still laughing quietly to herself. Everyone in love so certain that no one else has ever said the things they said, felt the things they felt. Everything new and secret, everything for no one but themselves.

She flipped through her records, pausing only long enough to reject each one. There seemed to be nothing she wanted to listen to. But that could not be true, she thought. She sat back on her heels and considered this. There had to be something. There was always something.

Her mind was full of noise—that was the problem. If she played a record, any record, the noise in her head might just grow louder, competing, making sure she paid attention to it. She pushed herself up off the floor—*All right, then. For once, let there be no music*—and walked the few steps to her chair. She sank down into it, cranked up the footrest, closed her eyes. Above her, she heard Alexander moving slowly down the hallway—no one home, she thought. She felt sorry for him.

But only fleetingly, only out of habit. It wasn't that she was angry with him. Or it wasn't exactly that she was angry with him. Honestly, she wasn't sure what it was she felt toward him—what it was she felt about what he had offered. Surprised, of course. But also…disappointed. He had meant well—he had always meant well, at least where she was concerned—but knowing this did nothing to soften her disappointment in him.

He would go with her to see her family, would he? They would hop on the D train and show up at their doorstep. The doorstep of her childhood. That was his plan! To take her there, after nearly thirty years. As if she could be sure there *was* a *there*. For all she knew they all were dead. For all she knew they'd moved away—her letters forwarded to someplace else where they could be unread, unopened.

Imagine her own child believing it would be so easy. Or (this would be more like him) believing that it would be hard but possible—because he could not imagine that it, that anything, was impossible. He had no idea. That joke of his—a conspiracy of silence. What did he know about silence? Three decades and not a word from them. Because *they did not forgive her.* Not even now. As if her life, the very life she had constructed—Alexander's own existence!—was unforgivable. As if time had stopped during that long-ago summer when she and Bartha had begun their "romance"—as if they had still to forgive her for that. As if they could not forgive her for having altered the course of her life.

They had not forgiven her or else they had forgotten her. Or they were dead—every one of them. Her mother and her father, Sylvia. In which case she'd been writing letters to a family that no longer existed. To no one, nowhere. And for how long?

Her eyes had filled again. She would cry today, she thought, until she had shed every single tear she had been holding back, holding on to, all these years. For Bartha's sake. For Bartha who did not want to see her weep.

I'm not saying it'll be so easy for you. I'm just saying that you can *do it, that I'll help you.*

She could hear him saying this exactly as if he already had. As if they had debated it. As if she'd given him the chance to make an argument.

Not possible, she heard herself tell him. *No. It cannot be done. I'm sorry.*

And Alexander saying, *No, Mom. Hard, yes, but not impossible.*

And this: *You have nothing to be sorry for.*

Whose fault was it that he understood her—understood who she was—so little? Whose fault that he believed that nothing was impossible? That all one had to do was set one's mind to it and anything was possible. All hers. He knew only what she'd taught him, and *she'd* taught him this. Taught him that he could do, could imagine, could make happen—could *be*—anything. She'd made sure he'd known that no one in the world was more important—not to her (but was she not at one time everyone? was *she* not the world?). He had no idea what *not loved* felt like—no idea that not loved was a possibility.

He knew nothing of what had made her. He knew nothing at all.

She imagined her parents, her sister—gone, all of them. She *tried* to imagine it, tried to imagine what the difference would be between them alive and silent, as they had for so long been—and no longer living. Was there a difference?

There must be, would have to be, a difference.

But they could not be dead. Someone would have written, called her. They would not have let death pass without a word to her, would they? But who were *they*? The world? The old neighborhood. Relatives. Relatives even if they were distant ones, ones she'd never met or heard of. A friend of the family from before she was born. A customer. Someone. Someone would have tried to reach her.

Unless no one had ever troubled to write down her address. Unless all of the letters she had written had been thrown out at the instant of their arrival.

But that was unthinkable. It was unbearable, she felt, and that it *was* unbearable was a surprise to her. But she understood now that she had been keeping in her mind all these years an image of the many letters she had written. They were stacked in bundles, tied with string. Kept in drawers or in a closet, in old cardboard boxes, under someone's bed. Saved for what—for whom, by whom— she could not have said. She knew only that although she had accepted, *expected*, that none of her letters would be answered, that they would not be read—even that they would remain unopened—her mind rebelled against the possibility that they had not been been *kept*.

She snapped down the footrest of her chair and stood up. She was too agitated to stay seated. She could hear Alexander in the kitchen. Dishes clattering, water running. The refrigerator opening and closing. Cabinet doors snapping shut. She heard his footsteps as he moved about the room. Taking care of things for her.

He was a good boy, she knew that. She wasn't angry with him—how could she be angry with him? A good man, not a boy. A good *son*. How many times had she told her family that in the letters she wrote to them? She had told them all about him, from the most important to the most trivial things there were to tell: his grades in school, and prizes he won, the kinds of games he played, something startlingly grown up or charming or amusing he had said. The names of his friends, the names of his teachers. Where he went to college, what he studied. What he told her, when he called, about his new life.

There had been years during which she'd written about little but him. Not in the first years—in the first years she had written out of loneliness, out of what had seemed at the time to her to be misery. During those years the letters had been a refuge—the one place, the one time, for her to confess what she felt, to speak truthfully of what was in her heart. Later, as she grew accustomed to her life, as she grew older—as Alexander grew older, old enough for conversation—she stopped needing to write so often. She stopped needing to air grievances, unhappiness. She was not unhappy then. She wrote about the house, the garden, Omaha, Clara and Vilmos—the ordinary business of her life. And Alexander.

She wrote once a month, then once every few months, then three times a year, then twice. For the past six or seven years she'd written just once yearly, in the days following Alexander's birthday. A tradition, she would tell herself as she sat down to write the latest news into the silence. There was very little to report but Alexander's news, although she mentioned when Bartha had given up his students and when he'd given up his Sundays out. She described what was coming up in the garden. One year—last year or the year before—she enclosed a snapshot of the garden as it looked just then. It was the end of summer, the *hibiscus syriacus* hedge in full bloom. To her family, the garden might have looked like it belonged in Florida, in southern California. Somewhere hot and sunny and beautiful, not here.

On the back of the photo, she had written the names of all the flowers: Echinacea & rudbeckia (pink, purple, yellow, orange coneflower), salvia, asters, helenium, *hibiscus syriacus* (Rose of Sharon). They would be amazed, she thought, that she had done all this herself. That she knew these names.

Once—another impulse—she had slipped into an envelope the instant before sealing it the brochure Alexander had sent her that showed the window gates he custom-made to earn a living between shows of his sculpture. They were gates for rich people, for people who needed to keep burglars out of their New York City apartments but would do so only *artfully,* he told her, laughing at them, at these people for whom ordinary hardware-store gates, like the one her father had installed so many years ago over her own window—hers and Sylvia's—which opened onto the fire escape (from which *she* had escaped, after unlocking the gate from the inside!) were not good enough.

Later she was sorry she had sent them the brochure. She could not ask Alexander for another copy of it, not without lying to him about what had become of the first one.

She had never sent on to her family any of the postcards that announced his shows, the cards that featured photographs of his sculptures. She would not part with these: she hung them all carefully, matted and framed, throughout the house. But she wrote about the art he made, describing it to them just as he had described it to her, telling them the highlights of his letters to her. That there was something queer about his writing to her from New York and her reporting back to New York with his news—that the news made a circle that never closed—she did not point out, of course. And what they thought of this, what they thought of anything, she would never know.

If they thought. If they knew.

She had begun to pace the room. She felt caged, jumpy. She went to her records again. There had to be something she wanted to hear, something that would suit her. There had never been a time when music had not helped her. It soothed her, or else it lifted her—it pulled her in whatever direction she needed to be pulled. "Like magic," she used to tell Bartha, who laughed—who always laughed at the faith she put in music. "Not magic," he would say. "When what is called 'magic' is made by human beings, it is only a trick. And music is not a trick."

Lecturing and teasing her, both at the same time. He had always talked to her this way. Lecturing or telling stories, but always teasing. And then the story-telling had stopped, and then the lecturing. And finally the teasing.

But long ago he'd said, "Real magic, my dear, if it were

to exist, would be something else. Sent by heaven. Made by the angels."

Could it be that he did not know that if not for her faith in music—her faith, her expectations, all her hopes—she never would have fallen in love with him?

Perhaps he did know—perhaps this was why he lectured her, why he teased her. To let her know he knew (for how often had his little lectures over the years seemed to be less about teaching her something than demonstrating that he knew it?) and to make light of what he must have understood, then, to be her great disappointment. For what had come of all that faith, that hope, those expectations? When *he* had turned out to be only himself—only human (no magic then, as Bartha himself would have said: only trickery)?

For Bartha, there had been no disappointment, no loss of faith, no dashed hopes. Or rather, such losses had long preceded her. From her, he had expected nothing. Or perhaps he had expected so little—hoped for so little, had so little faith—he could not have been disappointed.

She would never know for sure. How could she know? How little she knew him!

Had known him. Everything in the past now. *Had. Known.*

Indeed, as she knelt before the rows of record albums, she reflected that she had not only not come to know her husband better as the years had passed but had come to *un*know him. With each passing year, it seemed to her she had understood him less.

She drew back; she sat back on her heels. Yes, it was true. It was as if she had purposefully un-known him. As if this had been what she'd wanted, without ever knowing she had wanted it. She hadn't known *anything* of what she'd wanted, really, had groped blindly for it, without reason, without knowledge. She had chosen a mystery. Chosen unknowing.

Would she have preferred a husband she could have known through and through? she asked herself—but this was not a question, because she knew the answer without asking. Why would she have wanted such a husband? She had her son. It was he she had known, he she *knew*. Whether he wanted her to or not, and no matter how hard he tried to tug away from her and from that truth, she knew him.

And if he didn't know her as she knew him, if she despaired that he—that anyone—would ever know her as she knew him, well, hadn't she chosen that too?

All the choices one made, knowingly and unknowingly. One choice after another, and that was one's whole life.

Or not her *whole* life. Not according to her son. A period of time longer than *his* entire life, and he declared it hardly any time at all. *In the greater scheme of things.*

So how was it that she felt as if she had already spent her whole life—*spent* it, so that there was nothing left—on her marriage to Bartha? How was it that it felt as if *forever* was behind her?

And what stretched ahead—what came after forever—she could not imagine.

She reached out a hand and ran it over the spines of her albums. She had the sense again, just as she had had last night, that there was some one record in particular that she wished to hear—and again she found that she could not think of what it could be. But she did not have the heart to search for it—to try and fail and try again and hope that she would stumble upon it as she had last night. This time, it seemed to her, she would not be able to find it. This time she was certain that whatever it was, it was something she didn't have.

She set her hands on her knees. She couldn't think of what she should do now. For a little while she stayed where she was, sitting back on her heels before the long row of records. She ached—she had just noticed that. Her back ached, and her neck. Her shoulders too. She was worn out—how could she not be? And it could not have helped that she had slept last night in Alexander's chair. She rubbed her neck, tried to massage her own left shoulder. A stupid thing to have done, spending the night in a chair, watching over her son. Imagining that even as she slept, she could watch over him. She would suffer for this.

And now someone was knocking. Alexander—knocking on her door.

She pulled herself up slowly, with a groan, and went slowly to the door. When she opened it she saw that he had a cup of tea in his hand.

His eyes followed hers. "An excuse to knock," he said. "A sorry one, I know, when you wanted solitude."

She took the cup from him and said, "Thank you. That was thoughtful of you."

He hung his head. He looked like himself, age eight or nine. "You never got to drink the one you'd been wanting before. Plus…."

He trailed off, wanting her to interrupt him. But she had nothing to say.

Finally he said, "All right. Plus, what I wanted to say was—I don't know, I mean, I know you were kidding earlier. When you said you wanted to be sure I wouldn't, you know, abandon you? But even so, I wanted…."

He couldn't seem to finish this sentence either. She took pity on him. "Yes, I was kidding."

"Still. It made you cry."

"Everything has been making me cry. It's possible this

tea will make me cry." He looked alarmed. "I meant that to be a joke," she said.

"Well." He cleared his throat. "All I wanted to say was that, you know, you should know I won't."

"Abandon me?" Her laughter, which had slipped out of her without warning, caught her so much off guard that she laughed again. Her poor son was crestfallen. She took his arm with her free hand and drew him toward her.

"It's too late, you know," she said, as she lay her head on his shoulder. "You've been abandoning me little by little since the instant you were born."

This time it was Alexander who began to cry. She bent to set the cup down on the floor beside them, then straightened up and put both arms around him.

"It's all right," she said. "Hush. It's all right." She stroked his hair. "I know, I know." She spoke softly, meaninglessly, just as she had when he was a baby and couldn't have understood the words but only their reassuring sound. Sometimes Bartha, listening in, would murmur, "Ach, Esther, you know what? What do you know?" He did not say this cruelly, but with what sounded like wonder.

When Alexander lifted his head, she studied his face and saw flickering across it both herself and Bartha, that clamor of the two of them within him. "Why don't you come in and sit with me?" she asked him.

"Are you sure you wouldn't rather be alone?"

"I'm sure. Come. Keep me company in my solitude."

But as she bent to pick up her teacup he said, "Look, I want to tell you something. Don't be angry."

What now? she thought. She could not imagine. "All right," she said. "Just tell me."

"I meant it when I said that I'd go with you to see them. And then we could tell them together—"

243

"About your father." He looked at her questioningly. "That he's *gone*," Esther said.

"That, yes. Of course. But also—also, I don't know. Everything."

"Everything," Esther said. "Ah. That would be a lot."

"It would."

"Well, then." She sighed. "We'll see."

He followed her across the room as she moved toward her recliner. "In the meantime, I wonder…"

She stopped and turned to him, curiously. "What? What do you wonder?"

"Will you keep writing to them?"

"Ah," she said. "I don't know. I hadn't thought about it."

"It's just that, now that Dad's gone, I just wondered—"

"I wonder too," she told him. It was the truth. She took his hand and patted it before she sat down in the recliner. "Now, my darling, would you do something for me?"

"Sure—anything."

"Would you put on some music?"

"That's all?" He laughed. "That's easy. What would you like to hear?"

"Anything. Anything you like. You choose."

She watched him as he turned away from her and moved to the stereo, watched him kneel and bow his head to consider the rows of records and cassette tapes on the shelves beneath it. He might have been praying. Anyone who didn't know him, who didn't know that in Bartha's house one knelt and lowered one's head only to choose a record, might have guessed this. But her son, like her, had never been taught to pray.

Had Bartha? She had never asked; she would never know.

She thought of her own family, in the small apartment above the store where she had lived with them so long ago. There, one knelt only to scrub the floor, to pick up something one had dropped, to tie a shoe. Once when she was very young, after she had gone to church with Kathleen for her first communion, the first time she had ever been inside a church, the first time she had ever seen anyone pray, she had asked her father about the kneeling. This was before she had seen prayer in the movies, before she had come to take the kneeling for granted—although even then, watching the Marias drop to their knees in "West Side Story" and "The Sound of Music," or Queen Katherine interrupted mid-prayer in "Anne of the Thousand Days," she would think of her father's answer to her question: *They kneel because they fear God, because fear is a part of their religion. It's not a part of ours.*

Her father's answer had surprised her almost as much as the sight of Kathleen's family and everyone around them on their knees that day. Had her father not met with ridicule and anger every one of her mother's attempts to preserve what he called "the backwards habits" of her own observant childhood? *A part of ours*—she turned it over in her mind. When had it become *ours*—his? But she hadn't dared to ask him, and her father surprised her again—for once, reading the expression on her face and responding to it: *Even Jews who pray don't pray on their knees. Listen to me, Esther: nothing should ever bring you to your knees.*

Nothing had ever brought *him* to his knees. Nothing had ever cowed him, it was true. But nothing had ever humbled or awed him, either.

Had it never occurred to him that this was not necessarily something to be proud of, or to be passed on to his daughter?

And after she was gone, what had he thought about her refusing to be cowed by him? Or had he had too much pride to ever think of it that way?

"Listen," Alexander said. He was on his feet now. He put a record on the turntable and set the needle down.

She closed her eyes to listen. Music filled the room. It poured into every corner.

This was when she liked her room best—when it was full of music, when the music was like liquid all around her.

He had chosen well, she thought. Although perhaps it would not have mattered what he had chosen, only that he had.

It was a pity it could not go on forever, that what he had chosen for her would come to an end. That something else would have to be chosen. And something else again.

But for now the room was a container for her and the music that was everywhere around her in her room. *Her room*—and even now, even after all these years, it was a pleasure to think of this. *Her* room. A pleasure, she thought, that her son would never understand, a pleasure the very meaning of which would be lost on one who had had his own room for as long as he could remember. If he even troubled to remember, now that he had his own home.

As she did too. It struck her suddenly: her own home for the first time in her life.

She opened her eyes. There was her son in the corner, watching her as she listened, and watching not with curiosity or puzzlement or hope or concern or even ordinary interest, she could see, but only with love.

Not a pity, she thought, but a wonder. A wonder, and a glory—to choose, and then to choose again. And again, and still again.

Acknowledgments

I am no stranger to long incubations and multiplicities of drafts, but this book takes the cake. It was begun during a residency at Yaddo twenty-five years ago, in solitude and silence in a corner of the mansion, and a draft of the entire manuscript was not completed until six years later—by which time I had a husband and a lively three-year-old daughter, and we were living in a crowded, always under-construction one-bedroom apartment in Brooklyn Heights while I was on sabbatical from my teaching job. We had bartered my husband's considerable skills (it was he who was doing all that constructing) for the year's rent, and thus he spent part of every day recreating elaborate plaster cornices and rebuilding crumbling walls, and part of it making still lifes in a grand studio he had been granted in Tribeca for the year, and—from nine AM till one PM each day—while I worked on this book at the rear of the apartment, he and our daughter drew pictures and made paintings and built complicated block structures at the front end of the apartment, sitting on the floor on plaster-dusted and paint-spattered dropcloths. I wrote sitting crosslegged on the bed on a laptop (my first) for which my brother had "loaned" me the money.

Time passed. We returned to Ohio, the child started preschool, I periodically revised and put aside the manuscript of *Devotion* (its title, born at Yaddo, never wavered) as I wrote other books—as I published a collection of novellas, began to write and publish nonfiction for the first time, wrote another novel, taught, advised, edited a journal, took on administrative work, began voice lessons (and never once, surprisingly enough, paused to think of

Esther and Bartha as I did). My daughter grew up—started kindergarten, started high school, went away to college. As I write these acknowledgments to a book I began before she was born—before I'd met the man who was to be her father—she is about to graduate, to take her place in the world. The passage of time is as puzzling to me as it is to Esther Bartha.

Over the many years that I picked up and set down this novel, many people—writers and civilians both—were a great help to me. During my daughter's early childhood I drew upon the strengths of other mothers, several of whom I spent countless hours with while our children were in their dance classes (if I knew how to reach them now, to thank them in person, I would; all I can do is note how much their conversation and kindness meant to me and the effect it had on both my work and life: Laura, Elyse, and Linda—I believe this book would not exist without you), and the "Maudwomen," fellow devotees of the *Betsy-Tacy* books—the books that made me a writer—with whom I communicated feverishly by listserv and email (in those nascent internet years!). To Susan O'Doherty, who read a draft in the late nineties, I owe a long-deferred debt of gratitude. To my brother, Scott Herman, who never let me pay him back for that loan, I am (as I ever am) more thankful than I will ever be able to say. To Kate Nitze, who was my (smart, clever, kind) editor at the late, lamented MacAdam/Cage, who reminded me a decade ago why I'd written this novel in the first place—I now blow many kisses. To Marian B.S. Young, who ruefully called me her "very own Virginia Woolf" when she read the (first) finished "final" draft, and who has steadfastly stood by me for well over three decades now, there may be no sufficient words of gratitude. And to Jon Roemer, who rescued this book from the drawer where I'd put it (I thought) for good and inspired me to look at it anew—and then helped me make it better—I hereby swear eternal gratitude and love.

To my mother, Sheila Herman, and my husband, Glen Holland, for *their* devotion; to my daughter, Grace Herman-Holland, for her excellent companionship and wisdom, insight, and unfailingly interesting conversation—oh, and so much joy; to the Corporation of Yaddo and the Ohio State University and the Ohio Arts Council; to Stephanie Henkle, who taught me how to sing, and the Harmony Project and David Brown, who have kept me singing; and to my students, who for twenty-seven years have done a fine job of keeping me on my toes—I am immeasurably grateful.

About the author

Michelle Herman is the author of the novels *Missing* and *Dog*, the collection of novellas *A New and Glorious Life*, and three essay collections—*Like A Song: Essays*, *The Middle of Everything*, and *Stories We Tell Ourselves* (longlisted for the 2014 PEN/Diamonstein-Spielvogel Award for the Art of the Essay), as well as a book for children, *A Girl's Guide to Life*.

Her essays and short fiction have appeared in a wide range of magazines, from *The American Scholar* and *The Southern Review* to *O, the Oprah Magazine* and *Redbook*. Born and raised in Brooklyn, she has lived for many years in Columbus, Ohio, where she directs the MFA Program in Creative Writing at Ohio State.

CPSIA information can be obtained at www.ICGtesting.com
Printed in the USA
LVOW11s2245100216

474597LV00004B/109/P